Thank

Great job

Barcelona
2a/11/2017

GUINEA

By

Fernando Gamboa

First edition: October 2008
Revised and corrected edition for e-Book: January 2012
English edition 2017
© Fernando Gamboa 2017
Cover design by Fernando Gamboa

www.gamboabooks.com

*Dedicated to Africans in general.
To the people of Equatorial Guinea in particular.*

*To write for the fire,
for something to happen,
so that awareness does not die,
so that evil does not spread,
so that it does not remain unpunished,
so that it does not happen again.*

Alfonso Armada
African Notebooks

The meeting

I met Sarah Malik one hot evening in August. We were two strangers at the bar of a faded hotel which had known better times. I was passing through and she had stopped by to have a drink, while Julie London whispered *Cry me a river* on an old record player in the corner, sadness clutched to her throat. I went to the bar and offered to buy her another of whatever she was having, but she barely nodded, her gaze lost among the bottles on the shelves. Glancing discreetly at her reflection in the mirror in front of us, I noticed that she was an attractive young woman, with shoulder-length blond hair and brown eyes which revealed a strange, faraway pain and seemed to be looking for something beyond the walls of that bar. We sat on stools barely two feet away from each other, but in reality she was wandering very far in time and memory, and I was like a castaway watching her pass like a sail on the horizon.

Resigned, I downed my beer beneath the compassionate look of the waiter, left a couple of bills on the counter and, in silence, got up from my stool.

"Thanks for the drink," she murmured in a tired voice.

I turned in surprise and saw her eyes in the mirror, fixed on me.

"You're welcome," I said, offering her my hand. "My name's Fernando."

She swivelled on her stool, and after staring at me with the same boredom which seemed to colour her every move, she shook my hand indifferently.

"I'm Sarah," she introduced herself, and as if to complete a ritual, asked me where I was from.

"Spain."

"And what brings you here?"

"I was going to ask you the same question."

She said nothing, merely blinking a couple of times, seeming to let the conversation drop there.

"I'm a writer…" I said at last, afraid she would turn her back on me again. "I'm here looking for ideas for a new novel."

"A writer?" she asked with sudden interest.

"Well… yes."

"A novelist… in search of his novel," she muttered, turning to the bar counter again, giving the trace of a bitter smile as she put the glass to her lips. "Would you like to hear a good story… a true story, for your book?"

"Of course," I said sincerely, leaning my elbow on the counter.

"Then, listen to me carefully," she said, bringing her face very close to mine and lowering her voice, "because I'm going to tell you something which happened about seven years ago… in a little corner of Africa. A story of courage, love, hate, of…" She fell silent, once again with her gaze absent and the unfinished sentence suspended in the limbo of words that refuse to be shared. "A true story," she finished, taking my hand, "which sometimes doesn't seem to be that at all." She stared into my eyes. "I'm going to tell you my story."

And she told me her story, the most extraordinary one I have ever heard.

I have simply transcribed it here, word for word, just as she told it to me. I have just been the simple, spellbound stenographer of this amazing story, a link, in the same way that you, when you reach the last page of this book, might become another link in this same chain.

This book is a step forward on an uncertain path, and only time will show where it ends up leading us.

1

"Ms. Margarita! I'm back!" I called as I opened the wooden door, painted in sky blue.

"Ms. Margarita?" I asked when I did not get the usual welcoming response.

I left my small backpack on the floor and peeped into the kitchen, trusting I would find her, as every day, immersed in her fish stews and frittatas.

"Ms. Margarita? I called again, a little more intrigued at not finding her there for the first time in almost two months. "Where are you?"

I went to look in the toilet, a few yards away from the house and decorated as usual by the hairy tarantula on the white wall, which I had ended up naming Matilda after sharing so many private moments with it. Then I went to look in the little garden at the back, went back to the house and walked into the only room I had not looked in. And there she was, lying on her bed like a forgotten doll, in the gloom, in her old nightgown which stuck to her body from the sweat spreading in a patch on the sheets.

Alarmed, I ran to open the window, and thousands of droplets of perspiration on her dark skin reflected the afternoon light, and the woman's eyes half-opened in an effort too great for such a thin and exhausted body from too many difficult years.

"Sarah..." she barely managed to articulate.

"Yes, Ms. Margarita. I'm here," I said. I took her hand, trying to keep calm. "What's the matter?"

The old woman tried to smile, but the pain stopped her.

"I'm dying..." she whimpered.

"No way! Don't say that!" I protested without thinking. "I'll put you in the jeep and we'll go to the hospital in Malabo." I touched her forehead to check her temperature and had to bite my lip to suppress my horror when I realized she was burning with fever.

"You're having a bout of malaria. I'll bring your temperature down in the shower and then we'll rush to the hospital."

I picked her up, surprised at her lightness. It was like picking up a child. She had always been thin, but as I felt her spine and ribs standing out through her skin under the nightgown, I was aware of her sickly gauntness.

"Don't you worry, Ms. Margarita, you'll get well," I said, more to myself than to her, while the old lady allowed me to carry her like a dying bird.

I put her in the shower and stupidly turned on the tap. There had not been running water in the country for decades, still less in the little fishing village. I left the old lady sitting on the floor of the shower, leaning against the wall and almost unable to hold herself up while I went to the big blue plastic drum where we stored the water. I took a small bucket from the floor, filled it and began to pour water delicately over her head and body, in what I guessed was a vain attempt to bring down her fever one or two degrees.

The poor woman moaned weakly, but was unable to articulate a word or make the slightest movement, letting herself be handled, perhaps aware that her life was no longer in her own hands.

I could not tell how long we spent like that: she collapsed on the floor of the shower, me trying to cool her desperately under the faint light of an oil lamp, hanging from an equally useless wall lamp   there had not been electricity there for a long time either. At last, seeing I was not getting any results with that pathetic bucket of tepid water, I decided to take

11

her, wrapped only in a thin robe, to the hospital in Malabo, a couple of hours away by an infamous road.

I settled her as best I could on the back seat of the white Defender with the blue UNICEF sticker and trod hard on the accelerator, knowing that every minute I wasted on the road might be vital for her survival. I took the road which starts in Luba and runs along the western coast of the island, while the sun sank in the waters of the Gulf of Guinea. In the distance I could make out the gleam of the numerous oil rigs which had sprouted from the sea in recent years like dirty birthday candles.

The road was extremely lonely, and the car's lights made it more and more necessary to follow the sinuous road or dodge some animal determined to nap right in the middle of it. The Land Rover's tires squealed on the curves which were asphalted, and on the ones which were not it slid dangerously. A couple of times I nearly drove off the road, and beyond it there was the ocean. The old woman had stopped moaning a while ago, and that was not a good sign.

Suddenly I saw the beam of a flashlight on one side of the road, directed straight at me, and my headlights revealed a tree trunk across the road. I immediately thought of a robbery or a military checkpoint, or both at once, which was the usual thing.

I stopped the vehicle beside the light which never ceased dazzling me, fully aware that even with the Land Rover I could not have cleared the obstacle.

"Let me through!" I yelled from the window. "I have a very sick lady here!"

The person wielding the flashlight did not reply, but simply directed the light inside the vehicle, where Ms. Margarita was huddled shivering in the back seat.

"Papers," an authoritarian voice said. No identification was offered, but I guessed it was a soldier or a policeman.

"Please!" I insisted. "There's no time for this! Can't you see this woman is dying?"

"Papers!" the voice repeated, this time more urgently.

"For fuck's sake! Here you have my fucking papers!" As I mechanically reached for my backpack on the passenger seat, my heart skipped a beat when I realized it must still be by the house door, where I had left it when I arrived.

I looked toward the light. Conscious that there was a life at stake and it was in my hands, I decided to moderate my tone and try to get out of there as soon as possible.

"I'm sorry, but as I rushed out to go to the hospital I must have left my passport and permits in the house. I don't have them with me."

"Get out of the vehicle," was the harsh reply.

"Let's see..." I muttered, without opening the door of the car yet, trying to resolve the situation somehow, "I know I should carry all my papers with me, and I apologize for my mistake, but I have to get to the hospital in Malabo urgently or else this lady will die. If you want, I can leave my watch as a guarantee that I'll come back, and I'll bring you anything you want. It's a good watch, worth more than a hundred euros." I took it off my wrist and handed it to him through the window.

A hand took it brusquely from my fingers and shone the light on it. I saw the end of a khaki green sleeve. And once more the light shone in my eyes.

"American?" the voice asked, almost as if it were an insult.

"Yes, I work for UNICEF, on a field research study on—"

"I see" he interrupted me. "American... And where did you say you were headed?"

"To the hospital in Malabo! I've already told you!" I replied, unable to restrain my impatience.

The man with the flashlight turned the light onto the back seat, then the hood, the initials on the side of the Land Rover, and back at my eyes.

"All right," he said with what I sensed was mockery. "Get out of the vehicle."

"But…" I said in confusion, "the watch…"

"We'll keep it as evidence," he said without hiding his glee. "Now get out of the car or I'll get you out myself."

"But what are you accusing me of? Why? Don't you see that this lady needs urgent help?"

At that moment the door of the Land Rover was violently flung open and a pair of strong hands dragged me out of my seat by the arm and hair, throwing me onto the ground without any consideration.

I hit the door and felt a thread of warm blood running from my forehead. Lying there on the pavement I could not believe what was happening.

"Listen to me!" I begged. "You don't know what you're doing! I'm a representative of UNICEF, and an American citizen! If you hurt me in any way or hold me illegally, your superiors will cut off your balls! Do you understand what I'm saying?"

I don't know if they understood, but the reply was in the way of hearty laughter on the part of several men I could not see. Unexpectedly, a military boot came out of nowhere and kicked me on the side of the head. I lost consciousness.

2

I do not clearly remember the exact moment when I opened my eyes. I know there was a tiny barred window where a timid ray of sun came in to bump against the dirty wall, as if it too had arrived there without really knowing how, like me, and could not escape.

I was in a cell. A stinking, damp, dark and hot cell. Although it might be more accurate just to describe it as claustrophobic. The tiny space would barely have allowed me to lie on the floor and spread my arms without touching the walls. They were blackened by mold, and on closer inspection hundreds of inscriptions, pleas and perhaps a farewell could be made out on them, written one on top of the other with bare nails. There was also the stench of urine and feces, underlined by that of rancid sweat, which on top of the damp turned every breath of air into a disgusting experience.

What I remember perfectly well is my headache. A terrible pain focused on the spot where that boot had impacted on my skull – the day before? I had no idea how long I had been there. Actually I did not know anything at all. Where I was, or why I was locked there, much less what had become of Ms. Margarita. I remember sitting up, leaning on the grubby walls and shouting at the metallic door, and how my brain seemed to burst at the echo of my own voice inside my head. I remember banging uselessly on the rusty door, kicking it with my bare feet, cursing that piece of iron as if it had been directly responsible for my situation. I remember the pain. I remember the despair… certainly I remember more than I would like to.

At last, I gave in to exhaustion and the evidence that either nobody could hear me, or else nobody cared about whatever I did or failed to do.

From the darkness of my cell I tried to pay attention to every noise from outside, as if this could confirm there was someone out there, and in some way nourish the absurd hope that they would remember me. During those first hours of captivity I kept cheering myself by imagining that at any moment that metallic door would open and a man in a suit would appear, making excuses for the terrible misunderstanding, assuring me with much bowing that I might leave whenever I wished. Unfortunately the illusion retreated every hour I spent between those dirty walls. I had been in Guinea long enough to know how things worked in this unfortunate country. But I did not want to think about it. If I did, I was overcome by such anxiety and fear that my whole body shivered and I felt like vomiting.

I had landed at the recently inaugurated airport terminal in Malabo some weeks before, and the first thing I encountered on the airplane steps was a gust of hot wind. It felt like a welcome to paradise after leaving Boston hours before under an unfriendly overcast sky.

As the days went by I realized that first gust of hot air actually came directly from hell.

In the oppressive cell, where time seemed to stand still a couple of times I glanced unconsciously at my left wrist, where there was only a strip of white skin now   I had time to remember my parents seeing me off at the airport, whispering in my ear as they hugged me to be very careful.

"Don't worry. Someone from UNICEF will be waiting for me in Malabo, and I'll have their support as long as I'm there. I'm just going to do a study on the child population in the rural areas, and I have a safe-conduct from the Guinean government. What could happen to me?"

I nearly burst out laughing when I recalled that conversation.

While I reminisced that instant I noticed that outside things were beginning to stir. From the echoes of distant voices I guessed that on the other side of the tiny window there must be some kind of yard, where some men were shouting imperiously while others whimpered or begged for mercy. I must have been confined in some kind of police station or military precinct, and those, probably like me, were imprisoned men and women. Perhaps, also like me, arbitrarily detained and taken to…

The door opened.

Complaining on its hinges, the heavy iron door seemed to yawn until it bumped against the wall on its right, and a rectangle of diffuse light allowed me to glimpse the profile of a short fat man with what appeared to be a military cap on his head.

Bewildered, I took a step back. I had spent hours wishing for that door to open, but suddenly I was afraid, very much afraid. Like a frightened animal in its lair I did not want to leave that cell, however disgusting it was. I backed up against the far wall, trying to avoid being seen by that gloomy silhouette from which two yellow eyes glared.

"Bring her," he ordered in a hoarse, authoritarian voice.

Then the fat man turned away out of sight, and at once two younger soldiers burst in. Without any consideration they tied my hands behind me with a plastic strip, and each one grabbing one of my arms, they took me out of the cell. Instead of giving me the opportunity to stand, they preferred to drag me along the floor like a dead weight, grazing my elbows, shoulders, feet and neck horribly in the process.

"Please!" I called out. "Let me stand, I'm begging you! You're hurting me!"

The only answer was a sinister laugh from both of them.

When we reached the end of the corridor we passed a new door. Beside it another soldier, sitting in a chair, gave me a look which I wanted to think was compassionate, although it was probably just indifferent. After going through this last door we reached the yard I had imagined. It was surrounded by tall walls topped with barbed wire, and spotlights at the top lit up a scene which from my position, with my head twisted a few inches from the ground, I was unable to grasp; or perhaps my mind simply refused to accept it. Several soldiers stood in something like a circle, while in the middle two bodies seemed to be fighting on the ground, urged on by the standing men. It was not until I heard the terrified scream of a woman that I understood what I was witnessing.

I could not help a cry of horror.

Immediately one of the soldiers who were dragging me noticed what I was staring at, and bringing his face close to mine he leered, revealing a yellow line of dirty teeth.

"You like it, huh, you bitch? Let's go see it more closely…"

My fear turned to absolute panic, and I tried desperately to break away from the iron grasp of the two men, writhing in a vain attempt to stand. Then without thinking twice the soldier who was holding me by the left arm kicked me in the pit of my stomach, making me throw up bitter bile.

We crossed the yard, and the circle of jeering soldiers parted so that I could watch the terrible scene from the front row. Hanging from the arms of my captors, I found myself face to face with the terrified expression of the woman who was being raped. A shiver ran down my spine when I realized she was not a woman but a poor girl no more than fourteen or fifteen years old. Her eyes seemed to be on the point of bursting out of their sockets with terror. She screamed for mercy with her mouth full of blood, and I was not even capable of holding her gaze. I looked away from her suffering as she was forced again and again, naked, thrown on the dirty cement of the yard like a rag doll broken at the hands of monsters who kicked her amid insults and spitting. They had mutilated her, cutting off part of her ears, marking her like a steer, and on her breasts I could see little open cuts around her nipples, with the same shape teeth might leave when biting flesh.

I wanted to scream too, but no sound came out of my throat. I shut my eyelids as hard as I could, trying to escape from that cacophony of inhuman howls of pain and madness. But those horrendous howls drilled through my eardrums into the deepest reaches of my memory, and the wretched girl's eyes, unhinged with pain, were forever etched in fire on my retina, like scars that would never disappear.

Although I was convinced I would be, I was not next in line. I heard the soldiers arguing among them about what to do with me, until one of the two who were carrying me settled the matter. The Captain, he said, was waiting for me in the interrogation room, and they would have time to have their way with me later on. Once again I was dragged along the yard like a dead animal, and someone opened another door. We went into a room, though all I could see of it was the floor sliding before my face, then the two soldiers lifted me in the air and dropped me in a wooden chair which had been nailed to the floor.

I could see my bare toes bleeding from the dragging, and one of my right toenails had disappeared, leaving only a surface of raw flesh. They hurt terribly and I wanted to look away from them, but the kick had left me winded and I could barely raise my head.

Still looking down, I heard the soldiers withdrawing, leaving me alone in the room.

If I had not been overwhelmed by pain, I might have been glad at the thought that at least they were not going to rape me yet.

Several minutes went by, and the door opened again. This time only a single pair of shoes came into the room. I felt them walk in a circle around me fastidiously until they stopped in front of me. A pair of shining black shoes, in contrast to my own bare, dirty, blood-covered feet.

"Miss Malik…" said the rough voice of the man who had ordered me to be taken there. "Sarah Malik."

I raised my eyes as best I could. An unexpected spark of hope burst out in my chest at hearing my name.

"Yes! It's me!" I cried, stumbling over my words. "I work for UNICEF, I have a safe-conduct, I'm American, you have the wrong person, I was only taking an old lady to the hospital, I—"

"Shut up!"

"But—"

"I told you to shut up!" he repeated. He lifted my chin brusquely. "You will only speak when I tell you to… if you don't wish to end up like the girl in the yard."

The man released my face with a gesture of disdain and sat down at a wooden table right in front of me. I could barely manage to keep my head up, but I could make out a soldier of about fifty, with an ugly scar on his left cheek from eye to jaw. He made a show of reading from a document on the table. It was not until ten minutes of unbearable silence had gone by, only punctuated by the screams of the girl in the yard, that he seemed to be satisfied. He looked up, apparently taking in the fact that I was still there.

"What were you doing traveling alone on a restricted road at night?"

"What are you talking about? I was not alone. I was taking the woman who was putting me up to the hospital. It must be there in that report in front of you."

"The report doesn't mention anybody traveling in the vehicle with you," he said as he spread out the sheets of paper on the table.

"But it's true! Ms. Margarita was lying in the back seat shivering with fever!"

"Are you saying I am a liar?" he asked in an icy tone.

"No, of course not… maybe the report is wrong…"

"Then you are saying that my soldiers are liars?"

"I'm not saying anybody's a liar! I'm just telling you the truth!"

"Finding out the truth, Miss Malik, is why we are here. So tell me, why were you traveling alone on a restricted road at night?"

I began to fear for Ms. Margarita's fate. But at that moment it was me who was handcuffed in an interrogation room. There was nothing I could do for her, whatever might have happened to her.

"Are you thinking up the answer you are going to invent?" he murmured, bringing me out of my reverie.

"What? No! I'll tell you everything you want! I have nothing to hide!"

"Are you sure…?"

"Of course! I already told you I'm in your country doing a study for UNICEF. I haven't done anything illegal!"

"Then if you have nothing to hide, why do you travel at night and without papers?"

"For God's sake…I already explained that I was taking a very sick old lady to the hospital in Malabo, and in the rush the backpack where I keep my papers was left behind at the lady's house."

The soldier glanced at the report on the table again. "I see…" he murmured without looking up. "Very convenient."

"What do you mean? It's the truth!"

"The truth? Then explain to me why you were hiding subversive propaganda against the government of Equatorial Guinea in your car."

"Subversive propaganda? What the hell are you talking about?"

With all the calmness in the world the soldier got up from his chair, walked round the table and stood in front of me.

Then with all his strength he slapped me with the back of his huge hand, so hard it felt as though he was going to knock my head off.

I was stunned for a few seconds, unable to accept what was happening.

"Well, Miss Malik," came the voice again, but very distant and mingled with a buzzing. "Now that we have established some rules of respect toward authority, I will ask you the same question again. Who were you taking that propaganda to? Who is your contact?"

"I swear…" I muttered, my lip torn and bleeding, "I don't know what propaganda you're talking about…"

This time the punch came from the other side. It hit me on the jaw and I thought he had broken it when the burst of pain came together with a horrible crunch of bones.

"Lying is not going to help you… and I can spend the whole day like this."

I tried to open my mouth to reply, but the pain was so intense I could only whisper through my teeth.

"I'm… not…"

Then he grabbed my hair, pulled my head back fiercely and put my old personal journal in front of my eyes. The one I had been keeping ever since I arrived in Equatorial Guinea and which I thought I had lost a few weeks back.

"Do you deny this notebook is yours? Let me remind you, it has your name written on the cover."

"Where…?" I muttered, puzzled.

"Where was it? Under the passenger's seat, just where you had hidden it."

Repeated blows to the head have one virtue, they prevent you from thinking clearly. Had it not been for that I would have gone mad that very moment, convinced I was immersed in some Kafkaesque sadomasochistic delirium.

I did not know which to refute first, the fact that I had not hidden anything or that what he had catalogued as subversive propaganda was nothing more than my small journal. Although it might be that denying either of the absurd accusations would only bring on more blows and pain.

"My journal… it's only my journal…"

The man opened a page which had already been marked and read:"The government is a bunch of wretched pathetic thieves who remorselessly steal the bread from the mouths of the Guineans. They're supported by an army and police, real bloodthirsty sons of bitches who don't answer to any law or justice which is not dictated by their own depraved instincts. Only on the day the people rise in arms against the tyrants will the country regain hope."He closed the notebook with a clap and passed it in front of my face."Do you want me to go on reading?"

I did not know what to say. I was terrified. Obviously those words were mine, but trying to defend myself in any way would only mean more pain, the kind of pain I was already feeling, stabbing every one of my nerve ends and keeping me paralyzed. I simply shook my head.

"I see we are beginning to understand each other… Now, tell me who your contact is."

My head was spinning. I could not think. I could not defend myself. I could not confess anything, since there was nothing to confess."My journal…" I heard someone say through my mouth. "It's not propaganda… it's my journal… I haven't done anything…"

"Miss Malik, you disappoint me… I thought you had already understood your situation, but I see I was wrong. You're forcing me to do things you are not going to like…"This sounded terrible coming from that brutish man."Take your clothes off."

"No, please…"

"Then, tell me what I want to hear."

"But, it's the truth… I wasn't going to see anybody… I have nothing to hide…" I had to spit out the blood filling my mouth. "I swear…"

"You're trying my patience, young lady. Stop lying. Someone who has nothing to hide does not try to bribe an officer at a roadside checkpoint."

"Bribe…?" I realized what he meant as I remembered my bare left wrist.

It was madness, but from his macabre logic the supposed evidence pointed to my guilt. My bewilderment grew with every moment that went by.

"Besides," the soldier said, bringing me out of the quagmire I was in, "Malik, your surname, is Arab, is it not?"

"It's… Syrian," I replied, if possible even more perplexed by this question. "My father was born there and migrated to the United States as a boy."

"So, Syria…" The man chewed the name over, trying to remember where he had heard it before. "Ah, yes." His eyes opened wide in a gesture of comprehension. "The same place as the terrorists of ISIS. Isn't that right? And if there's something the whole world knows," he finished, pleased with his own insight, "it's that all Arabs are terrorists."

In that moment I realized I was dealing with an ignorant bastard, which is the worst kind of bastard.

"What do you mean by that…? You're not implying…"– I tried to gather strength from my incredulity – "that just because my father is Syrian I'm a terrorist? But we're not even Muslims!"

"You just admitted that your father is Syrian."

"So what? Steve Jobs's father was Syrian too. Are you going to tell me he was also a terrorist?"

"Steve Jobs? Who's that? An accomplice of yours?" His eyes narrowed in suspicion. "Your contact in the CIA?"

"What?" I had never been so confused in my life. "He… You don't…? Oh, shit." I bit my lips to stop myself from crying and shook my head. "This can't be happening to me. It's impossible…" I took a deep breath and looked up at the soldier. "All this is a mistake. A terrible mistake! You're totally wrong about me."

"I do not think so," he replied, absolutely convinced of his reasoning. "All this evidence points to the fact that you are an ISIS terrorist, sent by the CIA to overthrow the sovereign government of Equatorial Guinea."

I would never in my whole life have thought I would hear something as insane as that. In any other circumstances I would have fallen about with laughter at such a surreal accusation, but I could only articulate three words, and in the same moment I regretted them."You're crazy."

Inevitably a new punch swung across and impacted on my stomach, making me fall off the chair amid spasms of pain. Then the sole of a shoe crushed my neck mercilessly, choking me so that I almost fainted. With my hands tied behind my back there was nothing I could do to free myself. I thought I was going to die there on the grubby floor of a Guinean jail, strangled by the shoe of a soldier who believed that all Arabs were terrorists and that the members of ISIS were agents in the American secret service.

But just when I was beginning to feel I was lost, unexpectedly the pressure on my neck vanished and I was able to breathe again, gagging desperately for air, almost grateful to that monster for that act of mercy.

"I'll…" I managed to say once I had my voice back, "confess anything you want… but I don't know what to say…"

The soldier brought his face close to mine, making me breathe in his disgusting halitosis of rotting flesh."Don't you worry about that, Miss Malik. I have your confession already written out on my table. I only need you to sign it."

3

To call a trial the ten bare minutes they made me stand in a dirty room in front of a man in a toga would be a bad joke. No defense lawyer, no right to speak, and with a confession signed under torture and no idea what was written in it: the chances of being cleared of the insane accusations against me were rather slim.

Entrenched in downhearted stoicism, I heard the judge, in his alternative role as district attorney, read out the handful of accusations and then declare me guilty of the charges of incitement to revolt, espionage and aggression (I must have hurt the soldier's fists during the interrogation), contempt of court, attempted bribery, and as the final flourish, terrorism and conspiracy to assassinate president Theodore Obiang Nguema. In all, twenty years in prison with no chance of bail or appeal.

If I had not been so stunned and still in a state of shock from what had happened the day before, perhaps I would have collapsed right there and begged for mercy. But I felt as though I were on a cloud, looking down at a woman who resembled me and who had practically been condemned to die. True, I was sorry for that woman, but I could not relate to the fact that very possibly I would never go back to my native Boston and would die in an infested Guinean prison, either at the hands of the guards, from malaria or from hunger.

At least – I mused – my hands were not tied and I could rub the countless bruises which marked my body. In the end it seemed my jaw had not been broken, and when I was back in my cell I passed the time trying to clean the dried blood off my feet, knees and face with saliva. I was curiously calm, perhaps because I knew the torture was over, or else because I no longer had to worry about anything. The coin was flipped, and it had come out tails. I wished I had been a believer, so that I could commend my soul to God, but by this point I had too many blasphemies against me for anyone up there to bother lending me a hand. That is, if God himself wasn't getting even with me for ignoring him for so long. In any case, after the brutal beating they threw me back into my stinking cell   which I had come to miss   and left me there until the following morning, when they had entertained me with that minimalist trial.

As evening fell   I knew because of the diffused ray of light that came in through the tiny window   activity grew in the yard once again, and the door to my cell opened complainingly. A couple of soldiers, different from those of the previous day, came into my cell. One of them carried again a plastic bridle to handcuff me, although this time I was quick enough to put my hands in front of me to prevent them from tying them behind my back. They exchanged glances. After weighing up the few chances I had of escaping in any way, they handcuffed me in front and took me out to the yard.

A group of males were waiting there, sitting on the ground. The terrible scene I had witnessed the day before came back to my mind, and I was petrified, suspecting I might be next. I stepped back, but the soldiers pushed me to where the rest were and forced me to sit down as well. I noticed that all of them, like me, had their hands tied with the same white plastic bridles. We were all prisoners. The question was: what were we doing there? A gloomy silence reigned over the twenty-five or thirty males, among whom I was the only woman. There were old men, youngsters who I doubted could be older than fourteen, and a majority of middle-aged men, almost all covered in dried blood. Their eyes were bent on the ground, not daring to look up. But there was a very big and strong one who kept his head high in defiance and looked at the guards surrounding us with contained fury out of his one healthy eye. The other was so swollen I doubt whether he could see out of it.

Ten minutes or so later the answer to what we were doing assembled there arrived in the form of a military transport truck. At the same time the officer who had tortured me the day before appeared at one of the doors. I tried to hide like an ostrich when he passed beside me, but he did not even seem to notice me. "Get them on the truck!" he ordered.

Then the guards kicked us up and pushed us inside the vehicle. As I had arrived last, I was also the last to be taken to the truck. The Goliath with the swollen eye climbed on right after me. The truck was already full, so I could barely fit among the other prisoners and turn around to look back. The soldiers tried to close the gate of the truck, but the human crowd inside it made it impossible.

"Captain, sir," one of the soldiers warned, "it's too full. We can't shut the gate."

The Captain that is, the interrogating bastard approached the back of the truck. After assessing the situation, he addressed the big man who was right between the gate and me. "Let's see," he said. "You! Get off the truck for a moment."

The muscular giant, without moderating his haughtiness, jumped off and landed almost in the face of the torturer who, by his side, looked like a chubby dwarf disguised as an officer.

Without any warning, before anybody could guess what was about to happen, the chubby dwarf drew his pistol and shot the prisoner in the forehead. The giant fell backward with his head burst open, spattering blood and brains all over the dirty yard.

"That's what happens when you eat too much!" he mocked, his pistol still smoking and blood on his face. The rest of the troop laughed as if it was the best joke they had heard in their lives.

I was so horrified I could not even cry out. I had found out that same morning that there is no justice in Equatorial Guinea, but now I had seen with my own eyes that a human life had no value, and that all of us in that truck were in the sadistic hands of murderers who would not hesitate to pull the trigger on a mere whim. Behind me there was a faint murmur of horror, but nobody dared say a word for fear of attracting attention.

At last, with much heaving, they managed to shut the wooden gate, and the truck set off for a destination unknown to me.

It was already night when we passed through a big town, which must have been Malabo, and through the spaces between the planks of the gate I could make out the lights in the houses and some passer-by reflected in their brightness. I wanted to cry out for help, for them to call the American embassy, anything. But terror had me speechless; besides, I guessed I would have gained nothing except another beating, or something worse, when we reached our destination.

After a few minutes we left the town and took a road which I thought might have been the one that led to what had been my home for the past three months.

The truck kept bouncing up and down because of the bad condition of the asphalt, but we were so squashed against each other that it was impossible for anyone to fall on the floor. The limited amount of air coming in through the boards of the truck was hot and dense and stank of fear. We could barely breathe, and I was afraid that if the journey lasted much longer I would end up fainting.

"Does anyone know where we're being taken?" I asked, breaking the silence around me.

"To Black Beach Prison," said someone behind me, to my right. "It's the only one on the island."

"I don't think so, my friend..." another voice said. "Black Beach is chock-a-block. It's been weeks since they've taken anybody there."

While I was trying to imagine how full an African prison had to be for it to be considered chock-a-block, a boy's voice asked fearfully, "So... where are they taking us?"

Nobody answered that question, but I heard someone whisper in the boy's ear, "Don't worry, son... don't worry."

Another heavy silence fell over my partners in misery. Like resigned lambs on their way to the slaughterhouse, heads down, they seemed lost in memories of happier days, surely trying to forget, perhaps saying goodbye somehow to the loved ones they would never see again. Meanwhile, squeezed in among them, I was so overwhelmed by the succession of punishments fate was handing out to me that when I sensed those words suggested we were not heading for a prison at all but for some more ominous destination, it took several minutes before the thought became a conscious one.

The strangest thing is that I was not afraid. I simply gave in to the same despairing apathy the other prisoners in the truck had given themselves up to.

We went on bouncing in silence for more than half an hour when – whether from the exaggerated jolting or the pressure of bodies – suddenly, exactly the way it happens in the most improbable movies, the right panel of the loading gate, the one right in front of me, snapped its hinges with a dry crack and disappeared into the darkness behind.

For a couple of minutes nobody moved, unable to believe it had really happened. Then someone shouted and I was immediately pushed from behind. I fell off the moving truck as the other prisoners leapt into the night and freedom without looking back.

Thanks to the fact that my hands were tied in front of me I was able to protect my face in the fall, and although I fell hard on my shoulder when I hit the road, I was so stunned I barely felt the pain.

I raised my head, trying to sit up, and with horror I saw the brake lights of the truck go on as it stopped a few yards ahead of where I was. I looked around for a place to hide, but the shadows were all around me and I was paralyzed by indecision. I heard the truck doors open, and a moment later the rattling of a machine gun rending the night. I had barely sat up when I had to lie down on the ground as I realized the bullets were whistling over my head.

Then, out of the darkness, a strong hand grabbed my arm and lifted me into the air."Get up!" a male voice whispered in my ear. "If you stay here they'll kill you!"

Without my own will, allowing myself to be guided by that hand that would not let go, I got to my feet and began to run into the shadows.

4

I ran barefoot, unable to see anything in the complete darkness and borne along by someone I could not see either. I felt branches, trunks and leaves tearing my clothes and skin at each step. We were going deeper into the dense vegetation, running like a couple of blindfolded fools, and I prayed I would not hit my head on a tree or step on a sharp root with my bare feet. I was eager to escape, to get away from the road as fast and far as possible. I did not care where I was going or who was dragging me toward the forest. Nothing could be worse than to fall into the hands of the soldiers again.

After what seemed like an eternity, running and stumbling continuously, my guide in the darkness seemed to slacken his pace. Puffing, lungs burning, I stopped to breathe in the air which seemed to be in such short supply in that jungle. But the hand that seized my arm urged me to keep going, pulling me as if I were a doll.

"Wait… wait a moment." I panted. "I need to breathe."

The man's fingers grasped me even harder, and once again he egged me on to keep going.

"Please!" I protested, my heart in my mouth.

Then, still without being able to see him, I felt the man's face close to mine.

"We can't waste a minute," he whispered gravely. "And if you raise your voice again… I'll leave you by yourself."

The mere mention of that possibility made my pulse beat even faster. Despite what he had just said, my unknown savior waited a few moments before setting off once more, with me like an exhausted extension of himself. We went on like this for at least half an hour more until we stopped at last and in silence, surrounded by darkness, I collapsed onto the damp ground.

"It looks like they're not coming after us," the man muttered as he let go of my arm. "Now we can rest."

"Thank you for helping me, thank you… My name is Sarah," I said, fixing my eyes on the blackness.

"I'm Gabriel Biné," he whispered. "And it's too soon to thank me; we're not safe yet."

I looked around and knew that although he might be right, no one would be able to find us that night in the middle of the jungle.

"So… Gabriel, do you have any idea of what we could do now?" I asked the void expectantly.

I heard the rustle of dry leaves before he answered. "I don't know about you, miss, but I'm going to sleep a little," he said, trying to sound untroubled. "We need to get our strength back. Tomorrow's going to be a very long day."

Despite my fear of being found, despite sleeping on the ground beside a stranger in a place which for all I knew might be full of dangerous wild animals, and despite the physical pain which overwhelmed me from the sole of my feet to my battered jaw, I was physically and emotionally worn out and without realizing it, I fell asleep in a matter of seconds.

I would have sworn ten minutes had not yet passed when someone put their hand on my shoulder and I gave a start, opening my eyes in fright and looking all around me in confusion. There beside me, the face of a man who put his finger to his lips, barely a foot away from my own face, reminded me of the insanity of the night before. The stranger was a bit taller than me, and although he was thin, under his torn white shirt, there was a suggestion of strong muscles, accustomed to labour. His clean-shaven head and firm features reminded me oddly of my father's, with a combination of straight lines and angles framing thick lips, together with striking emerald green eyes which radiated calm and security, standing out in his ebony face. He definitely looked like someone one could trust.

"Good morning," I whispered, attempting a smile.

"Good morning," he replied in a soft voice. "How did you sleep?"

"Deeply... except that it seemed too short, my neck hurts and the mosquitoes have feasted on me."

"They took your shoes away," he said, pointing to where they should have been. "How are your feet?"

I sat up and studied the soles of my feet carefully."They seem okay, but I won't know until I start walking."

"Then we must walk."

"All right," I said, and stood up. "Have you any idea where we are?" I looked at the strange forest we were in, which seemed to have a curious symmetry about it.

"It's an abandoned cocoa plantation. There must be a path somewhere nearby."

"How do you know it's abandoned? Have you been here before?"

"No, never," he admitted nonchalantly. "But they're all abandoned."

"Of course, I forgot... Do you know which way to go?"

He looked around with his hands on his waist. "No," he said with a shrug. "What do you think?"

"Me?" I pointed at myself with my thumb, surprised."Are you serious?"

"Well... okay. Let's go that way," he resolved with feigned confidence and indicated one direction at random.

"All right..." I looked up at the sky as I tried to arrange my torn clothes into some decency. "You go in front, I'll follow."

Gabriel started to walk, looking at my bare feet out of the corner of his eye."Miss," he said, stopping for a moment. "I suggest you use your shirt to fashion some sort of shoes."

"With my shirt?"

"Sure. Put a layer of green leaves on the soles of your feet and wrap them in the cloth," he said, describing what he meant by way of gestures. "Last night you were lucky, but you might stab your foot on something and I'd rather not have to carry you."

It was a little embarrassing to be shirtless before a stranger, even though it was the sensible thing to do. And the suggestion that he would carry me if need be was reassuring. Although naturally I hoped it would not be necessary.

Once I had put my improvised shoes together with Gabriel's help, we set off again through the underbrush. I simply followed his footsteps, watching where I put my feet, and in the light of day it seemed a miracle that I had not hurt myself the night before. The thick cocoa bushes were still exactly where the Spanish settlers had planted them decades ago, but in between the orderly lines there now grew endless shrubs and thin saplings which struggled to find a gap under the thick canopy. Meanwhile in front of me Gabriel was forced to clear a way through them with his bare hands, cursing whenever some long sharp thorn scratched him.

I was less worried than I would have expected. I suppose the fortunate circumstances of my escape, getting away by the skin of my teeth from certain death, had made me strangely confident. I seemed to believe that my time had not yet come and that if I had escaped the night before it was not simply so that I could be captured the following morning.

"Why were you arrested?" I asked him, looking at his back.

"For being funny."

"What did you say?"

"Yes, for telling a joke about the president."

"It can't be…"

"I was having a couple of beers with some friends. Although one of them was not such a good friend as I thought he was… and the next day they came to arrest me."

"And they took you to that prison we were in."

"No," he said, still walking. "I wasn't at home, but they gave my father and mother a beating and took my younger brother. They said that if I didn't go to the Malabo precinct, they'd torture him until I turned myself in."

I do not know what shocked me more, what I had just heard or the casual tone he said it in."They kidnapped your brother in order to get you? For telling a joke?"

Gabriel stopped for a moment, turned and looked me up and down."You haven't been in Guinea long, have you?"

"Almost two months," I replied, trying not to sound like a tourist.

"The Guinean police take your family, that's what they do. Where have you been these two months? In a hotel for whites only?"

"Not exactly," I said, a little upset. "I've been working in all the Bubi villages of the island of Bioko, doing research for UNICEF."

"Are you a doctor?" he asked, setting off again.

"Anthropologist."

"Why were you arrested?" he asked, half turning.

"To tell you the truth, I'm not really sure. But yesterday, round about this time, I was facing a dickhead disguised as a judge who sentenced me to twenty years in prison for espionage, terrorism, incitement to revolt and, among other nonsense, conspiracy to kill president Obiang. Can you believe it? The assholes! I thought they were going to rape me or put me in jail for the rest of my life… They locked me up, beat me, forced me to watch them raping a poor girl in the yard… Oh God, what savages!"

Without realizing, my voice had been rising and for the first time I felt the rage making its way up my throat. Gabriel stared at me, tightening his jaw.

"Why are you looking at me like that?" I said, seeing his bloodshot green eyes fixed on me.

He did not reply. He observed me gravely, as if trying to glimpse in my eyes what was stored in my memory. Then he turned and went on walking with his fists clenched.

It must have been mid-morning when we discerned a small village and stopped at the edge of the jungle, looking out attentively.

"Well, miss, now it's dangerous," he said in a low voice. "The fewer people who see you the better. I'll go to the village, to find someone to take us. You stay here, and if you see someone coming, run and hide in the forest. Agreed?"

"Right, but what will you tell people when they ask? You look as if you'd fallen from a plane without a parachute."

"I'll say I had an accident." He pointed his finger at me and added, "But the most important thing is that nobody discovers you."

"I'm dying of thirst, and I'm so hungry I could eat a zebu, horns and all."

"I'll try to get some water and food," he said as he stood up.

"Oh! And if you could find a shirt and something to wear on my feet, please…" I spread my arms to remind him of my castaway appearance. "I can't go on like this, I'd attract even more attention."

"I'll try to bring you something that fits, but remember I've got no money." He raised an eyebrow and added, "Anything else?"

"Some eyeliner would be nice, and if you find some passion red lipstick…"

37

"I'll be back soon," he said as he turned to go. I was not sure whether he had understood I was joking. Stealthily, he left the thicket and disappeared among the huts of reed and palm.

5

Everybody knows that when you are bored, time seems to pass very slowly. What some people may not have had the opportunity to check is that when you add fear to boredom, time not only drags but seems to stop completely.

The sun was almost at its zenith, falling like molten lead between the leaves of the trees, and what with the hunger and thirst I was feeling and the myriad bugs and ants which seemed to have no other place to roam than my bare back and legs, I was going crazy. I was beginning to seriously contemplate the idea of leaving my hiding place and setting off by myself to look for what I needed.

What if they had caught Gabriel? I could be waiting for hours crouching in that forest, and in the end someone would find me and turn me over to the soldiers. Of course, that was why he was taking so long. He had surely been caught and was being tortured at that moment, and when he confessed where I was hiding they would come for me. Surely that was it.

It was decided. I could not spend one more minute in that place, I had to get away from there at once. But where would I go? Well, I would improvise, I was good at that. The important thing was to get out of there.

I stood up and began to walk, stooping, toward the nearest house. Before I reached it I came upon a clothes line stretched between two trees at the back, and without thinking twice I grabbed what looked like a lady's printed dress and a scarf to cover my hair. I also found a discarded pair of flip-flops, which I did not hesitate to change for my leaf-soled shoes.

Once dressed   there would have been room for three of me in that robe   I buried my rags by a tree and approached the house again. Stealthily, with my back to the wall, I began to slide toward the corner. I was just peeking around it when a hand grabbed my shoulder and pulled me back as a male voice behind me said, "Where do you think you're going?"

With my heart pounding, I turned instinctively and punched the man in the face.

"Well now!" he said, rubbing his cheek. "I'm glad to see you too."

"Fuck!" I cried as I recognized Gabriel. "You scared me to death!"

"Sure… excuse me for hitting your hand with my face," he muttered. "Thank goodness you didn't have a knife."

"I'd have left your face just like that of the man who tortured me."

Gabriel's expression changed subtly."Did Captain Anastasio interrogate you?"

"Is that the name of that cut-faced bastard?"

"Anastasio Mbá Nseng," he said, almost spitting out the name. "One of the worst officers in the army. Nobody really knows how many people he's killed. He's a psychopath who hates everybody, but particularly whites, and even more the Bubis. I'm surprised you came out of one of his interrogations alive."

"I have to say it wasn't exactly a party. And though he didn't get to rape me, I was pretty sure he was going to."

Gabriel smiled crookedly."That would have been hard. Rumour has it that he was castrated when he was young."

"You mean…?"

"They say that the Bubi manager of a Spanish plantation cut it off him when he discovered him with his daughter. That's why he hates Bubis and whites so much, but it's just a rumour nobody dares to repeat. To meddle with the ones who rule in Equatorial Guinea shortens life expectancy… By the way, nice dress. Did you go shopping?"

"I saw it in a shop window," I said, smoothing it out, "and I couldn't resist it. But tell me, where were you? I thought you'd been caught."

"I was looking for someone to take us, but I didn't have any luck."

"Great," I said, tired. "Well then, I'll have to find a way of getting to the American embassy on my own."

Gabriel looked at me as if he had just heard an orphan ask for her mom.

"To be honest, I don't think it's a good idea to go anywhere near your embassy."

"Why?" I asked in surprise. "Surely they're the only ones who can help me get out of this country."

Again the same look, this time accompanied by a slow shake of his head.

"Maybe, but most likely the embassy will be watched, since they know you've escaped. You wouldn't be able to go near." He shrugged. "I'm sorry if you had your hopes up, but it's not going to be that easy."

The logic behind Gabriel's words sank me in despair. My improvised plan of escape had just vanished into the jungle, with my spirit in pursuit.

Gabriel must have felt my distress. He hastened to take me by the shoulders. "Don't you worry, miss," he said with exaggerated confidence. "I'm going to help you out of this, trust me."

I lifted my gaze, and Gabriel's hopeful smile infused me with an optimism I would have thought impossible coming from someone I had just met.

"Thank you," I managed to mumble. And I leaned my head on his chest.

In the afternoon an old Lada with its bumpers tied on with ropes and no glass in the windows stopped a dozen yards away from us. A woman of fifty or so got out of the vehicle and went into a house, while a white-haired man at the wheel kept the engine running. After looking around, spurred on by necessity, I came out of the forest and ran toward the car, with Gabriel close behind me.

"Excuse me, sir," I said, leaning on the window. "We've had a car accident. Would you be so kind as to take us to…" I turned to Gabriel. I had no idea where to ask him to take us.

"I'm going through Luba," the man said. "I can drop you off there."

"That would be wonderful! Thank you so much!" I cried, opening the back door. We jumped into the car without a second thought.

The back seat was made of boards, like a bench in a park, but given the circumstances I would have gotten in even if it was a fakir's car.

"Thank you very much," I repeated, and offered him my hand over the back of his seat. "My name is Sarah, Sarah Malik."

He turned round and raised an eyebrow."Pleased to meet you, Miss Malik," he replied as he eyed me.

At that moment the driver's wife as I took her to be – returned. After the initial surprise and accusing her husband of being a Casanova, she had no objections to our presence and was pleased to take us. They introduced themselves as Dolores and Donato Balekia, and offered me some water which I accepted with delight.

"You're American, aren't you?" she asked, while I took a long swig from the bottle.

"Yes, ma'am."

"Whereabouts?"

"Boston, in the north-east."

"Our son Nuno lives in Philadelphia."

"How wonderful! Isn't it?"

"Oh, yes." She nodded emphatically. "If it wasn't for the money he sends us every month…well, you can see the state of the car."

There followed several minutes of silence, which the woman broke by laughing under her breath.

"Funny you should have addressed me as ma'am," she commented. "A white person would never have called me that in colonial times."

"What did they call you?" I asked candidly, and regretted my question at once.

"Oh… girl, nigger or stupid black. Depending on the kind of day the mistress of the house was having, where I worked as a servant."

"Oh…I'm sorry."

"Don't be, my dear. That was a long, long time ago. In fact, sometimes I miss it, you know?"

"Seriously?"

"Not the ill-treatment, of course," she said with a grimace. "Some Spaniards used us almost as slaves. They saw us as silly children and sometimes treated us worse than their dogs. Despite all that, sometimes I think we lived better."

"Now we live in fear," the husband intervened languidly, eyeing me in the mirror. "But on another note, there was no accident, was there?"

I turned a questioning look toward Gabriel, but he just shrugged.

"The truth is," I muttered, "that we… didn't have any accident."

"Problems with the military?" he asked nonchalantly.

"How do you know?" I asked in surprise.

The couple laughed in unison. "There are two types of people in Guinea," Donato explained. "The ones who have problems with the government and the military—"

"And the ones who're going to have them," Dolores finished.

"I think I'm already in the first group," I said.

"In that case," she said, "I have something here which might suit you."

The woman put her hand in her bag and took out a small can, flat and round.

When I understood what it was, I could not help a laugh and glanced skeptically at Gabriel, as if it was a joke.

Minutes later I was buried in the backseat of the rattling vehicle, wrapped in my multicolored dress, my hair hidden under a scarf in the same style, and hands, feet and face covered in shoe polish.

I had no doubt that if the police stopped us it would not take them a moment to see it was a ridiculous disguise. But they had convinced me that from a distance, covered with the scarf, I could go unnoticed and not give myself away as a westerner: something exceptional in Equatorial Guinea and consequently very noticeable. Drawing attention to myself was the last thing I wanted at that moment.

Beside me, scrutinizing the road over the driver's shoulder, Gabriel appeared calmer than he must have been. I was fully aware of how much those people were risking for me without knowing me at all, because driving me around in disguise on their back seat would mean the most terrible consequences for them if we were found out.

"I don't know how to thank you for all this," I whispered, sincerely. "You're the best people I've—"

"Easy, girl," Dolores said, half-turning. "You don't have to thank us for anything. We're just doing what we have to do."

"But you don't even know who I am, and you're—"

"My dear," Donato said then, looking at me through the rear view mirror, "it doesn't matter who you are or aren't. If we can help you save your life, we're not going to stop just because we don't know you. Can't you see that?"

"Anyway, I'll always be in your debt," I insisted. "I have no idea when or how, but I'll compensate you for what you're doing."

"Here we don't do things expecting a reward," Gabriel muttered with a hint of anger. "We don't expect anything in return; this isn't a commercial deal. It's done because it must be done, and that's it. It's enough for this couple and for me to know we're doing the right thing."

"I apologize, then. I didn't mean to offend anybody. I just wanted you to know how grateful I am."

"You're welcome, love," the husband replied with a trace of puzzlement, looking at me once again through the cracked rear view mirror which was tied to the roof of the car with wire.

I was trying to relax, gazing at the walls of thick vegetation flanking the dirt track we were following and which now and then closed above us like a green tunnel, alive and shadowy.

Every once in a while we passed by some nipa hut, always with the face of a child peeping out, curious to know who was driving along the forgotten road, and I had to hold back the impulse to wave out of the window at those who watched us every time this happened, as if we were royalty in a carriage.

"Not many cars pass this way, do they?" I said.

"Only soldiers and politicians when they come to steal," Donato clarified. "And as this isn't a military vehicle, they must think we're important people. In this part of the island hardly anyone can afford their own car."

"Now that you mention it, what part of the island would this be? I don't remember having ever been this way before."

"We're close to the old volcano, and if we follow this road we'll get to Luba in not much longer than an hour."

"And when we're there…" I asked raising an eyebrow, "what will we do?"

"Don't worry," he said half-turning. "In Luba you'll be safe. We have friends there."

In spite of Donato's soothing tone, my head was buzzing with questions. I have never been one to let myself be led by the hand like a good girl.

"Ah… I don't want to seem distrustful, but then what? With my skin color it won't take them long to find me, no matter how well I hide."

Gabriel watched me for a few seconds, as if only then noticing my paleness.

"We'll think of something."

"Yes, but—"

"Stop fretting about that," he interrupted me, and turning again to face ahead he added, "Everything's going to be all right. If we don't come across any patrols, we'll reach Luba without any trouble."

6

With twilight already giving way to night, we passed the first huts on the outskirts of Luba. The small village, once a port for loading cocoa beans and a harbor for fishing boats, was today no more than a broken memory of orphaned buildings and half sunken ships rotting behind the beach.

Although the only light in the street was that of our own headlights, I could make out a series of red X's painted on the façades of some houses.

"What do those marks on the walls mean?" I asked.

"They always make them when the president's going to go through a village," Donato explained.

"I don't understand…"

"Well, a civil servant comes and marks the houses that are old or dirty."

"To fix them?"

Dolores turned round in her seat and looked at me indulgently."No, my dear. They mark them to know which ones to pull down."

"But… aren't there people living in them?"

"Of course, darling," the woman agreed stoically. "Of course."

A couple of blocks further on, I tried to say something to banish the uneasiness which was oppressing me."Well, it looks like we've arrived without any trouble."

As if it were an agreed signal, at that precise moment a car behind us blinked its lights and honked several times for us to stop.

Convinced we had been discovered, I grabbed the upholstery of the front seat in terror. If I had been able to, I would have fled that same moment. But my panic only managed to paralyze me and I remained there, perspiring through the shoe polish in my absurd disguise, in the back seat of a car belonging to some strangers on whom my life depended.

Donato brought the car slowly to a halt.

The tension was unbearable. If it was the army, the police or the presidential guard, we were lost. All four of us.

The other vehicle, a veteran olive green Land Rover, caught up with us and stopped on our left. The driver stretched out to roll down the window closest to our side, looked inside the car and said, "Good evening. Do you know anywhere near here where I can buy some diesel?"

I still had not gotten over the fright when we stopped in front of a humble hut on the other side of the village, beyond the Mission of the Franciscan nuns. They could boast of having the only building in the village with electricity and running water.

When night falls, Luba becomes a ghost city. Despite being the second biggest settlement on the island of Bioko, it is utterly abandoned to its fate by a government that does not provide a single basic service there. I had visited the place a few weeks before. Apart from talking to the locals, eating a splendid fish meal at Jemaro's diner   a Lebanese cook who was reluctant to explain what the hell he was doing there   or having some huge Cameroonian "33" beers at a shop run by some Chinese   the only ones with a butane refrigerator in the whole village   there was very little to do there.

"We're here," Donato said, breaking the silence.

"Who lives here?" I asked, noticing how humble the structure was.

"A sister of mine with her daughter."

"Do they know we're coming?"

48

"Don't worry," he replied, guessing my uneasiness. "You'll be well received."

Luckily night had fallen, and the shadows helped me get out of the car without fear of being recognized by anyone, although there was really no one in the vicinity of the isolated house who might see us. The couple had gone in a moment before me, so that when I walked in they were all waiting for me.

In the light of an oil lamp on top of a small table, the tiny dwelling seemed smaller still with four adults standing there, occupying almost all the space of the one minuscule room.

Then the woman who was presumably Donato's sister stepped forward and took my hand in hers. "Welcome to my humble home."

I took her bony hand in mine and could clearly see the wrinkles in her face, her toothless smile and the aura of kindness exuding from her. The dirty dress she wore, full of patches, did not take away a shred of her dignity. A certain resemblance to the missing Miss Margaret awakened in me an inevitable wave of affection for her.

"Thank you, ma'am. You don't know how grateful I am to you for letting me into your house."

"Oh, girl, you have nothing to thank me for," she said with a wave of her hand. "I love visitors. And don't call me ma'am, you make me feel older. Best simply call me Maria."

"Well, thank you very much, Maria," I said, shaking her hand. "My name is Sarah. It's a pleasure to meet you."

"And this is Paula," she said, pointing to a dark bundle huddled over a mat in a corner, which I had not noticed at all. "But forgive her for not getting up. She's sick."

"What's the matter with her?" I could not help asking as I went across to her.

"She has AIDS," she replied with a subdued sadness.

"Oh," was all I could think of saying. "I'm so sorry."

"She's asleep now," she said as she bent over her and caressed her forehead with infinite tenderness. "She's better this way... so it doesn't hurt."

That woman, in that extremely humble house, with a daughter suffering from AIDS, was offering me her home without reservations. And in exchange I was putting her in danger.

I had no choice, but that did not make me feel less selfish.

"Are you unwell? Your expression has changed."

I raised my eyes. It was Gabriel, watching me intently.

"No... well, yes. The truth is I don't feel I have a right to be here. I can only bring these people a whole lot of trouble."

"You're back with that?"

"It's what I think."

"Well, you can forget about it. You're going to stay here until we find a way to leave the island."

"And you?"

"I have to find my family and, if I can, help them go into hiding."

"Why?"

"I already told you, Sarah. In Equatorial Guinea when they want to catch someone, in this case me, they kidnap family and friends of the person in question and lock them up until the one they're looking for gives himself up voluntarily. It's my duty to warn them and help them hide."

"I see, but... does that mean I'm going to stay here all alone?"

"Mrs. Maria will take care of you as if you were her own daughter."

Maria, who was looking at me with a puzzled expression, took my hands in hers. "Don't worry, girl, don't worry..."

Half an hour later Gabriel, Dolores and Donato left the house, got into the rackety Lada and faded away into the darkness of the Luba streets.

And I was alone.

7

"Come on, my dear, come inside," a voice said behind me.

I did as I was told. The sight of what was going to be my refuge for who knew how long could not have been more desolate.

Mrs. Maria motioned me into the house, but what with the yellow gloom of the oil lamp, the primitive table it stood on as the sole piece of furniture and the dark bundle on the floor which had turned out to be a severely ill woman, my heart sank to my feet. For a second I even thought about turning, running away and trying to solve my problems on my own.

During the weeks I had been in Guinea I had visited a number of villages lost in the jungle and had spent the night in huts even humbler than this one. I was now realizing that I had always done so – unconsciously – in my role as *the great white doctor*, watching everything as an object to be studied. I had seen this very scene before and had taken it in as another typical feature of the country, like the palm trees or the mosquitoes. But at that moment, for the first time, standing on that threshold, I thought I could glimpse the true meaning of the word *poverty* inside that house.

"Don't worry, girl, you'll only be here a few days."

Donato's sister seemed to have read my mind such must have been my look of distaste. Had it not been for the shoe polish which still covered my face, she would have seen me blush with shame.

"Oh, no, Mrs. Maria… forgive me. I'm infinitely grateful for your help. I'm delighted to be here…" I said as I took a couple of steps toward her.

"Come on, girl, you needn't lie to an old woman. I too look at my house and feel sad." She passed her hand over the top of the old table, her gaze distant. "We used to live in a pretty house in the center of Luba. It even had a small garden full of orchids at the back. That house was the legacy of my late husband and of the love we shared, and now... this table is the last thing I have of his."

I looked again at that worn out piece of furniture, and no longer saw it as a bunch of badly put together moth-eaten pieces of wood but as a living entity, an anchor for her memory.

"How come you don't live in that house anymore?"

"They took it away from me."

"The bank?"

"No." She shook her head bitterly. "We built that house with our own hands. We didn't owe anybody."

"So...?"

"Well, it was like what happens with some beautiful women. The day comes when their beauty becomes their doom."

"I don't understand."

"That means you haven't been in Guinea for very long..." she murmured to herself. "The retinue of the president's wife happened to pass by my house one day, the "first lady" liked it, and decided to have it for herself."

"What!?" I asked, incredulous. "Just like that?"

"Just like that. One day her bodyguards arrived and kicked me and my sick daughter out of the house, without even letting us change our clothes or turn off the stove where I was cooking dinner."

"I can't believe it... And didn't they give you anything in exchange? Compensate you?"

"Oh yes, a beating at the door when I tried to get back in."

"But... I don't understand..." I said in confusion. "I thought Obiang was one of the richest men in Africa. Why

53

would his wife want to take away your home if she could buy the Palace of Versailles with all the money she has?"

"How do you think they've become so rich, girl?"

"Yes, but—"

"They take everything," she interrupted me with the bitterness of years showing at the corners of her tired eyes. "Everything."

The old lady leaned back on the table, making a visible effort to recover her calm. She closed her eyes for a moment, and when she opened them again she was once again her kind self."Forgive this crazy old woman. You're fleeing from the military, and here I am telling you all this old woman's nonsense. Are you hungry?"

"I could eat a crocodile!"

"Well now… I've run out of crocodile, but I can make you a fish soup."

"Thank you, anything would be fine. I haven't eaten in days."

"Ah, then I'd better make you a *grombif* with peanuts."

"*Grombif?*"

"It's a forest animal. A trapper friend of mine brought me one a few days ago. I believe there's still some left," she said as she bent over and rummaged among some battered tin pans on the floor.

"Is it some kind of deer?"

"More like a kind of rat."

"Oh, gee…" I could not help myself. "I hope it's tasty, at least."

"Yes, very. As soon as I've taken the worms out I'll give you some."

At this point I really I must have moaned in disgust, because the old lady lost no time in turning round and smiling impishly.

"Relax, it's a joke," she said.

After reheating the food in a rudimentary wood stove, we sat on the floor, on a mat, and I began to gulp down the food with an eagerness I do not think I had ever felt in my life.

"Take it easy. If you eat so fast it'll make you sick."

"But I'm so hungry," I muttered with my mouth full.

"I can imagine. Unfortunately," she said, looking toward her daughter, "we're used to being hungry."

"Oh my God… and I'm eating the little you have!" I exclaimed in horror pushing the plate away.

"Don't worry, Sarah. My stomach's already used to it, and meat doesn't sit well with Paula."

It sounded to me like a cheap excuse to stop me feeling guilty, but in fact I was so hungry I pretended to believe her. That evening I discovered the point at which necessity will dissolve the most upright principles, as if they were sugar cubes.

"How old is she?" I asked looking at her daughter.

"She's just turned twenty-three… and God only knows whether she'll reach twenty-four."

"Is she taking any medication?

"Is there any medication for what she has?" Maria asked in surprise.

"There are some medicines that might delay or even stop the advance of the illness."

"Well, it's the first I've heard of it. But anyway, I wouldn't be able to buy them… I fear that for my darling it's too late."

I couldn't find the appropriate words, if they existed at all, for a moment like this. What could I say? Anything would have sounded clichéd or stupid. Like nearly all westerners who watch the news about other people's misfortunes with a pretence of interest, I was only thinking of filling my stomach, while right in front of me was one woman wracked with sickness, and another with sorrow.

"I'm sorry…" was all I could murmur.

Mrs. Maria simply shrugged.

I quickly finished the *grombif* and a couple of bananas as well, and with my appetite sated I lay down on the mat.

"Did you like it?"

"It was delicious, thank you," I assured her sincerely. "Were you by any chance the chef in a restaurant?"

A smile of forgotten pride appeared at the corner of her mouth. "No, girl. I was a teacher, like my late husband."

"You don't say! And you don't work as such any more?"

Mrs. Maria looked at me skeptically. "How long did you say you've been in Guinea?"

"Almost two months."

"And how many schools have you seen, not counting the ones at the missions?"

"Well… not many."

"There's your answer."

"Are you saying that there are hardly any schools in Guinea?"

"There used to be, darling. There used to be."

"So… what happened to them? Were they closed?"

"They didn't even bother to do that. The government simply abandoned them and stopped paying the teachers."

"To keep the money?"

"That, and to have a docile, uneducated population, easy to manipulate."

"I don't know why but that doesn't surprise me…"

"I guess all dictatorships work in the same sort of way," said the old woman as she rose and took away my plastic plate.

"In fact," I said as I gazed at the empty place my dinner had occupied, "I'd say that attitude isn't limited to dictatorships."

8

I could not say exactly when I fell asleep, but it was certainly quickly. Despite the discomfort of sleeping on a thin mat on that irregular floor of compacted red dirt, knowing I was safe within those four walls allowed me to rest for the first time and wake up the following day with something you could almost have called optimism.

"Good morning," I mumbled, my mouth dry, when I half-opened my eyes and saw Mrs. Maria squatting in front of the clay stove.

"Good morning, dear," she replied, turning to me with a smile. "How did you sleep?"

"I can't really remember, which means I slept well, I guess."

"I'm glad, I'm glad. Look," she said, pointing to the other end of the room. "Let me introduce you to Paula."

I turned my head, and in a corner, like some absurdly elongated ebony figurine, a young woman as tall as I am but terribly skinny was staring at me in silence out of yellow eyes which at another time must have been full of life.

"Hello, Paula. I'm Sarah."

She did not answer, but there was no need. In those pupils you could read the clear story of suffering and the certainty that social conventions were futile when one is on the brink of death. She kept her eyes on me for only a few seconds more. Then, dragging her feet, barely covered by a ragged t-shirt, she opened the door and went out of the house.

"Excuse her," her mother said. "She doesn't feel very well."

"There's nothing to excuse, but where's she going?"

"To the toilet. Well, it's really nothing but a hole in the ground, but it's what we have. It's behind the house, near the banana tree."

"Good to know… but what I need first is some water to wash. I stink of shoe polish."

"Of course, here's a washing bowl. But remember, if you need to go out, even for a moment, you'll have to paint yourself again and try not to let anybody see you."

"Yes, I know. It's horrible to have to hide like this," I said, going to the basin and trying to clean up a little.

"Better not think about it. For the moment you must only think about getting your strength back. And by the way, you haven't told me the reason for your arrest."

"Well, to be honest, I don't know either." The paste was hard to clean off, and I rubbed hard as I talked. "They stopped me at a road checkpoint not far from here, then took me to some kind of police station with soldiers and after they'd tortured me they made me sign a fake confession so as to sentence me. It was like a grotesque nightmare I couldn't escape from."

Mrs. Maria shook her head as she listened to my story. "What a terrible impression you must be getting of Guinea."

"On the contrary," I said, looking up. "Here I've found the most wonderful people I've ever met in my life. The fact that you're saddled with a government of ruthless bastards isn't your fault."

"You tell me whose fault it is, then."

"You didn't choose Obiang. He just carried out a military coup and eliminated anybody who might oppose him."

"True. But he and his clique have been in power for more than thirty years, and if we don't shake him off our backs he'll go on for another thirty. If we Guineans don't do anything about it, nobody will do it for us."

"It's not easy to get rid of tyrants. You need international pressure and an organized opposition within the country itself. From what little I know, Obiang has the support of all the foreign powers, and his opponents end up fattening the local crocodiles."

The old woman gave a bitter grimace. "I see at least you have some idea of the state Guinea's in."

"I've spent most of the time I've been here working in rural areas, but not under a stone. In fact I think my personal journal, where I recorded what I was seeing and my opinions about Obiang's *democraship*, was one of the reasons why I'm in this situation."

"*Democraship*..." she repeated with a slight smile. "I like the word."

"I didn't know any word to describe a dictatorship disguised as a democracy, so I decided to make one up. I think I'll register it as soon as I go back to..."

Unexpectedly, as I was on the point of mentioning my hometown, my memories took me down the lanes of the Boston Public Garden, breathing in the cool air of a fall afternoon, the mellow cafés and the smell of wet cobblestones after the rain as I walked toward my parents' house on a Sunday afternoon.

A wave of nostalgia ran from my battered feet to the corners of my eyes, so that the tears I had not known were there began to fall. I hastened to wipe them off with the back of my hand, but Mrs. Maria had already noticed.

"You miss your home, little one, don't you?"

"Until a second ago I thought I didn't. But... it seems..."

Unable to hold back, I suddenly wept as I had not in many years. The old woman squatted beside me, offering me comfort. I hugged her as though she was my own mom and broke down in her lap, shedding on her skirt all the tears of fear, pain and despair which had built up during the worst days of my life.

Hours later, with my unhappiness diluted like salty water, I helped her prepare lunch. Mrs. Maria had gathered together all her meager resources – or so I suspected – and gone to the fishermen's market. To my amazement, she had returned with three enormous lobsters, still alive, in a plastic bag.

"But…" My jaw dropped when I saw them. "How…?"

"You have to treat guests with love," she replied to my stammering question. "And especially girls who feel a long way from home."

I glanced at Paula for a moment. She was back in her corner, barely covered by rags, oblivious to everything, and once again I felt terribly guilty."Mrs. Maria, I'm infinitely grateful for this, but please don't do it again. I can't let you spend so much money to please an American cry-baby."

"Bah!" she replied, waving this aside. "Lobsters are very common here, and as we used to say, they were going for a song."

After boiling the lobsters with bay leaves and some other spices I could not identify, the three of us sat down on the floor, each with our plastic plate, ready to enjoy the scrumptious lunch. We did not have enough cutlery, so we made do without them and attacked the lobsters in the traditional way. Even Paula, forever in limbo, seemed to come back to the house to enjoy the exquisite delicacy, and for those few moments, perhaps for the first time in many years, whispering and laughter lit up faces and eyes. We felt surprisingly happy to be there. To have someone to look after us, or to look after. Happy to be alive.

Satisfied with laughter and seafood, the three of us relaxed amid looks of complicity and unfinished jokes, lying down on the mats we had put out for the food.

"Mrs. Maria?"

"What is it, darling?"

"You wouldn't happen to have a mirror, would you?"

The old woman looked at me in surprise. "What do you want a mirror for?"

"To have a look at my face. Since I was beaten in the interrogation room I haven't checked it out, and my jaw and temple are still sore."

"Ah… no, I don't think we have a mirror."

Judging by the expression on her face I thought she was lying, although I did not understand why.

"It doesn't need to be big, a small one will do."

"I don't know—"

"Come on, Mrs. Maria. I want to see my face. I refuse to accept there isn't a mirror in a house with two women living in it."

"All right, then." She got to her feet.

She rummaged in a small wooden box where she kept her personal toiletries and brought out what must have been a corner of a big mirror.

"This is all I have," she said handing it over, "but be careful you don't cut yourself on the edges."

"Don't worry," I said. And straight away I went to the brightest part of the house and held the piece of mirror up to my face.

"Oh my God, I'm a complete mess," I muttered after a few seconds, the time it took me to identify that swollen, bruised face as mine.

Mrs. Maria came up behind me and put her arm around my waist.

"You were tortured," she said in an attempt to comfort me in the face of evidence. "You can be thankful there's nothing broken, and those ugly bruises will disappear in a week or two. You've been lucky, very lucky."

She was right. I could consider myself lucky to have survived the experience with no more than a beating. But the face the mirror showed me, with its left temple grotesquely deformed by the swelling, the jaw equally bruised, small cuts in forehead and cheeks, and the remains of shoe polish which made me even more unrecognizable, drove me once more into a state of despair.

That despair turned into panic when a second later someone banged on the door and an unknown male voice cried loudly, "*Potoo! Potoo!*"

9

I grabbed Mrs. Maria's arm in a reflex move, muffling a cry of terror which nearly came out through my teeth. I looked from side to side trying to find somewhere to hide, but that house with its bare walls and the single table offered no shelter. In the end I turned to my host. Apparently calm, she was looking at me with a finger on her lips.

"Yes?" she asked at last, raising her voice, not moving from her place.

"Can you lend me your machete, Mrs. Maria? I have to do a bit of clearing in front of the house; the weeds are too tall."

"Of course, Antonio. But it's high time you got your own, you've been using mine for over a year," she said, standing up and gesturing me to hide behind the door.

"You're right, ma'am. In exchange I'll do some cutting in front of your house too. Is that all right?"

"That's fine." She took the dented machete she kept leaning against the wall, opened the door halfway and handed it to the man I couldn't see. "You needn't bring it back; I'll call by to pick it up later."

"Many thanks," the man said. "How's Paula?"

"Tired, poor thing."

"Huh… well, if you need anything, you know you just have to ask me or my wife for it."

"Thank you, Antonio. See you later." She waved him goodbye and closed the door. The house recovered its comfortable semi-darkness.

"He's my neighbor," she said in a confidential voice. "Good people."

"He scared the life out of me," I said trying to regain my normal heartbeat. "By the way, what does *potoo* mean?"

"It's a Bubi greeting. If someone greets you saying *mbolo* you'll know they're Fang. And if they say *potoo*, they're Bubi. Although in your case, being white, they'll always say *hola*, or *hello* if they know you're a *gringa*."

"You're both Bubi, aren't you?"

"Yes, we are, dear. With pride but also with sorrow."

"Sorrow?"

"Yes, of course, you know."

"No, I don't," I admitted.

The old woman looked me over, assessing me, genuinely surprised at my ignorance."Do you mean to tell me you don't know anything about the abuse of the Bubis by the government?"

My silence was enough to make her snort softly and shake her head.

"Well now, girl," she said, sitting back on the floor and inviting me to do the same. "In Guinea there are several ethnic groups, but the majority are Fang and Bubi." Judging by her studied gestures, Mrs. Maria seemed to be remembering her days as a teacher. "The Fang people come from the continent; it's thought they originated in Sudan, but they crossed Zaire and Gabon, fleeing from the Muslims, and arrived at the west coast of Africa centuries ago, and at the island of Bioko only decades ago. The Bubis, though, have lived on this island for more than two thousand years and here we're still a majority. The problem is that the population of continental Guinea, like the government, belongs to the Fang ethnic group. Fearing that the island with the capital and the oil rigs might try to break away from the continental region, with which it has little in common, Obiang Nguema has put in place an even more repressive regime of terror and abuse against the Bubis than against the rest of the Fang population, which is saying a lot. He has institutionalized a rivalry between the two groups that is unfortunately setting in."

"Actually," I said in my own defense, "I had heard something about this rivalry. But I had no idea it was the government that encouraged it."

Mrs. Maria made a face."Before, during the Spanish time," she said, looking up at the ceiling as if searching for memories among the dry palm leaves, "the Bubis were a little better regarded than the Fangs. Sometimes they were made foremen in the plantations, and some were even in charge of Fangs. But with independence they took power, and I believe some are getting their own back—"

"Mrs. Maria," I interrupted her, "to be honest, I don't know much about your history or the rivalries between the ethnic groups, but I do know about the use and abuse of *us* and *them*, and those distinctions have never brought about any good. Ever."

The old woman nodded emphatically."There I totally agree with you. But now the one using that argument to blame us for all the evil that's happening in Guinea, and to deflect attention, is the government. For us Africans, ethnicity or clan is a statement of cultural identity in the face of the borders arbitrarily imposed by the European settlers. The downside is that there's always someone trying to take advantage of it, and turning it into an excuse to bring about conflicts which only end up filling the graveyards."

"And do you believe that's going to happen in Equatorial Guinea?"

"I hope not, my dear," she replied, raising both eyebrows in a mixture of hope and stoicism. "I hope not."

There was no point deciding who would wash the dishes. The fact that one had to go outside to use the wash basin and get water from the rusty oil drum with the Exxon Mobil logo which was used as a water tank prevented me from helping Mrs. Maria; and Paula, poor Paula, had more than enough with her constant fever and the pain which sometimes drove her to clench her fists until her hands bled from digging her nails into them. It was hard to imagine a more desperate situation than knowing you are dying, without hope of any cure or of getting hold of painkillers to lessen the suffering. I felt sorry for her, and as we stayed alone inside the small hut and I could count the ribs on her body and every section of her spine, I saw in her the absolute abandonment which most African people are doomed to. She was only one of the tens of thousands of people who suffer in a way we cannot even imagine: helpless, fragile, innocent, horribly aware that her life was coming to an end and that she would never dance again, make love, or have children to take care of and give all her love to. But Paula was right in front of me at that moment, not behind some aseptic television screen. She was as real as her mask of pain, her sweat, or the intangible halo of death that had already settled around her, which although not visible was nonetheless there.

"Sarah…" she mumbled to my surprise, in a halting voice.

"Tell me, Paula," I said getting closer to her.

"Is it true than in America people can be cured of AIDS?"

The question took me so much by surprise, and her voice was so unexpectedly hopeful, that I had to take a few moments to choose my words carefully."As I told your mother, there really isn't a cure yet… but sometimes they can delay the effects."

"And do you think I could go to your country… so that they could give me that medicine?"

This was a terrible conversation. I did not want to lie to someone who was dying, but neither could I choke off that breath of hope which seemed to shine in the depths of her jet black eyes.

"I don't know," I said at last. "But if I go back to the States, I swear I'll do the impossible so you can get the treatment, even if I have to pay for it myself."

A tear ran down the dark skin of that young face, worn out by sickness."Thank you," she murmured lowering her head.

I still did not know what to say, so I held her shriveled body between my bruised arms and we merged into a disconsolate embrace which shared fear, pain and a distant hope.

I knew then that I would never be able to forget that embrace, and that somehow I was sealing a pact, not only with Paula but with a whole continent. In a way I was putting my arms around Africa and letting her into my heart forever.

10

In the few days after landing in Guinea I had noticed that sunsets in this part of the world are minimal, brief as nowhere else. Perhaps because there is no room for romanticism and the sun decides to plummet on to the horizon every day at seven p.m., punctual in a way nothing else in Africa is.

Inside the hut, the difference between day and night could be guessed at by the streaks of light filtering through the framework of canes which made up the walls. So when those vanished, I knew the day had come to an end. OI smeared shoe polish on my face, feet and hands; borrowed some of Paula's clothes she was huddled in her corner once again – and, taking advantage of the shadows that shrouded the village, went outside, oil lamp in hand, to the hole in the ground at the back by the banana tree.

On my return, I heard a vehicle approaching. Its headlights swept the street and stopped in front of the house where I had been shut up for two days. Gabriel had returned at last, and I was surprised by how exaggeratedly happy that made me feel. I had never suspected that I could look forward to the return of a stranger so eagerly.

I was going round the house with a smile on my face when the blood froze in my veins as I heard several male voices speaking among themselves. I recognized one of them in particular. A voice which was inseparably linked in my brain with pain and fear.

In terror, I flattened myself against the wall, put out the oil lamp and slipped round to the back of the house without making any noise.

"Open the door!" the voice shouted.

"Who is it?" I heard Mrs. Maria ask in a frightened voice.

The reply came in the form of a crash of splitting wood. They had kicked down the door of the house.

"Who are you?" the old woman asked again, trying to give some dignity to the question so as not to betray her fear.

The unmistakable sound of a slap made my hair stand on end, and I imagined gentle Maria thrown onto the floor, bleeding, and poor Paula shrinking in her corner, scared to death.

"I do the questioning here. Where's the white woman?"
"I don't know."

Another dull blow, and the gasp of the air being sucked from somebody's lungs.

"I'll ask you for the last time. Where's the American? We know she was here after she fled from justice. You know where she went."

The old woman had a hard time catching her breath and answering."I… don't…"

Someone must have seen me go into the house and had not hesitated to warn the military. Most probably their attention had been caught by the clothes I was wearing or my evasive attitude. It seemed that the warning I had been given repeatedly, ever since arriving in Guinea, about the ubiquity of the secret police and their informers was not so exaggerated after all.

"All right," the despicable captain said. "We'll take you to the Malabo police station. I'm sure you'll feel like talking there."

"But… my daughter… I have to take care of her…"

"Your daughter's dead already," he said mockingly. "Just look at her."

"But I swear I don't know where that woman is," Mrs. Maria said pleadingly. "Yes, she was here, but she left right away and didn't say where she was going."

"I don't believe you. But we're going to do something better than taking you away," he said with a sinister laugh. "You'll stay here in your house, we'll be watching you closely, and you won't be able to go out, even to the toilet, until she comes back."

"And... if she doesn't?"

"In that case," I heard him reply, almost laughing, "we'll make bets on who lasts longer without food or water... you or your daughter."

I had no idea where I was going, but once again I was running barefoot in the middle of the night. Panic spurred me downhill, and I ran with the useless oil lamp still clutched in my hand along a narrow path on the edge of the village. A warm yellowish light filtered from some houses, and more than once I was tempted to knock on one of those doors asking for help, but I could not risk it. It was obvious that some neighbor had reported Mrs. Maria; I was not safe in this village, still less with Captain Anastasio roaming about. I continued my heedless race, tripping now and then, until suddenly I felt the water up to my ankles. I had reached the beach.

I dropped on my back on the sand, panting, and looked at the starry equatorial sky. It was the first time in days that I had been like this, alone in the open air under the studded African sky. Gradually my breathing returned to normal. Even then I decided to stay there, resting, contemplating the way the diffuse Milky Way seemed to be born from the womb of the Atlantic Ocean and lose itself above my head, amid silhouettes of palm trees swaying in the sea breeze, like a glittering umbilical cord joining sea and land. It was beautiful, really beautiful, and that thought stopped my mind darting back to Mrs. Maria's hut. I did not want it to. If I let myself be carried away by panic I would go crazy. I had to recover my calm at all costs, and this beach was as good a place as any for that. I breathed in and out. In and out, in and out... Oh God, why me?

I searched, up in the sky, for whoever was responsible somewhere in the vicinity of Orion.

"You must be having a blast with me! Aren't you?"

I had shouted without realizing it, but quite honestly I was past caring. I was convinced that I could not get rid of this nightmare, trapped in this sort of Alcatraz Island, fleeing from an implacable pursuer, and now absolutely on my own and hating myself for having fled, leaving in the hands of a sadistic murderer the two women who had sheltered me.

"Oh well, kiddo," I said out loud. "Enjoy this night on a beach out of paradise... because it might be the last one."And with a stoical sigh I dug my elbows in the sand and followed the line of the horizon with my eyes, as far as the edge of the village.

A dark band stretched into the sea, presumably the old, now abandoned loading pier. Then the shape of the houses along the shore where the fishermen lived, and inland, set in the middle of that pattern of shadows and stars, a flash of light appeared from the center of the village. Puzzled, I tried to guess what it might be. As far as I could remember, there was no electricity in the village and there was only one building with its own generator: the Mission of the Franciscan Nuns.

11

I walked along the beach, bent almost double, avoiding noises and people like a frightened cat. After twenty minutes of jumpy anxiety I found myself in front of the religious mission, whose lights were out by now. I stood by the wall of an abandoned building on the other side of the street. Then, commending myself to the mercy of all the saints in heaven, I crossed the road and, once I was by the door of the mission, proceeded to hammer at the knocker with desperate urgency.

A couple of minutes went by. I was afraid there would be no one there, or that they might prefer to ignore any call once night had fallen, or else that they would be asleep and would not hear me, or…

"All right! Coming!"

There was the sound of footsteps approaching from the end of a corridor.

"Who is it?" the sleepy voice of a woman asked from the other side of the door.

"Hello…" After what I had been through, I had still not thought of what to say. "Could you please open the door?"

"Who is it?"

"I need help," I murmured, fearing to call the attention of some neighbor or passer-by.

"Are you sick?" the voice asked, sounding worried.

"You could say that. Please let me in and I'll explain everything."

"All right, all right…" she said at last, and I heard her opening the inner lock. "But this isn't the usual thing at this hour of the night."

The door opened, and in the gloom, candle in one hand, a small elderly nun appeared like a familiar, protective figure.

As soon as I crossed the threshold I closed the door behind me, leaned on it, overcome by weariness, and slipped down to the floor, immensely relieved to feel safe.

"My dear, whatever is the matter?" she asked, bringing the candle close to my face.

I raised my eyes. I could imagine my tears carving rivers in my grotesque make-up. The amazement of the Franciscan nun at discovering she was before a white woman, her face painted with shoe polish and covered in cuts and bruises, was so great that she muffled a cry. Without needing any explanations on my part, she turned and ran in search of her sisters.

Minutes later I was sitting at the dining room table, with the three nuns who ran the mission across from me, leaning on the flowery oilcloth and insisting that I had some strong spirit to soothe my nerves.

When I had regained my calm, I accepted a couple of shots of the famous Spanish anisette Anise Mono and gave them a detailed account of the circumstances which had brought me to their door that night.

"Poor thing," Sister Julia said for the fourth or fifth time. She was the one who had opened the door. The other two missionaries, Cecilia and Antonia, remained silent, as deeply absorbed as if I were telling them the plot of a horror movie. In a way, that was exactly what I was doing.

"And then, walking along the beach, I reached your door, and well... here I am."

"So we see, yes."

"I'm so, so grateful to you for taking me in. Really, thank you so much."

The nuns exchanged questioning looks.

"You're welcome, dear," Sister Cecilia said, thoughtfully scratching the oilcloth with a nail. Although I don't

73

know what we're going to do if that Captain Anastasio should come looking for you at the mission. We don't have anywhere to hide you, and obviously you can't pass for one of us: the three of us are old and short, and you're young, tall and pretty."

Reality crossed my path once more, and the fantasy of safety in that place vanished in the air like a puff of smoke. The spirit I had got back for myself moments before gave way again to fear and anxiety, and it must have been so clearly reflected in my expression that the other two sisters hastened to come round the table to hug me, fearing I would burst into tears again. They did not know that I was running out of tears.

"Relax, Sarah," one of them said in my ear. "With God's help everything will be resolved. Now don't you worry and rest, we'll help you take off all this shoe polish and then you'll go to bed. You'll see how different everything looks in the morning."

I let them lead me like a sleepwalker along the corridors of that house in shadows. After a much needed shower, they changed my ragged clothes for a nightgown which did not fit or look much better, and the three of them accompanied me to my designated room, where I rediscovered the longed-for pleasure of sleeping in a bed.

That night I dreamt about my mother. My father and brother were dozing in the garden at home like lizards in the first warm weather of May, while she, as usual, was busy around the house, but with that calm which made it look as if she was not doing anything. She brought a tray with cool lemonade from the kitchen and placed it on the garden table, then turned toward my bedroom window upstairs and called me to come down and join the rest of the family.

"Sarah… Sarah…" I even thought she was shaking my shoulder to hurry me up. Although her voice was not exactly her voice. "Sarah… wake up…"

Then I opened my eyes and found myself facing the round face of Sister Antonia.

"What? What's going on...? I asked, not really remembering where I was.

"The military," she said, her eyes wide. "The soldiers have come."

The Franciscan's expression was the one she would have worn if she had been announcing the appearance of Satan, and my reaction was even worse than if that had been the case. I leapt to my feet in terror, trying to imagine how to escape from that nightmare, for the umpteenth time."Is there a back door?" I asked, grabbing the nun's shoulders.

"No, and all the windows have bars."

"Well then... where can I hide?"

"I'll take you to the chapel. We have a little room for the Bibles and song books; you can hide there. Follow me quickly."

Sister Antonia ran down the hallway with me right at her heels. She opened a door and I found myself in a room like the one I had slept in, but here the bed and furniture had been replaced by prie-dieus and a small altar. On one side of the room, a narrow door with a lock opened in front of me, revealing a tiny storeroom with shelves full of holy books.

"Come on," the nun urged me in a whisper. "Help me take all this out."

Between the two of us we emptied the little storage space and took out the shelves, and after I got inside and realized there were neither windows nor light, I heard the sister shut the door behind me and lock it.

"Don't worry," she whispered through a tiny breathing hole. "The sisters are talking with the officer and, God willing, they'll convince him they can't come in. I'll be back presently, but above all, don't make any noise."

With that unnecessary order and the faint hope that those bastards would have some kind of respect for the missionary nuns, I was left in the darkness, sweating, swallowing my fear in that tiny space where oxygen did not reach.

12

The minutes dragged by, and the feeling of asphyxia grew as what little calm I had left ebbed away. Not that I had ever thought of myself as some movie heroine, or even *brave*, as my girlfriends had called me when they had come to the airport to say goodbye every time I went on a trip, but I had never been keen on others solving my problems. Less so if I was hiding inside a closet.

Instinctively I tried to find a handle, but there was no such thing on that door, and in any case without the key it would not have been much use. My patience had drained away through that narrow breathing hole long ago, and I was already beginning to think about pushing the door down when footsteps echoed in the corridor.

I heard the door to the chapel open. Someone cleared their throat loudly, took a few steps inside and stopped just on the other side of the thin wooden door.

I thought I sensed hoarse breathing and bit my lips to avoid making even the tiniest noise, although my heart seemed to want to betray me by beating so hard I was sure its hysterical thumping would be heard from across the street.

Then, just when I feared my escape had finally come to its end, a key was pushed into the lock, the door opened, and in front of a blinding rectangle of light I made out Sister Cecilia's small silhouette."Don't worry, dear," she said taking my hand, "it's all over."

"The situation isn't very good," Sister Julia warned me as she sat across from me with her fingers clasped on the table.

"It seems that somehow they made the woman who took you in confess you'd been at her house until last night, and now they're looking for you all over the town."

I could not help shivering at the thought of what that *somehow* might have involved."Do you think Maria and Paula will be all right?"

The nuns exchanged glances.

"Sarah," the sister went on, "what should concern you right now is your own safety." She took my hands in hers. "You can't do anything for them. Their fate is in God's hands."

"But they… it's my fault…"

"No, Sarah. Others are to blame."

"But I'm responsible for—"

"You're not responsible for anything," she cut me off. "You're just one more victim of this madness. If you hadn't been lucky enough to have been outside the house when the military arrived you'd have been captured as well, and Maria's fate and her daughter's would have been the same."

In spite of the nun's words, I felt overwhelmed by the responsibility and certainty that in some way I had betrayed those two women. And now I was here, with a cup of coffee before me in the mission dining room, while God only knew what might be happening to them."Like in the movies…" I muttered absentmindedly.

"Excuse me?"

"Huh?" I was surprised she had heard me. "Nothing. I was just thinking out loud…that in the end, just like in the movies, the blacks end up in deep trouble and the whites get away scot-free."

Sister Cecilia nodded gravely."You're right, dear. But the poor always end up badly regardless of the color of their skin, while the rich and powerful, who also come in all colors, get away with anything. It isn't true in your case, however, and if they caught you and killed you, God forbid, your corpse would stink just like any African's."

"I know… but isn't there anything we could do for them?"

"Sarah," Sister Antonia said firmly, "what you have to do is worry about staying alive yourself. The soldier who came was a nobody, and we were able to get rid of him on the excuse that this is holy ground. But make no mistake, he'll run to tell his superiors, and in a little while they'll be back at our door and there'll be nothing we can do to stop them."

"So… what can I do, then?" I asked wearily.

The Franciscan nuns looked at one another again, and their silence was clearer than anything they might have said.

Searching through the closets with Sister Cecilia, we came on some religious clothes belonging to nuns who no longer lived there. Although they made me look pretty funny, not being anywhere near my size, at least they would be something clean to wear.

"What we don't have are shoes in your size," the sister said, "so you'll have to carry on with your rubber sandals."

"Don't worry about that," I said as I changed into the clothes. "You've already done a lot for me."

"There, there," she protested, shaking her head. "I only wish we could do more, but it won't be long before the soldiers come back, and by then you need to be a long way away from here."

"It's funny," I said in front of the closet mirror. "Who'd have thought that one day I'd see myself wearing a nun's robes?"

"The ways of the Lord are inscrutable…" Sister Julia said with good-natured humor.

"And remember," Sister Cecilia said behind me, "we're risking ourselves by letting you wear the Order's robes. If they find out at the Holy See, we'd be admonished most harshly. And if the military came to the conclusion that we helped you escape, then it's not only we, but this mission that's been so hard to create and which is so important for these people, that will be in serious trouble."

"I understand perfectly. I can assure you that as soon as I can I'll get rid of these clothes and nobody will know that you've helped me. Thank you again and—"
Several powerful knocks on the street door cut me off in mid-sentence.

13

There was no sense in hiding now. They must know I was there, and they would search meticulously as far as the last corner of the mission. It would be no use hiding in any closet.

I was frozen, petrified, in the middle of the room, and it was not until the banging on the door sounded again, even more insistently, that one of the sisters went out into the corridor with a last look back at me.

"He's here," said Sister Julia.

"Who?" I asked in alarm.

The nun put her hand on my back soothingly. "Don't worry. It must be Antonia, who's found Dionisio."

"Dionisio?"

"A good friend. We believe he can help you get out of Luba."

"But… how? When did…" I was still puzzled.

"While you were asleep Sister Antonia went to contact some trustworthy people, to try and get you off the island."

I was so stunned I could not manage to say anything with some sense in it.

"Before you say anything," Cecilia went on, raising her hand, "please don't thank us any more."

At that moment, Sister Antonia came into the room, closely followed by a short, chubby Guinean man with salt-and-pepper hair, tightly fitted into a set of greasy blue overalls and with thick pebble glasses which enlarged the brown eyes I saw studying me curiously.

"Dionisio," said Sister Antonia stepping aside, "this is Sister Sarah."

"Sister," he said shyly.

I was about to shake his hand, and he offered me his own with the fingers closed, as if he did not want to get mine dirty when he squeezed them, or else he thought it was an inappropriate greeting between a man and a woman.

"Dionisio is absolutely trustworthy," the nun who had brought him assured me in a confident voice.

"And this is for you," said Sister Cecilia. She took my hand and put something in my palm, then quickly squeezed it shut.

I realized in surprise that she had given me a tight wad of bills."Oh no… Thank you, but I can't accept it," I protested, and tried to give it back.

"Holy Mother of God… don't be foolish, child. You need this money a lot more than we do. I wish we could give you more, but it's all we have."

"But—"

"Say no more," Sister Julia interrupted firmly. She put her finger to her lips. "Now go with Dionisio and do whatever he says, he'll take you off the island. And don't worry, we'll try to contact your embassy to let them know your situation. You'll see," she added with exaggerated confidence, "in the end, everything will be all right."

"Now you must leave," Cecilia intervened, taking my arm and leading me to the door. "There's no time to lose."

"But… where am I going?" I asked. I was a little embarrassed and definitely afraid as I glanced at Dionisio from the corner of my eye.

"Trust him, there's no time for explanations now. You go with Dionisio and do what he tells you."

Undecided, I stopped at the door of the mission, shivering at the sight of the darkness outside.

Sister Cecilia must have sensed my fear through my arm."Relax, dear, everything's going to be all right. The Lord will protect you," she said in a deep, calm voice. Looking into my eyes, she hugged me with surprising strength.

Then the two other sisters came forward and we joined in a warm embrace.

"I'll always be grateful to you." I sobbed. "Thank you, all three of you, and… even though I have to confess I'm not much of a believer, well… God bless you. I hope we'll be able to meet again in better circumstances."

I was already outside the door when I remembered I was still wearing the nun's robe."Wait!" I said, and started to turn back. "I have to take all this off. I'm not going round dressed as a nun."

"On the contrary," Sister Julia replied, looking me up and down. "It's the best disguise you could have. In Guinea the only white women are nuns or doctors, and you'll attract much less attention dressed like this."

"Well, yes, but…"

At this point Dionisio took my arm to stop me going back."Don't worry, Sister Sarah. I help you get out of here. Trust. Okay?"

Blind trust is not one of my strong points, but given the situation I had no choice but to accept.

"Yes, sure… I just hope they know what they're doing."

Dionisio turned and headed down the street without answering, but I could hear him muttering something under his breath."Me too…" he said to himself. "Me too."

As soon as we left the mission we headed in the direction of the city's derelict docks, walking nonchalantly, with exaggerated calm, so as not to raise any suspicions. My heart was beating furiously as I walked beside my guide through the lonely and dusty streets of Luba.

"Where are we going?" I asked in a whisper.

"To the old docks."

"Am I going to hide there?"

"No, the sisters asked me to get you off the island."

I was thoroughly intrigued; I could see no ship for us to board, but apart from that the harbor was so dilapidated, with even a half-sunken boat rusting away, it seemed impossible that anything could even dock there.

"And where's the boat?"

"You wait," he said calmly, as if he was taking me to a surprise birthday party.

I decided to keep my anxiety under control, grant him a well-earned vote of trust and wait to see how things developed.

A trust which evaporated when we looked out over the edge of the concrete pier and Dionisio waved a hand at what was going to be my escape boat.

"You've got to be kidding me!" I cried, pointing at what was below.

"No, sister," he said very seriously. "That ladder to go down, I go behind you."

"But… it's just an old canoe. And it doesn't even have a motor!"

"It matters that it floats, and this floats."

"B… but…" I stammered in pure incredulity. "How do you think I'm going to get out of here in *that*? There are hundreds of miles between here and dry land!"

"Yes, many miles," he said, nodding imperturbably.

"I'll never make it!" I cried. I was convinced the guy had lost his wits.

He looked at me in confusion. "You think you row to the continent?"

"I…well, I…"

Dionisio shook his head, I would guess in amusement, and urged me to go down the rusty ladder.

Perhaps under the influence of the robe I was wearing, I took a leap of faith and embarked – not without a few doubts – in the worm-eaten canoe, carved out of a single tree trunk.

I sat on the seat at the prow as Dionisio told me to, and as soon as we were both on board we began to row vigorously. A chubby African dressed as a mechanic and an atheist in nun's robes heading toward the open sea. What a sight.

14

"Where are we going, Dionisio?" I asked, turning to face him.

"You'll see," he replied, panting. "Now I need you row hard."

"Sorry, I didn't know we were in a race," I said breathlessly.

Dionisio let out his breath with a trace of annoyance."It's no race, sister. But if you not row, the current drag and we end in the middle of sea."

"Okay, okay... I'll row. But I'd like to know where you're taking me. I'm tired of always being one step behind events, and I need to have some feeling of control over my future."

"We go to beach for the night."

"A beach? Will it be safe?"

"I think," he said, puffing with the effort. "Now, please, row. I answer questions later."

Once we were far enough from the coast so that in the distance nobody could tell us from any other fishing canoe, we set course toward the south. On our right the rough sea began to strike the side of the boat swaying it like a tumbler doll. The mere few inches which separated the edge of the canoe from the surface of the water made me fear that any small wave might end up flooding us.

So we rowed for what seemed to me like an eternity. Although the white Franciscan wimple protected me from the rays of a relentless sun, I sweated as never before in my whole life, and I came to the conclusion that religious robes were not designed for rowing a canoe in tropical seas.

"Are we there yet?" I asked. I was exhausted, and enormous drops of sweat were running down my forehead.

"Almost there now."

"Phew... you have no idea how much I'd love to get into the water right now," I said, dipping my hand in and mopping my face.

"I... don't think good idea."

"Why not?"

"Look behind."

I turned, intrigued. Dionisio followed my example, and after examining the sea behind us for a few moments he pointed at a spot about ten yards away. At first I did not understand what he was trying to point out, but when I followed the direction of his finger I saw a dark shadow and two small wakes, one in front of the other, which betrayed the presence of a dorsal fin and a tail fin barely broking the surface of the water.

"Fuck! It's a shark!"

"It's following us."

"But... why?"

"Perhaps it wants your blessing..."

"You don't say."

"Don't worry, sister," he added a few moments later, more seriously, "shark probably believes we fishermen and waits for leftovers. Don't put your hands in the water and nothing will happen. We're almost there."

That said, he put his oar in the water on the port side, and at once the canoe turned left toward the coast of the island.

What can I say about that luxurious vegetation which, with the perspective of distance, revealed itself to me as a green cloud of infinite shades covering all the horizon, evaporating in the distance as it rose abruptly along the side of the Luba volcano, eternally shrouded in mist? Perhaps if you have never been to Africa, there is no point in describing it. Like that tired old saying that you can't explain colors to a blind person.

In spite of everything that had happened to me, in spite of being in a canoe with a total stranger, disguised as a nun and stalked by a shark, I was dazzled by that place, by Guinea, in sum by Africa. No other corner of the earth can compare. Those two months there had been the most extraordinary of my life, and in the Guineans I had found the most generous and hospitable people I could ever have imagined. I saw the coast before me and felt an inexplicable attraction, which like a magnet pointed to that coast as the only north possible for me. If that canoe had had a mast, I would have had to ask Dionisio to tie me to it.

"Sister!" a voice shouted behind me, bringing me out of my reverie.

I turned. "What is it?"

"Forgive me, but this black man gets tired to row alone. Can you help so we get to beach before sunset?"

"Oh, yes, so sorry... I was distracted."

"I see... Come on then, row hard. The sooner we arrive, better."

It did not take us long to reach the shore, mostly thanks to the current which at that moment was in our favor. The beach where we landed was small, protected at both ends by rocky outcrops and an impenetrable green curtain which rose five or six yards from the docile surrender of the waves that came to die with a whisper on the fine black sand.

Dionisio picked up a plastic bag from the canoe containing two mangoes and some huge brown pods, like giant peas, which had black seeds inside covered in something white, juicy and extremely sweet; *lampaka* I think it was called. I guessed this was going to be our lunch, along with one gallon of bottled water which at that moment he was leaving on the sand.

And then, to my astonishment, Dionisio pushed the boat back into the water and jumped inside.

"Hey!" I shouted in sudden fright as I ran toward the canoe. "What are you doing? Where are you going?"

"Relax," he said picking up the oar. "I go back with wife, but they come for you tonight."

"Tonight? And I have to wait here all alone?" I looked right and left along the small beach of black sand, surrounded by a wall of vegetation. "I don't even know where I am…" I felt desolate.

"It's called Beach of Silence," he said. "You safe here."

"Don't leave me alone here, please," I pleaded. I was almost in tears as I held on to the edge of the canoe. "Stay with me."

"I can't."

"Please… I beg you."

"Trust. It is best way," he said, shaking his head.

"No, please…"

"Remember," he emphasized, ignoring my pleas. "You don't move from here in all night." He began to row slowly, moving away from the shore.

"But… who's going to come for me?" I asked anxiously, following him until the water came almost to my chest.

"Friends," he said, half-turning. "Wait here, and don't go in water… in case shark follows." When he was a dozen or so yards out, he seemed to remember something and turned to me. "Good luck, Sister Sarah. May God protect you!"

Downcast, silent, I watched the canoe move away slowly, while I grew correspondingly more scared. My spirit didn't stop shifting from despair to hope and back to despair, which was precisely the state I was in just then.

I was deeply grateful to the nuns, and to Dionisio, who had helped me generously, risking his own safety, more than anybody had ever done before. But I could hardly overlook the point that I had been abandoned on a beach with only the promise that someone would come for me.

For one second the terrible possibility that they had decided to turn me in to the militiamen in exchange for Maria and Paula's freedom crossed my mind. *But no,* I thought, *if that's what they'd intended they'd have just left me at the mission and I wouldn't have been able to escape.* In any case, no matter how incomprehensible their actions might be, I could not deny that they had shown an almost inexplicable generosity, and as they had insistently told me, perhaps the best thing to do was trust and hope everything would come out well. At any rate, I had no choice.

It was then that I realized I had not even said goodbye to that man. As he was a long way away by now I put my hands to my mouth and called him, "Dionisio!"

He stopped rowing and turned to me expectantly.

"Thank you!" I yelled. "Thank you very much!"

And after a glance back, he waved his arm in farewell and rowed on.

The evening languished, and the sun was barely a hand's-breadth above the Atlantic waters, tempering the burning fury it had shown that corner of the world, taking its leave with the orange flash given it by the Sahara sand, which after wandering for thousands of miles finally reached that coast and touched the incomparable African sunsets with unreality.

I lay on the sand, summoning up a deliberate stoicism, dressed only in my underwear with the hot religious robe in a bundle serving as a pillow for my head. Only the birds and tree frogs came to disturb the hypnotic rhythm of the waves breaking on the shore, and even the mosquitoes seemed to respect that moment, because I could not hear one single insidious whine.

"It's unbelievable… the peace you breathe here…" I murmured to myself, "this silence—"

"That's exactly what this place is called: the Beach of Silence," a man's voice said behind me. I was startled into leaping a couple of feet across the sand.

There was Gabriel, standing at the edge of a small path I had not noticed.

"Fuck!" I cried in delight. "Where did you come from?!"

He jabbed his thumb behind him. "From the village."

"Thank goodness!" I ran to him and hugged him wholeheartedly. "But... how did you find me?"

"I asked Dionisio to bring you here. It's a safe place."

"Was it your idea?"

He smiled."Don't you like the place?"

"Stop kidding. What are we doing here?"

Gabriel saw my frightened expression and sat down on the sand beside me."You needn't worry, Sarah. We're going to get off the island."

"Dionisio told me that already. But how?"

"You'll see."

15

With the coming of night I had no more doubts.
The noise of an engine from out at sea grew louder, and the beam of a strong flashlight swept the surface of the water as it approached the shore.

"Sarah Malik!" a voice shouted from the darkness.

For a moment I hesitated about answering. But if this was some subtle trick by the militiamen to catch me, it certainly did not make a lot of sense.

"Here!" I said at last, standing up and trusting I was not making a mistake. "I'm here!"

The beam wandered about until it found me and dazzled me. I put my hand in front of my eyes and waved, still unable to see anything.

"Are you Sarah Malik?" the voice asked again.

"Yes, it's me!"

"Get on board!" it urged, very close now. "There's no time!"

I hesitated again, but Gabriel took my arm and pushed me into the boat.

Once on board, we moved on in almost complete darkness toward a yellowish light in the midst of all that blackness, which could easily have been a single mile away or a hundred. The outboard engine was noisy rather than effective, but even so we made good speed and the invisible spattering of spray hit me full in the face. Meanwhile behind us the Beach of Silence had vanished into the shadows, and the only light coming from the ever more distant Luba was that of the oil lamps in the houses, some bonfire or other and the electric generator at the Franciscan mission. I had not thought about them for hours, and now, bouncing against the waves toward a solitary light-bulb in the middle of the night, I prayed nothing would happen to them and that they would not have to pay for putting me up and helping me. And in a chain of memories I thought of Mrs. Maria and her daughter Paula, and my silent tears of impotence mingled with the water of the Gulf of Guinea.

"Do you know what might have happened to Maria and Paula?"

Gabriel did not answer, and I repeated the question.

"I'd rather not talk about it now," he replied, raising his voice above the noise of the engine.

"But—"

"Sarah," he said with a sharp sigh, "I said I don't want to talk about it. Please forget it."

Although I was surprised by his gruff attitude, I had no choice but to swallow my unease and look ahead once more, watching the steadily approaching light of what was certainly our destination.

It was not until we were quite close that I was able to make out the silhouette of a cargo ship thirty yards or so long, illuminated only by the pale bulb guiding us to it, rocking gently with the waves. As we approached what looked like a sinister hulk of rusty metal, we stayed close to its side and the silent man who was steering the boat gave a whistle. A few seconds later it was answered in the form of a rope ladder.

"Up you go," he urged me.

I grabbed the shaky ladder as best I could, and although I banged my knees and knuckles repeatedly on the side of the hull and almost lost my sandals, I managed to climb until two pairs of hands came out of the dark, took my arms and lifted me over the gunwale, leaving me sitting on the deck.

Still in that fleeting light, I saw the two men who had hoisted me up throwing a couple of ropes overboard, and as soon as Gabriel had climbed up the same ladder they used them to raise the boat that had brought us there.

Then, while I was still slumped on the steel deck, the three men exchanged a few words I did not understand. After this a fourth man turned to me and said, "You're Sarah Malik, right?"

"That's right."

"Welcome aboard," he said, and held out his hand. "They didn't tell me you were a sister."

"Well... I'm really an only child."

The sailors looked at me in confusion, then suddenly burst into soft laughter. I still do not know whether it was because they caught the joke or because they thought they were dealing with an outlandish nun.

The important thing was that without more ado they led us along the ship's dark corridors, almost feeling their way as they went. After endless twisting and turning and going down steep ladders, they opened an iron door and we went into what I guessed was to be our cabin. In it a dirty porthole allowed me to see the reflection of the moon on the sea, faintly illuminating what looked like a couple of berths and a locker.

"There are clean sheets and dry clothes in the closet, and if you need anything there's always someone on duty on the bridge. We'll arrive tomorrow at noon," the sailor informed me from the gloom. "Have a good night." He closed the cabin door with a dull thump.

"Well, Gabriel," I said as I sat down heavily on one of the lower berths. "Are you going to tell me what I'm doing on this ship?"

He sat down beside me and let himself fall back on to the bed. "We're escaping," he said putting his hands behind his head as a pillow.

"Seriously?"

"What I mean to say is that we're escaping from the island of Bioko."

I must have gained ten years of life when I heard those words, which relieved me of much of the anxiety I had been suffering ever since the whole insane business started. At last there seemed to be a light at the end of the tunnel.

The soothing balm was so welcome that I leaned back in turn with a sigh, and as I closed my eyes I imagined myself back in Boston, walking along the cobbled streets, protected by a cloud of safety and sanity.

"The bad news is—"Why does there always have to be bad news?"that I think this ship is going to Bata."

"What?" I could not believe what I had just heard. "Are you telling me that all this is just to get from one part of Equatorial Guinea to another? What I want is to get out of this country once and for all!" I exploded. "What's the use of going from the island to the continent, if we never leave Guinea?"

"Sarah, don't shout. I'm right here beside you."

"How do you expect me not to shout? I thought we were safe, and a moment later I find out we're not!" I was letting loose some of the anger built up inside me, and now I was no longer lying on the bed beside Gabriel but had leapt to my feet and was howling and waving my arms, a gesture which of course was wasted in the darkness. "Fuck, fuck, fuck!"

"Calm down…"

"Calm down? How am I supposed to calm down? As soon as we dock, the Bata Port authorities will wonder what a white woman's doing in a cargo ship, and five minutes later I'll be in jail again. Why in hell didn't we take a ship going to Cameroon or Nigeria?"

"Because this isn't a taxi service. We were lucky that the nuns knew the captain of this ship, and he's risked bringing us with him on his route between Malabo and Bata."

"Okay, that I understand," I replied trying to calm down. "But I don't get what we stand to gain by going from the frying pan into the fire."

"For the moment what we gain is the fact that they're not looking for us in continental Guinea. It may be the same country, but the hundreds of miles of ocean between the two mean that for a while they'll only be searching the island."

"But what are we going to do once we get off at Bata? How are we going to avoid the militiamen at the harbor?"

"Sarah, I said the ship's going to Bata, not that we are."

"I don't follow. What do you mean by that?"

"Tomorrow, Sarah," he said, stretching himself out along the whole length of the bed. "At the moment I'm very tired, tomorrow I'll explain everything."

And a minute later, while I was still standing in the middle of the cabin trying to settle down, Gabriel's first snores mingled with the rattling from the engine room, and I felt the sea beginning to slip away under the merchant ship's hull.

16

"Good morning."

"What…?" I replied, half asleep and opening one eye.

"Time for breakfast," said a familiar voice in front of my face.

"Gabriel?" I barely recognized him through the mists of sleep. "What… what time is it?"

"It's already six o'clock, and if we don't hurry there'll be nothing left to eat."

"Very early…" I protested weakly.

"Stop whining and get your missionary body off that bed."

"I warn you," I said raising a finger as I stretched, "that joke stopped being funny a long time ago."

"Well, that might be open for discussion," he replied with a mocking grin. "The thing is, though, that the lie might come in handy."

"I'm not so convinced."

"Well, you should be. There are dozens of missionaries in Guinea, and with those clothes on there's more chance you'll go unnoticed. And it'll make it more difficult to connect you with an anthropologist who escaped from a truck of prisoners outside Malabo."

"I don't know…"

"Believe me. It's either this or covering you in shoe polish again."

"No way. You have no idea how much it made me sweat, and it stank, not to mention how ridiculous it looked."

"Then that's decided. From now on you'll be Sister Sarah."

"All right…" I said, although I was not too happy with the prospect. "But if you start mocking me, I'll break my vows and all hell will break loose."

Gabriel shook his head. "We might be able to pass you off as a nun… but with that attitude you'll never make a saint."

I guess we arrived at the dining room too late, because there was nobody there and no trace that breakfast had ever been served.

"I'm afraid we aren't going to be able to eat anything till lunchtime," Gabriel said, confirming my suspicions.

"And if we go down to the galley, won't they give us something?"

"The cook is also the chief engineer's assistant, and when he leaves the galley he puts it under lock and key."

"How do you know that?"

"This isn't the first time I've traveled on the *Queen Elizabeth*."

"*Queen Elizabeth?* That's the name of this ship?"

"Exactly. I guess the present owner thought it would be amusing to call this pile of scrap after the most luxurious ship in the world."

"Okay, but we'll get there, right?"

"Of course we will. It hasn't sunk, so far."

I was still turning Gabriel's unsettling last words over in my head when he suggested I go up to the bridge to introduce myself to the captain.

I went out onto the deck, where a spotless blue sky without a single cloud on the horizon dazzled me after the gloom of the interior. I climbed a completely rusted metal ladder, pushed open a creaking hatch and went on to the bridge. A man of fifty or so, dressed only in ragged shorts and flip-flops, was at the helm with a cigar stub at the corner of his mouth.

"Hey, Sister Sarah! At last we meet!" he cried when he saw me. He waved his hand around. "Do you like my ship?"

"Yes, of course," I felt obliged to say. "It's very nice."

"I'll sell it to you!" he said, and laughed uproariously. "I still don't understand how this piece of rusty iron can even float. It's a fucking miracle!" He laughed again. "Oh… and please forgive my language. I forgot you're a nun."

"Don't worry. Even I forget sometimes," I said getting closer to shake his hand. "I'm very grateful for your help."

"My name is Diego Nsue, the captain," he said, taking the cigar out of his mouth as he took my hand. "And don't mention it, although I trust your boss will take it into account when the time comes to collect the bills."

"My boss?"

"Your boss, sister," he said pointing his finger at the ceiling. "The one above."

"Oh yes, of course. You can be sure that the next time I speak to him, I'll give him the best references."

The captain stared at me for a moment, trying to work out whether I was making fun of him. He finally burst out into laughter again."Blimey! I didn't know nuns had a sense of humor."

"I'm a rather special missionary," I said trying to change the subject. "But tell me, how's the voyage going?"

"Like a dream," he said enthusiastically. "We're making about fifteen knots, and around noon we'll get to Bata."

"And then…?"

"Don't you worry, I'll tell you what to do when the time comes."

I raised an eyebrow. "You all like mysteries here, don't you?" I said, but when I got no answer I did not insist. "Oh well, changing the subject, who do I have to excommunicate on this ship to get something to eat?"

The captain let out again his easy laughter."I'll call the cook right away and ask him to prepare you something. You'll need your strength for what's in store for you."

"Thank you, captain. You're very kind."

"You're welcome, sister. And now if you'll excuse me, I have a ship to manage. Make yourself at home and enjoy the voyage."

I left the bridge, and as soon as I found Gabriel I went up to him with a question on the tip of my tongue. "Why do I always have the impression that I'm the one who knows least about what's going on, or where we're going?" I asked with my hands on my hips. "Would you mind putting me up to speed?"

Gabriel put a finger on his lips and took my arm. He led me to the stern, where a discolored Guinean flag fluttered in the breeze. "What do you want to know?"

"Everything. What your plan is, assuming you actually have one, and where we're going."

"My plan is to reach the continent, and from there cross the border into Gabon."

"Gabon?" I asked in surprise. "If I'm not mistaken, the border with Cameroon is a lot closer."

"True, and it's also more carefully watched."

"All right, let's say we're heading for Gabon. But when we get there, how are we going to avoid the militiamen at the harbor in Bata?"

"Easy. We'll get off before we arrive, the same way we got on."

"In that boat again?"

"I'm afraid so."

"Dressed as a missionary nun?"

Gabriel's smile was an explicit enough reply.

17

Just as he had promised, the captain told the cook to make us some food, and shortly afterward we were sitting beside each other at the least dirty table in the dining room, gulping down scrambled eggs with boiled rice.

"Gabriel," I said with my mouth full.

"Yes?" he replied without looking up from his plate.

"What's happened to Maria and Paula?" I asked, not looking at him.

A heavy silence delayed the answer. "I don't know…" he said in an unsteady voice.

I was afraid of the answer he might give, but the doubt was even worse. "Please," I insisted, "tell me whatever you know."

He looked at me out of the corner of his eye and breathed out heavily through his nose. "I believe they took both of them to the police station."

I knew what that meant from my own experience, and unfortunately I could guess what it would mean for an old woman and a sick girl. "And… can't we do anything about it?"

Gabriel shook his head slowly. He was visibly upset.

"Maybe," I said without thinking, "if I turn myself in—"

"Nonsense," he interrupted before I could finish the sentence. "Even if we both turned ourselves in they'd still keep them as accomplices, and their sacrifice would have been useless."

"Sacrifice? I don't want them to sacrifice themselves! What I want is to help them. They're in this mess because of me."

"You didn't know what was going to happen."

"So we're not going to do anything?"

Gabriel stared at me, frowning."Do you think you are in an adventure novel? This is real life, Sarah. Here the ones who play hero get a bullet in the head. If you want to make the most of your robe, pray for them. If not, try to forget about it."

"How can I forget about it? Those two women… I can't just do nothing now they're in trouble."

"So what are you going to do?" he asked bitterly. "Attack the Malabo police station? Go on a hunger strike? Set yourself on fire like a *bonzo*?" There was frustration in his voice, along with a lot of despair. "I'd be the first to risk my life to help them, but believe me, we can't do anything for them any longer. In this country there aren't any judges to appeal to, or newspapers to make accusations in. The fate of those two women has been cast. Now all we can do is wait and see."

I shook my head one last time, but I did not know what else to say. Rage washed over me, and I felt wretched at not being able to help the people who had helped me. I did not feel I could get all this hatred out of my chest, this hatred which gnawed at the bones of my soul, this impotence, this uncontrollable wish to kill with my own hands the culprit of all that unnecessary pain.

"I know how you feel," Gabriel said in a low voice. He reached out and stroked my hair tenderly.

"Why do you think you know?" I asked, suddenly sobbing, desolate.

Gabriel hugged me tight and put his lips to my ear."Very simple," he whispered. "Because I've been feeling like this all my life."

After the meal, back on deck, looking out from the prow to get a respite from the equatorial heat by the sea breeze, we watched the dark strip of the continental African coastline widen gradually.

"Tell me about yourself," I said without taking my eyes from the horizon.

Gabriel looked aside at me."My family is from Luba, although I was born in Malabo, and my parents sent me to Nigeria when I was young. First to study Mining Engineering at Lagos University, and later to work on the oil rigs there. After a few years I came back to Guinea, and when a big oilfield near Bioko was discovered, I found work on an Exxon rig. Then there was the incident at a bar in Malabo" – he shrugged – "and you know the rest."

"Did you work on an oil rig? It must have been tough."

"A little, but for a Guinean it was as if I'd won the lottery. I was lucky to have experience in prospecting from my time in Nigeria, and to speak enough English to become a foreman of the other Guinean workers, under orders from the American bosses. I'd have made a good living if it weren't for the fact that the contracting company which acted as intermediary kept eighty per cent of my salary."

"They took eighty per cent of your salary? Why?"

Gabriel shrugged."The company that was supposed to pay me," he said with a rueful smile, "is the property of one of Obiang's sons." This piece of information meant no other explanation was needed.

Even trying to talk about other things could not make me forget the uncertainty, which kept growing at the same rate as the land on the horizon. We had managed to escape from the island of Bioko, but we still had a long way to go before we could escape from the country itself.

Gabriel looked calm as he leaned on the rusty gunwale, but I was sure the same doubts were haunting him, and that he had the same aftertaste of fear in his mouth, no matter how confident and optimistic he might seem.

Africa, the continent of prejudices and set phrases which I had deliberately tried to eradicate, appeared to me now as a succession of clichés and fears. Descriptions like *the mysterious continent* or racist statements along the lines of *Africans only know how to do two things properly: kill and die* did not seem so far from the truth at that moment.

The truth was that I was afraid. I was terrified.

"Do you think we'll make it?" I asked, with my gaze fixed on the overwhelming green of the coast.

The answer never came, but looking at him out of the corner of my eye I saw the muscles tense in my traveling companion's jaw.

18

Nearly a mile from the coast, before there was any chance of being discovered, and with the help of some of the members of the *Queen Elizabeth*'s crew, we launched the lifeboat. Once again I found myself sitting in it with my nun's robe hitched up getting dirtier and smellier all the time on a narrow wooden plank. This time, though, we were not going out to sea in the darkness as we had done the previous time, but steering a diagonal course toward a dazzling beach shaded by palm trees. We were gradually leaving the modest silhouette of the city of Bata to our right, and it was not until we drew level with the control tower of the small airport to the north of the city that we set a course heading directly toward the coastline.

We moved forward with the engine at full throttle, trying to arrive as soon as possible. The sea we were cutting through looked calm enough, but when it reached the shore it was transformed into threatening clouds of white surf.

"It seems to me that we're going to have a rough landing," Gabriel said at my side.

I simply nodded, trying not to think about the huge waves I could see breaking strongly less than fifty yards away. I only hoped the beach was completely sandy, because if we ended up capsizing, those waves were going to give us quite a tumble, and any sharp rock might send us straight to hell without passing through the toll-booth.

"Hold on fast, sister!" the sailor said. "When the wave catches us, hold tight!"

I didn't quite understand what he meant to do, but we were already in the area where the great waves were forming. They could easily reach six feet, and instead of turning and asking I decided to act on faith   appropriately enough, as I was wearing those robes   and do as I was told.

A rising crest passed under our small boat, lifting it up nearly three feet, and for a second I was aware of the enormous strength of the masses of water which came to crash on that coast after building up energy over thousands of miles of ocean. I turned, feeling more than uneasy, and at that precise moment I saw a small blue mountain beginning to grow right behind us.

"Now, sister!" he called out. "Hold on as tight as you can!"

He did not need to say it twice. I grabbed the gunwale with the strength fear can give, and at once the boat began to tilt forward until I thought it would turn a perfect somersault with us inside it.

"Lean back! Lean back!" the voice at my back shouted.

I did so, and the boat immediately stopped tilting forward. Instead it picked up terrific speed and we shot off, out of control, toward the shore. We were riding the wave.

I could not   nor did I wish to   see the bulk of water which was driving us on, but judging by the deafening roar it made when we reached the breaker, it must have been enormous. Then a chaos of surf caught up with us and flooded into the boat. I heard Gabriel shouting something at me, but I could not understand what it was. I remained where I was, lying down, trying not to swallow water, getting myself ready for the moment we capsized, which seemed more than likely.

But in spite of my worst fears, disaster was avoided. I discovered we had reached dry land when I felt beneath my back the unmistakable friction of the sand against the keel.

I got to my feet in the boat with great difficulty. "I think… I'll get off here," I muttered with my stomach upside down.

"Don't you want to do it again, sister?" he asked me.
"You did it very well… but remember, pride is a sin."

"Quite honestly," he said, scratching his head shyly, "I didn't think you would..." He saw me shaking my head and laughing quietly. "But what are you laughing about?"

"Nothing... nothing... I was just remembering all the times I turned an ex-boyfriend down when he invited me to go surfing with him. And I was thinking: it's really funny that I've finally done it in Africa, on a lifeboat, dressed as a missionary."

The lifeboat had already begun its journey back, and the two of us had been left lying exhausted under a coconut palm. Unlike the beach in Bioko where we had been twenty-four hours earlier, this one was of fine white sand, and if it had not been for the amount of driftwood, branches, coconuts and plastic bags scattered all over the shore it would have been worthy of a place in any travel catalogue. The sun hung from its zenith, and my damp clothes, which I had spread out on a fallen trunk, were dry in less than ten minutes.

"Well," I said, leaning on my elbows. "Now what do we do?"

"First we rest a little longer. Then we'll head to a fishing village called Utonde, a short distance from here, we'll get hold of transport... and afterward, God will provide."

"Wow, a perfect plan."

"It still needs a bit of polishing."

Half an hour later, when we felt recovered, we started to walk along the beach heading north. A few paces away we saw a small group of wooden houses with palm roofs and, feigning normality,, we went in among them looking for someone to ask.

We found a group of men mending their fishing nets, and I went ahead to talk to them.

"*Mbolo*!" I said with a nod.

"*Mbolo*!" the fishermen replied as one.

"Do any of you know of a bus or country taxi that goes to Bata?"

The fishermen looked at one another inquiringly. "Late in the evening," said the older of them, turning to his companions. "Tomas 'with the shop' usually goes to Monbasi to visit his…ahem, you know."

The youngest, looking amused, pointed his thumb at me. "But do you think he'll want to take a nun in his car when he goes to visit his *ahem*?"

"Ah, that's true," the other admitted with a smile.

"Don't worry about that," I said, and came forward. "We Franciscan nuns are quite liberal, and that won't be a problem."

The fishermen exchanged looks again, this time of puzzlement.

"All right," the first man said, and nodded toward the end of the street of sand. "Tomas' shop is a bit further on. Talk to him, you might convince him."

"*Akiba*," I said in Fang, wishing them good fishing, leaving them behind with their gossip and malicious laughter.

Twenty yards ahead we reached the shop. A house like any other house, its door closed, different from the rest only because of a rusty orange advertisement for the legendary Mirinda. Gabriel knocked on the door, but there was no response. He tried again three times, each time more insistently, until a voice on the other side of the door asked us what we wanted.

"We're looking for Tomas," I said.

"That's me," the voice said. "What do you want?"

"They told us you might take us to Bata."

"Who told you that?"

"Some fishermen in the village. They told us you often go to the city, and you might be able to take us with you."

"Well, you can go back and tell that gang of gossips," the invisible speaker burst out as he opened the door abruptly, "they can go to—"The man, unkempt and wearing only a pair of underpants with holes in them, was left dumbfounded at finding himself face to face with a nun who was looking at him reproachfully."Oh, excuse me, sister," he said, looking abashed and partially hiding behind the door. "I didn't know you… you were a—"

"Would you do us a great favor and take us to Bata?" I interrupted, trying to take advantage of this sudden attack of prudishness.

"Of course, sister. But I only go to Monbasi, although from there you can catch a bus to the center."

I looked questioningly at Gabriel, and he nodded.

"All right, Mister Tomas. My name is Sarah… Sister Sarah," I said, shaking his hand. "When do we leave?"

In less than an hour we were on our way out of Utonde on a dirt road lined with palm trees and bushes in a patched-up Peugeot 504 sedan. The poor old car complained at the slightest opportunity, and even with the whole back seat to myself I could not find a single spot without a broken spring.

After a few miles we left behind the leafy strip close to the beach and came to the wide green grassland which surrounds the small airport at Bata.

"What a change," I said, just to set the conversation in motion. "I guess they cut down all the trees to avoid accidents, right?"

"Well, no," said Tomas. He was gripping the wheel as if it were the reins of a racehorse. "There was no need to cut anything down. It's always been like this here, a desert."

"A desert you say?" I looked right and left. "Where?"

"Well, all this," said our driver. He jabbed his chin at the green grassland.

"I'm sorry, I can only see a huge field of grass."

"Exactly what I'm telling you," he said, plainly stating the obvious as far as he was concerned. "A desert."

In some puzzlement, I refrained from explaining what a real desert was. I guessed that for anyone who had spent his whole life surrounded by thick tropical forests, a flat stretch of land without trees must seem a real wasteland.

Less than half an hour after leaving Utonde, we reached our destination. It was a neighborhood of humble houses, some of adobe, some of wood with zinc roofs, a few of brick. The streets were of compacted red dirt, furrowed by the dry beds of small streams and flanked by garbage and weeds. We passed a group of fifteen or twenty kids playing soccer in the middle of the street, all barefoot, kicking a ball which was no more than an enormous bunch of plastic bags stuck together. One of them was wearing a dirty t-shirt with David Beckham's face on the chest, and without really knowing why, I felt ashamed. Perhaps because part of me, as a westerner, saw myself responsible for selling printed blond dreams in exchange for smoke. I thought things had not really changed so much since the days when we bartered gold nuggets for colored glass beads.

"I'll leave you here, sister," Tomas said, stopping the car at a crossing. "If you wait at that corner you'll be able to find someone to take you to the center."

Gabriel opened his door. "Thank you very much. You've been very kind."

It took me a couple of seconds more to come out of my reverie. "Thank you, Tomas," I said as I got out of the vehicle, "and God bless you," I added, getting more and more into my role.

Our driver nodded. Waving goodbye with one hand, he started off again, on his way to his *ahem*'s house.

Gabriel and I looked at each other, then looked around, establishing that we were somewhere on the outskirts of Bata, but without the least idea of exactly where. One thing was clear, though: night was coming.

We could see no car either to right or left, apart from the one which had dropped us off there and which at that moment was turning a corner, winking its tail-light in farewell.

"I don't think even God passes this way," I said, looking from side to side.

In the deepening twilight I saw Gabriel's teeth shining as he smiled."Hearing you say that in that costume is even funnier than usual."

"Well, forgive me for not joining in the laughter, but in case you haven't noticed it doesn't look as if there's a lot of traffic passing this way, public lighting is notable by its absence and it's getting darker every minute."

"Scared?"

"A bit. I know there's very little crime in Guinea, but I'm not mad about being lost in a dark street on the outskirts of an unknown city."

"Well then," he said looking ahead and in a rather different tone of voice, "I don't think you're going to feel any better when you see what I'm seeing."

I turned around, following his gaze, and saw a police car coming straight toward us, trailing a cloud of dust behind it.

The police vehicle, a dilapidated blue Toyota pickup, stopped just in front of us. We had been waiting in vain for it to pass, but now two policemen were getting out of the car, both with handguns in their belts and one of them carrying an old machinegun.

"Stop right there! What are you doing in this neighborhood, nun?" said the one who looked to be the senior officer. "Are you looking for someone to fuck you?" he added scornfully, and winked at his partner.

"What sort of way is that to address a nun?" I asked, trying to hide the fear I felt. "Don't you know that our Lord hears everything and judges everything you say?" I had gambled on not letting myself be intimidated and appealing to their beliefs, trusting they would be God-fearing Christians.

The policeman hesitated, surprised that I had spoken so firmly. But after a second's indecision he took a step forward, thrusting his face so close to mine that I could easily smell the beer on his breath. "The only god in Equatorial Guinea," he said defiantly, raising his finger to the level of my eyes, "is our beloved president Theodore Obiang."

So, no: he was not a God-fearing Christian. Or at least not the God I had in mind.

"Come on, identification," he demanded, putting his hand out bad-temperedly.

Gabriel gave me a look of ironic gratitude.

"Officers," I said, sugar-coating my tone. "Forgive me. I've just arrived from the United States and I don't know the rules of the country."

"That's not my problem. Show me your papers."

"You're absolutely right, officer," I said calmly. "But it so happens… we've left our papers at the mission."

"Then you'll come to the police station with us."

A shiver ran down my spine when I heard those words. I had to summon up all my courage to avoid running away. "Now," I suggested in an unsteady voice as I took out some of the money the nuns had given me, "isn't there some way we can sort all this out, so as to make things simpler for everyone?"

The older policeman looked at the crumpled wad of notes with ill-concealed greed.

I held out my hand. After exchanging a glance, they took the money and counted it without the slightest shame.

"It's not enough," the younger one said. "You're coming with us."

"Wait a moment!" I said. I put both hands in my pockets and took out everything I could find. "It's all we've got!" I turned my skirt pockets inside out so that they could see it was true.

Gabriel did the same, and this seemed to convince the police there was nothing else to be had from us. They grabbed the few notes I had in my open hands. Then, hitching up their belts as if this were some ritual movement they had learnt at the police academy, they turned round and got into their vehicle again. They started the engine at the third attempt, looking at us out of the corners of their eyes without saying another word.

19

The rickety bus's only working headlight wobbled, so that it shone alternately on either side of the wall of vegetation the road snaked through. We were alone in the last row of seats, sharing the bus with an enormous woman with a chicken on her lap, a couple of children and an old lame man who was snoring fit to bust. We had left the city of Bata behind more than an hour ago, we were making good speed, and what was even better so far there was no wood to knock on in that vehicle we had not come to a road checkpoint.

Perhaps because of that brief relaxed interlude I felt I could allow myself to recall my encounter with the police, turning away as I did so from that gloomy landscape without a horizon.

Without realizing, I gave a brief snort.

"What's up?" Gabriel asked, not taking his eyes off the road.

"Nothing," I muttered shaking my head. "It's just that I remembered what one of the policemen said."

"What do you mean?"

"That nonsense about Theodore Obiang being the only god in Guinea. I didn't imagine the guy was so popular."

"It's not nonsense," he said sadly. "They simply follow the official policy."

"What?" I turned to him. "Are you telling me the official policy in Guinea consists of making the president into a god?"

"I know, it sounds like a bad joke, but it's a message that's repeated ceaselessly in the government media. And some people are beginning to believe it."

"You've got to be kidding me."

"Yeah, sure. Look at me laughing."

In all honesty, I was not that surprised. I had been in Guinea long enough to realize the statement was perfectly feasible. In fact I remembered, with a grimace the argument they had used to sentence me was not much more sensible.

I put my head out of the window to let the air clear my mind and strip away the unease that had been glued to my eyes for weeks now, leading me to see everything through a gloomy prism which was getting darker with each passing day. The problem was that the thick, lifeless air inside the bus was not helping. Instead it was making me feel suffocated and strange.

Anxiety had let in fear, which in turn had left the door open to something very close to weariness. I had arrived two months before overflowing with enthusiasm, imagining that I was going to save something or someone, that I was going to be useful, that the heart of darkness was going to be charmed by my devotion and generosity and that in turn I was going to fall in love with the country, and the day I went back home, I would say farewell amid the tears and promises of a crowd of grateful Africans.

Reality had decided to put me in my place. Which was, to be precise, on the back seat of a rackety bus making its way through the jungle night, fleeing to save my life.

"What a load of crap," I said under my breath.

Gabriel only half-turned to me. He gave the trace of a grin. "I totally agree."

"Hell…" I muttered. "It's just that when I stop to think about it, I get all worked up. But not only because of what's happening to us, because of everything in general. I swear I don't know how you put up with it."

"Who told you we do?"

"Well… I mean, it's enough to drive anyone crazy." I said. I tapped my temple. "It's a nightmare of soldiers and criminal police, led by brainless psychopaths."

"I see you're getting to know them."

"And you think it's funny?"

"What do you want me to do? Cry? Shoot myself? Organize a revolution?"

"Well, maybe that wouldn't be such a bad idea," I said heatedly. "Wouldn't you like to get rid of this crappy government?"

"I'd rather go on living."

"But this isn't life! Better to die on your feet than live on your knees."

Gabriel's expression lost the kindness I had seen in it a few seconds before. "Look, Sarah. First, don't raise your voice. And second, don't shout slogans at me. If you're going to start coming out with words you've seen written on t-shirts, you're in the wrong continent."

"Slogans? Do you really think living like this is normal?"

"Normal?" he said with a grimace. "Come on, Sarah, what's normal for you? Does having clean water seem normal to you? Electricity? Sewage? Hospitals? Food? Those aren't normal things, they're luxuries. The thing is that the minority of you, privileged people, who can enjoy them are convinced it's *normal*, and that the poor of the world are *weird people*. And the most pathetic thing is that you believe it's a question of merit that we live the way we do and you live the way you do. You miss the overwhelming truth: that you are the exception. That the immense majority of humans lack everything you think is essential, and that the number of poor people is increasing and the number of rich is decreasing."

"Now, don't you give me that typical African victim culture stuff about how the whites are the bad guys and everything's our fault. We all share some of the responsibility, but the ones who're robbing you are your own countrymen. Besides," I added angrily, jabbing a finger at him, "I don't only mean material things, but rights like justice and freedom."

"How lovely... shall we get off the bus, hold hands and start singing?"

"Go to hell, I'm being serious."

"Serious?" he said, and arched his eyebrows theatrically. "Do you really believe you're being serious? The only freedom you can find in places like Equatorial Guinea is the freedom to choose how to die, and sometimes not even that. It's typical of the whites to spout off about high-and-mighty concepts, but when it comes to making sacrifices or real efforts, they all look elsewhere or click on *like* on Facebook and feel good about it, convinced they've done all they could. Freedom and justice are beautiful words, but they don't put food on the table, or help vaccinate the children." He paused, breathed out loudly and looked up at the ceiling. "The only thing the revolutions in Africa have achieved is to dye the soil even redder, while foreign multinationals and governments arm and finance the different factions, with the sole aim of harvesting economic benefits when the conflict's over. And in the meantime, we shed blood so that a company or a bank can see a point two per cent rise in profits. And in the end, as always, the plates are still empty and there are no vaccines for the children."

I shook my head, denying his arguments. "But you've got to do something! Why don't you try to get rid of this dictator?"

"Do you believe the next one will be any better?"

"How should I know? But you ought to try, right? If you can put a genuine democracy in place, then you'll be able to—"

Gabriel interrupted me with a bitter laugh. "A democracy?" he repeated, as if it were the most amusing word in the world. "By all the spirits, you haven't understood a thing."

Then, as if the discussion had influenced the weather, it started to rain as I have only seen it rain in that part of the world.

Not one of your well-bred American rains which get your shoes wet and put the traffic lights out of order, but a furious rain which hurls itself against the windshield and roof, violent and implacable. The same rain that paints Guinea with lush green, and that I have seen more than once turn dirt paths into racing streams in a matter of minutes.

The beams of the headlights were diluted in the dense curtain of water and the windshield wipers were unable to cope, leaving a very limited field of vision which forced the driver to go much more slowly. Meanwhile the road went on zigzagging interminably, and an uncomfortable silence fell between us after that bitter argument.

"Have you thought about where we can spend the night?" I asked to break the tension.

"No idea, we might have to sleep in the street," he replied briefly. He was still upset with me.

"I see…" I leaned my head on the backrest. "I'm still not really convinced hiding in Bata would have been more dangerous than traveling on this road in the middle of the night."

"I explained that before," he said impatiently. "Despite being the second city of the country, but Bata is no more than a big village where it's not easy to pass unnoticed. Even more when at any moment they might start searching for a fake nun with a Guinean guide."

"All right, maybe in the circumstances this might be the best option, but heading inland on this bus, aren't we getting further away from the Gabon border instead of getting closer?"

"Don't worry," he said in a kinder voice. "We're taking a little detour, but we'll get where I want to all the same."

"What about the roadblocks?"

"As you'll have noticed, in the continental region there are fewer than in Bioko," he said, as we passed the umpteenth trailer loaded with huge trees from the jungle. "Usually there aren't any until Niefang crossroads."

"And we've got no choice but to stop there?"

"I'm afraid so."

"So what will we do, then?"

"Improvise. It hasn't turned out so bad, so far."

"I'd rather discuss it beforehand and agree, so as not to mess things up."

"Yes, that would be good," he said, but then after a brief pause he added, "Unfortunately, it seems we won't be able to."

"Why not?"

Gabriel jerked his chin forward at a dirty sign, half invisible in the rain. On it we could just about make out the words: POLICE CHECK. FOR A BETTER GUINEA.

20

Walking through the jungle without really knowing where you are or where you are going is stupid, doing it at night is simply insane, but if the rain is coming down in torrents you have to be absolutely desperate even to try. And yet this was our best chance of staying alive.

We had asked the driver to stop the bus just before it reached the checkpoint, and with nothing more than a wink he let us know that as far as he was concerned he would say nothing about our presence. We had been walking in silence for about ten minutes, getting away from the road, and by now we had lost sight of the lights at the checkpoint and hence of any point of reference to indicate where we were or where we were headed. I walked with a lighter in my right hand, trying to protect it from the rain with my left. Gabriel followed me, carrying a plastic canvas full of holes which we had found under our seat on the bus. For fear of falling in the hands of the militiamen again at some checkpoint, we had decided not to tempt fate and go into the jungle, no matter how unpromising it might seem. If the jungle by daylight might seem daunting, at night it turns into the most horrific place imaginable.

The useless gleam of my lighter barely managed to do more than light up the fleeting drops of rain that sparkled in front of me. I cheered myself by thinking that at least under that thick canopy of leaves the rain was less intense, and in some places we were almost sheltered from it. What could not be ignored was the brutal blast of the downpour on the overhead vault of the jungle, which I felt in my chest like a dull, deep vibration.

My sandals were sinking in the thick layer of humus and I had already slipped a couple of times, falling on my face in the mud, pestered by Gabriel's voice at my back, urging me to go faster and not stop.

"But I have no idea where I'm going!" I protested. I was breathless from that irrational escape in the dark.

"That doesn't matter," he said sharply. "We have to get away from the road."

"But—"

"Sarah," he interrupted me, "listen to me. For all we know, some passenger on that bus might have gotten nervous and told on us. I don't want to give them the chance of finding us by following our trail."

"Our trail? Are you serious?" I looked down at my feet. "With this downpour they wouldn't manage to find the trail of a herd of elephants!"

"Don't be so sure. The police and militiamen use hunters to follow trails, and you can be absolutely sure they'll find ours. I only hope we've got time to get far enough."

To make things worse, the terrain was always steep, so I was forced to hold on to trees and lianas all the time, as much to help me pull myself uphill as to stop me sliding on the downhill stretches. Although there was no way I could avoid this with only rubber sandals on my feet in that unbelievably slippery mud.

We had just gone down a second hill when the moment I put my feet down on the other side of a raging stream, my legs decided they had had enough. I stopped to breathe, leaning on my mud-covered knees, and saw Gabriel stop beside me. He too was panting heavily.

"Don't stop, Sarah," he urged me for the umpteenth time. "We have to keep going."

"No," I said breathlessly. "I'm not going on... I'm dead tired."

"If we don't keep going," he insisted gravely, "we will really be dead."

"Well…" I was fed up with the whole business by now. "You keep going if you want to. I can't take another step."

In that dense darkness I could not even see Gabriel, but for a few endless seconds I feared he would start wondering whether to stay with me or not.

"All right, "he conceded. "Let's look for someplace to spend the night."

"Now we understand each other."

"But before dawn comes," he warned me, "we'll set off again, and we won't stop until we reach safety."

"Very well," I said. I was happy at the thought of a rest. "I'll ask the receptionist to give us a call at six."

Gabriel did not laugh at my joke, and from the shadows, laconically, he gestured to me to follow him. We had to build ourselves a shelter.

Now it was he who held the feeble flame, while I carried the branches and leaves he passed me. I dragged or carried various huge banana leaves, others in the shape and size of hats in the style of Ladies' Day at the Grand National, all kinds of branches and flexible lianas, and a small palm tree which Gabriel had stripped of leaves and roots (I had no idea how or why) and given me to carry. I fell my whole length a couple of times, each time dropping a few branches which I tried hopelessly to find again by touch. When this happened Gabriel simply shone the lighter on me to make sure I was all right, then went on with his peculiar harvest. I followed the faint light, knowing full well that if I got lost in the dark, with the noise of the rain on the trees echoing like a million crazy drums, Gabriel would surely never be able to find me. And certainly nobody else would.

"We have enough," he said when I caught up with him again.

"I'm glad, 'cause I can't go on any longer."

He said nothing, simply stood up and went on walking while I wondered where on earth he was going.

For twenty or thirty yards we followed the course of the stream where I had put my feet down a few minutes before, until the light came to a halt and illuminated a strange silhouette. At first I did not recognize it, but then I made out the spectacular base of an imposing ceiba tree. Its unmistakable buttresses, like those of a Romanesque church, prop up an immense trunk which can easily reach a hundred and thirty feet tall, and whose base is perfect for setting up a shelter. In addition its massive upper branches would act as an umbrella and disperse a great deal of the rain, which was as heavy as ever.

"First we have to clear the ground," Gabriel said. "But be careful, use one of the branches. You never know what's under the leaves."

"What do you mean exactly by *you never know*?" I asked warily.

"Well, in Africa *you never know* might be a lot of things, and not many of them are nice ones. Although you'd better not think of that and concentrate on being careful."

With our limited light we might have overlooked an aardvark, but even so we cleared the place reasonably well, and if there had been a previous tenant there I was sure we had frightened it in our frenzy of cleaning. Next we tied the branches together using thin, flexible lianas, making a flat structure roughly six feet square, covered this with the enormous leaves we had collected and leaned it against the steep buttresses of the ceiba, creating a spartan but effective shelter for the night. Once we had fixed this substitute for a roof, we spread the plastic Gabriel had brought and immediately sat down on it. Of course all this was just an improvised canopy, and we could see the rain pouring down on both sides as well as at the front, but we were reasonably well-protected. Considering our situation, this was a lot more than might have been expected.

I gazed up at the ceiling, where a few drops of rain were filtering through. "Well," I said, "not bad, even if the quality of the finish leaves something to be desired."

"So sue me."

"Maybe I will," I said, relieved that he had recovered a little of his good humor. "And now I come to think about it," I added, seeing the trunk beside him, "why did you make me carry that chunk of palm tree all this way?"

"It's our dinner."

"Do you think I'm a beaver?"

"Does that mean you don't want any?"

"I'm not so hungry as to eat a tree," I retorted dismissively.

"All right... but don't come asking later on."

Then he pulled off the bark with his hands and began to peel the trunk with his teeth, leaving only the white core, which he proceeded to chew on calmly and without a word.

It took me a few seconds to realize, then I lunged at him and grabbed it from his hands.

"You...! You could've told me it was heart of palm!"

Gabriel smiled, and broke the delicious palm in half."By the way, do you usually sleep with your mouth open?"he asked as he chewed.

"I... well, I have no idea," I said in puzzlement. "Why do you ask?"

"Oh, it's nothing," he said, playing it down. "It's just that during the night some spiders love to crawl into the first hole they find."

21

At some time during the night the rain stopped.

A strange silence followed the cacophony, waking me suddenly with the unpleasant feeling that I was now deaf. My hearing took a couple of minutes to get used to it, rather like when you leave a brightly lit room and for a few moments everything seems darker than it really is. Slowly the noises of the jungle made their presence felt, or perhaps they had been there before and it was me who was gradually regaining the ability to hear them. First, as usual, the tireless, irregular croaking of the tree frogs. Then various unknown birds joined in the chorus, hooting or clacking their beaks in a baffling symphony. Next came distant *uh-uhs* mingled with the swish of branches bending and the movement of bodies in the crowns of the trees, many feet above our heads. And lastly, most disquieting of all, the sounds from the foliage around us: stealthy footsteps which might equally well have been those of a shy antelope or a lurking leopard. Although what really made my hair stand on end was the barely audible whisper of long scaly bodies slithering through the dry leaves, only inches away from me.

I huddled into a fetal position. Strange as it might seem, although I was in the midst of the equatorial jungle, I was beginning to feel a touch of cold. I had nothing to cover myself with, and the soaking wet clothes which were stuck to my body were so uncomfortable that I was beginning to consider taking them off. But instead of that I did something much more sensible: I hugged Gabriel in search of his body heat and, I must admit, the assurance I felt at having him by my side. Night-time in the jungle was terrifying, every shadow and every noise meant a bloodthirsty predator waiting for me to fall asleep, and without him there beside me dispelling my fear with his confident snores, that night would have been the longest in my life. So I hugged the only thing that was anchoring me to sanity, shooed away the monsters that were harassing my imagination, and tried to sleep.

And it was then, like a growing tide of varied resonances, that the insects appeared. First there was just an isolated buzzing beside my ear which I simply waved away with my hand, but then the buzzing grew progressively until it was an insolent murmur overwhelming all the other noises of the night. At the same time, I suppose unavoidably, my bare legs, ankles and arms began to itch. The mosquitoes were having a feast.

I hardly felt I had managed to shut my eyes at last, exhausted by the mortal tiredness which cramped every muscle of my ill-used body, when a hand shook my shoulder lightly and urged me to wake up.

"What's the matter?" I asked in sudden fear, convinced that some kind of danger was lurking.

"We have to leave."

"What, now?"

"Yes, now."

"But I've only just fallen asleep," I protested, rubbing my eyes in the dark.

"That's what you think. Dawn's about to break."

I looked in all directions and could see nothing remotely like an early morning gleam. More precisely, I could see nothing whatsoever. Everything was as dark as it had been when I had fallen asleep.

"Come on," he insisted, standing up and moving the roof aside.

I was sure he had gone mad and, having lost track of time, he was set on walking in the middle of the night. The drawback was that I had no choice but to go with him, so I got to my feet in my turn, shivering, half-dead with drowsiness and exhaustion.

"You're wrong, Gabriel," I said as I stretched. "It can't be any later than midnight."

"Whatever you say…"

"What do you bet?"

"A cold beer if it's dawn in less than an hour's time."

"Now I'd rather have a black coffee… but, okay, I'm on."

And so we started to walk again. Gabriel went behind me carrying the plastic sheet with me in front, trying to illuminate the ground under my feet with the lighter. I was half asleep, and the previous day's exhaustion was taking its toll with each step I took. As a result I did not pay much heed to a curious optical phenomenon taking place before my eyes, assuming it was the product of dim light and exhaustion.

The fact was that the ground seemed to be alive and moving under my mud-covered feet.

To my surprise, when we reached the rounded summit of the first hill of that day a little later, I glimpsed the first light of dawn. I was fantasizing about a warm sun that would dry my damp nun's clothes, without taking my eyes off the red promise of daylight, when Gabriel passed me without stopping.

"You owe me a beer," he said.

And I was very happy to have taken on that debt.

As the day grew, my spirits rose. The hills seemed less steep, the descents less dangerous. Slowly, the jungle revealed its confused and tangled shapes. Cyclopean trees like incredible columns rose from the earth and lost themselves in that green dome, as if they had been given the task of holding up the sky with their branches. If Tarzan had really existed   I thought with absolute conviction – there was no doubt he would have made his house in one of them.

A multitude of smaller trees filled the spaces between these giants. Most of them, if not all, were unknown to me, and although the diameter of their stems was ridiculous in comparison with their bigger cousins, they easily reached fifty or sixty feet. Like drowning men stretching their necks out of the water, they seemed to stretch to the limits of physical possibility in order to reach the few rays of sun, which were greatly esteemed amid that hyperbole of lush growth. What also surprised me was how relatively easy it was to walk through that jungle. There was no need to wield a machete to clear a path for ourselves, nor to leave our clothes and skin in rags on sharp thorns. If the ferns and smaller trees were to disappear and the layer of dead leaves on the ground were replaced by a well mown lawn, it could easily pass for a nicely maintained – if rather dark – park to have a picnic in.

I was about to pass my hand nonchalantly along one of those small trees with soft bark, thinking about nothing in particular, when Gabriel gave a shout behind me. I froze with shock.

"Don't move," he said, almost in a whisper.

"What? What's the matter?"

"Don't move a muscle."

"But what—" And then I saw it.

It looked like a thin liana coiled round the trunk. A bright green liana, no thicker than my little finger, flattened at the end. An end with two fixed spots on each side flanking a fine dark line. Out of this, for a tenth of a second, there poked a tiny appendix, pink and forked.

My hand was less than ten inches away from it.

"Now, without moving your arm, start walking back very, very slowly."

I began to move without taking my eyes off the snake, and realized I was holding my breath.

"Come on, Sarah, don't be afraid."

Like hell, don't be afraid, I thought. *That's easy to say when you're three yards away.*

I managed to take two steps back as slowly as possible, but my heart seemed to want to play tricks on me by beating so hard my ears rang. I could have sworn those heartbeats were making the leaves vibrate. At last I bumped into Gabriel, who seized me by the shoulders.

"There now," he said. "Calm down, you're trembling like a baby bird."

"How else am I supposed to tremble? That was not fun at all."

"It's a green mamba," he said before I could ask him. "And be grateful it was still lethargic at this hour, because if not, you and I would be saying goodbye right now."

Needless to say, from then on I kept my hands in my pockets and eyed all the trees I went past distrustfully, as well as the ground I walked on. And that led to another worrying discovery.

The strange sensation that the ground was a living entity was still there, so I decided to get down on my knees and look at it more closely. And what I discovered left me frozen, because far from what I had thought, it was not an optical illusion due to tiredness or the ingestion of hallucinogenic heart of palm. The ground was genuinely alive.

Millions of insects were moving through the decomposing dead leaves, making it undulate like the surface of a grey-brown sea. At first glance I could make out legions of ants following each other and crossing each other's tracks, beetles of different sizes and colors, unpleasant centipedes, millipedes and whoknowshowmanypedes. But above all, occupying almost the entire space in a density I could never have imagined possible, an uncountable number of spiders of all sizes flickered through that rotting substratum, rapidly and mysteriously, as if the anxiety to find something had set them all crazily in motion at the same time, passing over one another, ignoring each other and the countless other insects whose paths crossed with theirs.

The spectacle would have been hypnotic if not for the fact that the moment I stopped, those hairy or chitinous creatures of six, eight or more legs began to crawl up my bare legs and under my skirt.

I shouted like a madwoman as I jumped, trying to rid myself of the disgusting insects, until I found myself in front of Gabriel, who was watching me with one brow arched as if he were waiting for me to get tired of playing. So I tried to recover what dignity I had left. Concentrating on not leaving my foot for more than a second in any single place, I went on. I moved aside so as to follow my companion's steps, while he walked on as if he were simply taking a shortcut home.

While we walked, Gabriel would sporadically go up to a tree, study it closely and now and then stretch out his arm or use a thick branch he had taken as a staff to pick mangoes, papayas or bananas. These he put in the oil-cloth, which now served as a shopping basket. He also recited the names of some, pointing at them with his staff.

"This," he would say for example, "is a *palorojo*, and from its heart you can get a dye which is used in religious rituals, and also in medicines that only the healers know how to prepare. Also, the wood is useful for making tables and chairs. And that one over there" he would go on, enjoying his role as native guide "that one losing itself in the heights above is an *ukola,* and it can reach more than two hundred feet."

As the day wore on, the heat became more suffocating. It was as if we were going through a shadowy abandoned greenhouse, since though we could guess there was a splendid equatorial sun above the jungle canopy, down where we were the sunlight barely reached us. In any case, when it did it was reflected through a myriad leaves, which absorbed most of it. But that did not stop the unbearable humidity from making me sweat buckets underneath clothes that had never fully dried and I could not take off, unless I wanted to be bitten all over by the mosquitoes permanently harassing us. They had had a good go at me the night before.

Where they were not protected, my arms and legs were practically covered in tiny red spots, which when I sweated itched unbearably. Oddly enough, these bites were not slightly inflamed, as is the usual thing; there were only those little red marks. Gabriel eased my mind, assuring me they were gnats, not the Anopheles mosquitoes that transmitted malaria. On the other hand he pointed out that the area we were in was a high malaria risk, and that one bite from an infected mosquito would be enough to pass on the terrible illness.

That reminded me of the information I had read in a dossier given to every UNICEF member before taking any action in the field. A whole chapter was devoted to prophylaxis and treatment of malaria. I recalled the basic preventive measures: not leaving stagnant water near the house, taking a dose of chloroquine daily, always using a mosquito net to sleep, and if you were without one, smearing yourself with a repellent high in diethyltuolamine. I grimaced when I remembered how I had slept the last few nights, without any kind of protection and each day adding dozens of fresh bites which I had gotten used to ignoring. I remembered too that the cause of the illness was not a virus or bacteria but a parasite called *plasmodium* or something which flowed from the blood of an infected individual the appalling mosquito loves human blood so much that it ignores all other animals to a healthy one, and that it uses the *Anopheles* as an involuntary means of transport from one to the other. A parasite which, unbelievably, is impossible to eliminate. Which means that once you get malaria, you get it forever.

And perhaps under the influence of that thought, I found I was beginning to feel a little weak and that my joints were aching: the first symptoms of the illness.

22

We walked all morning through a mountainous region where the jungle was rather thicker, and even less sun penetrated as far as the layer of humus we were moving across with difficulty. The acrid smell of rotting vegetation, which I found so unpleasant in the first hours of the day, had already taken up permanent residence in my nostrils and I barely noticed it. What I did notice was that my feeling of sickness was growing, with symptoms like the onset of flu, so that I felt increasingly tired and needed more and more effort to move. We stopped to eat the fruit Gabriel had gathered along the way, in a clearing where an enormous ceiba had yielded to the ravages of time and the strangling creepers. After collapsing, it had left a small gap far above, and through this the sun fell warm on my face.

"How are you?" Gabriel asked with a certain unease.

"Tired… and I have a headache."

He frowned before saying, not very convincingly, "Don't worry. We'll take a break, then when you feel better we'll go on."

"I feel like dropping down on the ground and sleeping till tomorrow."

"I'm afraid there's no time for that. But if you want to take a nap for ten minutes, go ahead."

"Yeah…" I did not bother to hide my annoyance. "By the way, do you have any idea where we're going in such a hurry?"

"I think if we keep going southeast we'll reach the road again."

"The road again? Aren't we running away from it?"

"We're running away from the militiamen and their checkpoints. Once we've cleared those, we need to get as near as possible to the road until we come to a village."

"Won't that be dangerous?

"Not as much as going on walking blindly through the jungle."

"I thought you were an expert."

Gabriel raised his eyes to the heavens for a moment, as if he were summoning up his patience."Look, Sarah. The fact that I know a few of the trees and can recognize a poisonous snake doesn't in the least mean that I'm capable of surviving in the jungle for very long. The thing is, hardly anybody in Africa lives in the jungle. People never go into it unless they're forced to, and the villages are always found in cleared areas."

"Excuse me," I protested. "Although I haven't been in Guinea very long, I've been to several small villages that were buried in the jungle."

"No, Sarah, you're wrong. You've only been on the island of Bioko, where what you call jungle is no more than wet forest, and in many cases just old overgrown cocoa plantations. The true jungle is here, on the continent. On Bioko there are no leopards, green mambas, killer elephants or trees that can kill you just by brushing against them." He was staring at me, trying to make sure I understood what he was saying. "Even though in the white men's movies it might seem different, Africans fear the jungle as much as you do, and for perfectly good reasons."

"But... you seemed so confident walking along."

"Confident?" he repeated, and laughed in disbelief. "That's funny. I've spent the whole morning trying not to look scared."

With Gabriel's disturbing revelation still going round my head, we set off again shortly after finishing our frugal lunch. I was still tired, even more so (if that was possible) after our stop, but we could not just sit there forever. And in any case, when ants, beetles and spiders started crawling up my legs all over again I suddenly felt the urge to get up and keep on walking.

As the few rays of sunlight that managed to get through the vegetation were vertical by now, I guessed it had to be noon, and this discouraged me considerably when I realized that it did not dispel the shadows around me. It was like dwelling in an eternal twilight of strange, menacing shadows. Since Gabriel had given me his speech about the dangers of the jungle I had begun to see the place, which at first I had thought fascinating, in a very different light. It was now no longer an immense botanic garden lacking only a lawn. Instead I was walking through a gloomy forest where death might be lurking coiled around a tree, or under a pile of dry leaves, or watching me at that moment from the branch of some tree waiting for the right time to launch itself at its prey.

I followed Gabriel's footsteps, trying to put my feet where he did, without touching anything at all and constantly looking back, with my heart in my mouth when some shrub moved or I thought I saw a fleeting shadow crossing behind me out of the corner of my eye. Otherwise the jungle remained absolutely silent. An unreal silence, that I had not perceived until that moment and accentuated even more the oppressive loneliness of that jungle without daylight.

"Gabriel…" I said as we climbed up a steep hillside.

"Yes?" He too sounded tired.

"Why is there so much silence?"

He stopped and strained his ear, looking in all directions."It's true… There isn't even a bird to be heard."

"And that's… not good, right?" I asked, fearing the answer.

He turned to me with the trace of a smile."Far from it," he said, sounding almost cheerful. "It's a good thing."

"Why's that?"

"Easy. Where there's a lot of animal life, it means there are no humans to hunt them, which means—"

"If there aren't any animals, it's because we're close to a village where there are humans who hunt them."

My guide's satisfied expression was enough to tell me this was the correct conclusion.

Sure enough, a few minutes later we smelt smoke, and following the trail like hungry predators we reached the side of the road we had left behind the night before. In front of us a small hamlet of houses scattered along a dirt road looked to my eyes like an island of civilization in this green ocean. What was more, one of the humble huts with its planks and tin roof bore a rusty Coca-Cola sign, and out of its rudimentary chimney came the smoke which had led us there. It seemed to be a very modest roadside diner, and without stopping for a moment to think I started toward it in search of food and water.

But to my surprise Gabriel grabbed my arm and pulled me back. He pointed at the place, and without understanding what on earth he could mean, I looked at the small diner closely.

At that moment a man I had not noticed came out of the hut. The first thing I saw coming out of the darkness of the hut was a pair of olive-green pants, then a shirt of the same color and finally, to my horror, a flat cap above a pair of eyes that were staring fixedly toward where I was: the eyes I will never forget as long as I live.

23

I put my hand over my mouth to muffle a scream. How could *he* possibly be there? We were hundreds of miles of ocean and jungle from Malabo, we had just poked our heads out from the asphyxiating jungle for air in the middle of nowhere, and against all odds there was Captain Anastasio Mba, in all his disgusting reality.

I looked at Gabriel almost pleadingly, and he in turn stared back at me with the same incredulity. He was as confused as I was.

We stayed there watching in silence, without moving a muscle. Meanwhile the soldier stretched in the doorway of the hut, then with a wave called someone we could not see. A car engine started and stopped in front of the captain so that he could get into the vehicle, a pickup which apart from the driver was carrying six soldiers in camouflage seated on two wooden benches.

We knew straight away that these men were after us.

"What are we going to do now?" I asked in a whisper, more to myself than to him.

He remained silent. He watched the military truck move away along the road. "We have to go into the village," he said after a few seconds.

"What? They'll find us out straight away! By now half Guinea must know the army's looking for a white missionary and a Guinean, and someone will end up warning the militiamen, even if it's out of fear."

"Yes, you're right… clearly we can't both go together."

"And anyway, it'd be too much of a risk if you went on your own—"

"Actually," he interrupted me, "I was going to suggest that you went alone."

I was stunned. "What did you say?"

"Think about it. If they know we're in this part of the country, the militiamen will have all the roads under surveillance. The best way… the *only* way we have of getting out of here is by hiring a hunter as a guide to lead us through the jungle. And who better to hire one than a white tourist?"

"Do I, by any chance, look like a tourist?" I said opening my arms.

"A very devout tourist."

"You're very funny, but your plan sounds like a mess to me."

"Don't worry, it'll work."

In fact I could not have said which of the two possibilities I found more frightening: that the plan would work, or that it would not.

"Hell…" I thought out loud. I considered the dense jungle behind me. "I can't bear the thought of spending another day back in there."

"There aren't many options open to us, Sarah. And pray that you find someone who's prepared to guide us."

Finally, trembling with fear, I had no choice but to get to my feet and head for the village on the other side of the road.

With my ill-used missionary uniform, like a Franciscan castaway in that all-engulfing jungle, I crossed the road and went up to the small shop-diner the soldier had come out of, moments before.

"Hello, is there anybody here?" I said as I peered into the doorway.

In contrast to the blinding light outside, the place appeared lost in shadow. A couple of fly-covered plastic chairs was all there was in the way of furniture, and almost more disconcerting than the absence of any table to sit at was the decoration of the shelves. They were completely filled with empty Coca-Cola bottles and tins of sardines in tomato sauce. Dozens of them, as if the people of that village only fed on that sort of thing.

Then an old woman with skin that might have been mummified, dressed in rags, came out of the back. She pulled back a curtain.

"Hello," I said again. "Good morning."

The old woman looked up and stared at me for several seconds with narrowed eyes, scrutinizing me.

Then I thought this had been a big mistake. I had decided to ask about a guide, at the place I supposed would be the one most frequented by the population of that roadside village. And now it dawned on me that if Captain Anastasio had been there, that old woman might know they were looking for a Guinean escapee and a fake missionary nun: tall, with brown hair and a face covered in bruises and scratches.

"Can I help?" she asked at last with unexpected friendliness.

"Well now, you see, we… I'm looking for a hunter, someone who could be a guide through the jungle for me."

The woman glanced behind me. "For you alone?"

"Uh, yes. Just me."

She looked me up and down, obviously skeptical. "Are you a nun?"

"A Franciscan missionary."

By the expression on her face I might equally well have told her I was Batman. "Aha…" she muttered with a trace of scorn. "I have a nephew who can take you. Very good at tracking."

"Tracking?"
"Animal trails."
"Oh, right. Of course."

"Come," she said, taking a few stumbling steps. "My nephew's name is Renato. He lives just nearby. Good man."

I went out after the old woman, who stopped after a few yards and looked from one side of the road to the other.

"Sister," she said in puzzlement, looking up and down the road. "How did you get here? I don't see a car…"

"Um… it broke down a few miles down the road, and we had to walk here."

"We?" she asked raising an eyebrow. "Weren't you by yourself?"

My throat was so dry I could not even swallow."Well, actually…" Blank, my mind was a total blank.

"Bah, it doesn't matter," she said to my surprise, and winked at me. "You're pretty. If I were younger, I would also…"

Baffled by the conclusion the old woman had come to, I simply nodded in agreement and went on walking beside her.

Just as she had promised, her nephew's house was quite near, and when she banged on the doorframe a man dressed only in the briefest sports shorts and a pair of flip-flops came out. He certainly did not look like a daring hunter.

"Hello, auntie," he said to his relative, but he was looking at me.

"Renato, this young woman wants you to guide her through the jungle."

"Renato N'Dongo, at your service," he said shaking my hand. "Do you want me to be your guide?"

"Yes, that's right. I'd like to get to Oveng or Acalayong," I said, remembering Gabriel's instructions.

The hunter snorted."Gee… that's a long way, sister. Do you think you'll be able to hold up?"

"Don't you worry about that," I said firmly.

The guide took a step back to study me. He seemed satisfied with what he saw. "All right," he said. "But remember, there aren't any taxis in the jungle to go back in when you're tired."

"In my country I love to go hiking in the mountains. I won't get tired before you do," I said with a touch of bravado. I hoped I would not have to eat my words later on.

"So... tell me, how many days do you have?"

"As many as necessary."

"Wonderful, then we'll surely find them."

"Find them?" I asked, distracted. "Find who?"

Renato opened his eyes wider and laughed heartily. "Who do you think, sister? You've come to see the gorillas, right?"

24

From a distance our group would have looked, to say the least, colorful. Renato led the way with his satchel of vegetable fiber, his ragged clothes, rubber boots, a machete at his belt, and a battered-looking shotgun hanging from a cord on his back. Gabriel followed, with the big oil-cloth folded under one arm. And at the end of that bizarre procession the nun, that is to say, me: with my robes an eyesore, dirty, gaunt, covered in mosquito bites and surely -although Gabriel denied it still with the marks of a beating on my face. But the most surreal thing of all was the fact that the background of this picture was one of the least explored areas of virgin jungle on the planet, and I had no idea yet of where we were headed.

We walked at a good pace, along an invisible path that Renato seemed to be following without hesitation. To me, on the other hand, everything came to look more and more like the same. Oppressed by a headache which was increasingly getting worse, I had stopped looking up a while ago, and was concentrating instead on my feet and where I put them at each step. Nevertheless, in contrast to that morning, when it had just been Gabriel and I, I now felt safer under the guidance of a true connoisseur of the jungle, who moved confidently through a green labyrinth that seemed to be repeating itself ad infinitum.

On top of this, the mud made our progress very difficult, particularly when we had to go uphill. Invariably I ended up slipping and falling on my face on the muddy ground. This did not seem to affect Renato's lively pace; he walked on without any apparent effort while Gabriel and I were barely able to follow him.

In one of those moments when we lagged behind, I went to Gabriel's side. "Hey, Gabriel," I said. I lowered my voice so that our guide would not hear. "I don't want to sound like a demanding tourist, but...would you mind telling me what's this joke about looking for gorillas? Oh, and that village—"

"Oveng."

"Yeah, that's right. What are we supposed to go there for?"

"It's our best option," he replied curtly. "Don't think about it."

My headache was getting worse, my legs were getting less willing to respond, and without either a voice or vote in the matter I found myself once again entering that dark and threatening jungle when what I really wanted to do was get out of it as soon as possible.

"I don't know... I guess all this has to make sense in some way. But it's got to be very, I mean *very* convincing, to make me understand why we're going into this fucking jungle again."

Gabriel nodded ahead. "Renato is a hunter and jungle guide. We can't risk going by a road watched by the militiamen, so the only way to get out of here is by crossing the Alem Heights until we reach the village of Oveng, on the other side of the mountains."

"And what do the gorillas have to do with all this?"

"The Alem Mountains," he said, breathing heavily with the effort of talking and walking at the same time, "are one of the last refuges of the western gorilla in this part of Africa, and it's not unusual for white people to come from the other side of the world just to watch them. So we have the perfect excuse for a Guinean to accompany an American through this part of the country without things looking too suspicious."

"Okay, I see... but doesn't our friend find it strange that instead of being a biologist or a specialist in primates, I'm just a shabby missionary nun?"

"Look, in this part of the world being white is strange enough. You could be dressed as Dracula, and it would only be one more western eccentricity. When it comes to you, we don't pay much attention to clothing." He looked aside at me. "In Africa, skin in itself is a social category."

"All right. Maybe the plan isn't so absurd," I admitted, "but how are we going to survive several days without water or food?"

"Well, that depends on Renato. What I don't know is what we're going to pay him with."

"Don't you worry about that," I said confidently. And with a conjuror's gesture I put my hand into my bra and took out a small wad of CFA francs.

"Where…? How…?" Gabriel asked, surprised.

"You don't think I'd have given all the money we had to those two policemen in Bata, do you?" I said with a swagger as I fanned myself with the notes. "I always keep a reserve hidden for emergencies… in a safe place."

The almost continuous ascent was a torture which went on for the whole afternoon, and we did not stop until close to twilight, when we reached a small construction of dark wood in the middle of nowhere.

"Who does this house belong to?" I asked Renato as he hastened to open the door.

"I don't know," he said with a shrug. He seemed to be surprised by my question. And without any more ado, he walked into the musty dwelling, followed by Gabriel and me.

The inside of the house did nothing to improve the impression it had given from the outside. In fact there was so little light inside that it was only after a few seconds that I could start to identify the furniture. Three of the four walls held a series of bunk beds, carved with the same esthetic aspirations as the façade, and a couple of tin pots hung from nails fixed on a tree trunk serving as a supporting column. These made up the entire decoration of the place. Without needing to be told, I guessed this was a hunter's shelter.

"Are we spending the night here?" I asked. I was aware of the absence of anything resembling a mattress.

"Or you can sleep outside if you like," Renato said innocently.

"The place is perfect, thank you," I hastened to reply. "But I'd like to know when the restaurant opens."

"Are you hungry?"

"Do you think nuns don't eat?"

"Don't worry, sister," he said, taking one of the pots and going out of the door. "I'll get something ready straight away."

I took a look around, feeling desolate, and the only thing that comforted me was the thought that it could not be worse than the previous night.

"What wood is the house made of?" I asked Gabriel idly as I ran my hand over the dark surface of the wall.

"Mahogany."

"The whole house is made of mahogany?"

"Well, I think the beds are okume."

"Are you teasing me?

"I do tease you as often as I can," he said trying not to smile. "But in this case I'm serious."

"Do you have any idea of the fortune all this wood would cost in the United States?"

He shook his head, as he almost always ended up doing when speaking with me. "Why do white people always put a price on things? This is worth so much and that's worth so much else… This is just a hunter's hut, and they needed to make it with the best planks so it would last years. Who cares how much this wood would cost if you can gather it for free?"

"Are you accusing me of seeing everything in terms of commerce?"

He spread his hands wide. "Okay, you're right. But... are you sure you don't? Perhaps you ought to take a look at yourself and the way you live. You might be surprised."

At that moment in our conversation Renato appeared at the door with the pot full of water in one hand and in the other, hanging by a leg from what looked like a length of fishing line, a small porcupine: dead since who knows when, stinking of putrid meat, with a revolting mass of white maggots coming out of its snout and eyes.

"We're lucky!" he said happily. "We have meat for dinner!"

25

To call the process of skinning and cleaning that porcupine nauseating would be an understatement. The poor animal, Renato explained, had fallen into one of the many traps surrounding the shelter. They had been put there so that the hunters would have something to eat when they came that way, and were apparently spread out all over the jungle. The hunters only needed to follow the marks on the nearby trees to find them, or in their absence simply follow the unmistakable scent of decomposing flesh.

"Sometimes, with luck, a deer falls in, and then there's meat for a whole week," he said.

"But the fact that there are maggots in the dead animal," I said wrinkling my nose, "isn't a bad sign?"

"Bad sign?"

"Yes, I mean, aren't they bad?"

"Ah, yes! No, maggots aren't good," he said nonchalantly. "It's best to leave them aside and just eat the meat."

Once a small fire was lit in the center of the house over some blackened stones which had been arranged there for that purpose, he added a couple of handfuls of rice and a touch of some mysterious spice to the stew. The three of us stayed there watching the pieces of meat bobbing up and down in the pot amid an eddy of rice.

This was not the first dubious stew I had eaten in Guinea I still remember my first visit to the market in Malabo and the uncontrollable nausea it gave me as I vowed to become a vegetarian for the rest of my life but having been an eyewitness to the whole process, from trap to plate, made me hesitate to sink my teeth into our dinner even though I was famished.

Renato pointed to my plastic plate with its two pieces of meat and mountain of untouched rice. "Don't you like the *chucu-chucu*, sister?" he asked.

"*Chucu-chucu?*"

"It's the local name for a porcupine," Gabriel clarified for me. He had no problem with the meat. He even licked the bones.

"Or is it a sin to eat *chucu-chucu*?" our guide asked in a slightly worrying tone, with a piece halfway to his mouth.

"Well, to be honest, I'm not very sure," I said, staring at my plate.

"Come on, sister," said Gabriel as he chewed. "We're in the hands of God, and if you've been a loyal nun, He'll never let this food harm you."

I answered the joke with a savage glare. Renato urged me with renewed enthusiasm to try his stew, and Gabriel supported him, trying hard not to laugh.

Compared to the night before, it was like staying at the Hilton. Perhaps because of sleepiness and accumulated tension, I slept like a log and was not even bothered by the hard wooden mattress, or the button of the woolen jacket I used as a pillow, which ended up tattooed on my cheek, like a smiley without the smile. Renato also put a termite nest in the fire which he had taken off a tree. It was an unbeatable natural mosquito repellent, he said, and in spite of my initial skepticism and the amount of smoke that filled the hut, I had to admit that it was.

The downside of that night was that my increasing muscular pains were getting worse, along with my headache, and that earlier hint of a feverish attack turned into a real fever, although for the moment only a slight one.

By the time I woke up Renato had already gathered half a dozen tasty mangoes *ondoh* in the Fang language, as he explained while he peeled one which we breakfasted on with relish. And after cleaning the pot and leaving everything as we had found it, including the animal trap, we left the small shelter behind and set out on our vigorous hike once again.

Even though I was feeling slightly worse than the day before, my spirits rose considerably. For two reasons in particular. The first was that even going back down practically every slope we had gone up, following sinuous paths I never managed to guess in advance, we gradually went up into the Alem range. This meant on the one hand that the air was getting cooler all the time and breathing was not like inhaling hot soup, and on the other that the vegetation changed slightly. More and more clearings appeared in the jungle, with the light of day bursting in through them: islands of light and dry heat, which attracted me like a moth and gladdened me like sunny days after a long winter.

The other reason which cheered my spirit was that I caught up with Renato and, first just to make conversation and then out of genuine interest, he began to translate some words from English into Fang."Thank you is *akiwa*," he explained.

"And please?" I asked.

"*Ngongo*."

"*Akiwa... ngongo*," I repeated like a diligent student. "And good morning?"

"*Kirimbong*. And good night, *bumbalú*."

Then we started on the numbers: *mbo, bobein, bilá, bení* and so on… And in this way the morning flew by, so that if my stomach had not started to rumble I would never have remembered I had to eat. Luckily we did not find any other maggot-infested animals on our way, so we lunched on a quantity of mangoes, papayas and bananas which Renato had been gathering along the way and putting in his satchel as if it were a shopping basket.

We ate and set off again. We had got no further than the personal pronouns when Renato stopped abruptly and put his arm out to stop me. He pointed at the ground, where all I could see was three lumps of some kind of dung, besieged by half a dozen beetles. I looked at our guide, puzzled at the way he was squatting beside it and observing it with great concentration, as if this were the Mona Lisa of stools. He stuck a twig in it and smelt it, then when I was starting to fear he was going to offer me some, he stood up and looked around the thicket.

"Gorillas..." he said. His expression had changed, and there was a mixture of respect and unsteadiness in his voice. "And they're very close..."

26

"The Lord God must owe you a favor, sister," he said in a low voice as he scanned the surroundings.

"Why do you say that?"

"Because I've never found such a fresh trail on the second day. It always takes much longer, from two to three weeks at least."

"Do you mean to say that this poop is a gorilla's, and that if we follow its trail we'll come on them?"

"That's right. And besides, it's so recent, they must be very close."

Even though the excuse for our excursion was to look for gorillas, I had never really thought we were going to find them. We were escaping from the Guinean army, not setting off on a nature walk. But at that precise moment, when Renato looked around as if expecting to see one of the giant apes appear from behind a tree, my priorities changed completely and I felt an unexpected, irrational wish to see those animals. From one moment to the next I had stopped worrying about all the Captain Anastasios of the country, and was only thinking about following that presumed trail wherever it led.

"Do you really think you'll be able to find them?" I asked excitedly.

"Of course I will, this is full of tracks," he said with complete confidence, pointing at some marks on the ground that were invisible to me.

"But... can they be dangerous?" I asked with some anxiety.

This time Renato took a couple of seconds to answer. "You never know, sister," was his laconic reply. "You never know."

Our jungle guide advanced very slowly, in absolute silence, moving aside the leaves on the ground with the tip of his machete. He had asked me to follow him several yards behind and to stop whenever he did. Gabriel came up to me, inquiring wordlessly what on earth were we doing, but I chose to ignore him. Perhaps aware that this was a once-in-a-lifetime opportunity and that since we were here, no matter how difficult our situation might be, I felt it would be a sin   a smile came to my mind at the odd comparison – not to do whatever might be necessary to see those legendary hominids in their natural habitat.

Renato stopped at any broken stem, slight depression in the layer of dry leaves, or any sign that might suggest the direction the apes had taken.

"How many gorillas do you think we're following?" I whispered when I found myself beside him.

"It's a big group. I should think about fifteen or twenty… there aren't often more than ten or twelve."

"And is it the breeding season?" I asked. I was thrilled at the prospect of seeing a baby gorilla.

"Gorillas don't have a set breeding time, sister," he said with the trace of a smile. "They're like humans, they have children when they want to… or when they can."

"Wonderful, I hope we're lucky and see one," I muttered.

Renato grimaced. "Well, I'd rather we didn't," he said, shaking his head. "When they have little ones they turn more aggressive, and if they feel we might harm them they won't hesitate to defend themselves. And believe me, an adult male can kill a man with one blow of his hand."

"Are you trying to scare me?"

"No, sister." He smiled condescendingly. "I just want you to know this isn't a game. Two years ago a rich, pushy executive from the Texaco company in Malabo hired almost all the guides of Alem Mountain. He wanted to see gorillas, just like you, and in spite of the warnings he tried to get close to a baby."

"So what happened?"

The guide looked at me very seriously, then lowered his head. "The dominant male, the silverback, attacked him. Then the females, and finally the young males." He was idly playing with the handle of his machete, presumably remembering the incident. "We had to kill them all. Nine gorillas dead because of a stupid tourist," he murmured in a broken voice. "Only the baby survived… to die of sadness a week later."

Thoughtful and rather less confident, I followed Renato's footsteps. He had gone back to his task of tracking. Gabriel walked behind me in silence, somewhat distant from the experience, and – so it seemed to me – rather reluctant to waste so much time on something which for him was no more than an excuse.

Although this area of the jungle was better lit, it was still dark and gloomy, and knowing those gigantic and potentially dangerous creatures were close made me walk with all my senses alert. I was conscious of every noise, every leaf which stirred without any apparent reason.

We crossed a stream, passing into an area which for some reason appeared rather more heavily trodden and the dry leaves on it more worn down than a few yards behind.

Suddenly Renato stopped abruptly and turned to us with a finger on his lips. He signaled to us to crouch low, then pointed to a vague spot in the underbrush, ahead and to the left of where we were.

My heart skipped a beat. We had found them.

27

I half-closed my eyes in an attempt to glimpse the black silhouette of the gorillas in the foliage, but was unable to see or even guess anything at all. In the jungle, sight is the most useless of all the senses. What with the surrounding darkness and the army of trees closing ranks around us, it was impossible to be clear about anything more than a few yards away.

And it was then, just when I was beginning to feel frustrated at my inability to glimpse anything, that the unmistakable sound of a branch breaking revealed an unusual agitation in the foliage, and behind it a fleeting shadow, black and huge.

It was about twenty or twenty-five yards from me, but even so it looked enormous. Although I could only partially glimpse its back, I could feel the calmness of its movements and the magnitude of its power in what was its domain.

It appeared to be sitting on the ground, eating nonchalantly. Every once in a while, when it reached out to grab fresh shoots, the plants around it shook, and that was what had given it away.

I could not take my eyes off that hairy back, fixed to the spot, ignoring the obnoxious mosquitoes whining around me and the insects which insisted on crawling up my legs. It was a magical moment, and I did not want to miss a single second.

Then Renato retraced his steps and came back to us. "It's getting late," he whispered. "We have to leave."

I heard the guide's words, but refused to believe them."What? Now?"

"Don't fret, sister. They'll still be here tomorrow."

"How do you know?" I asked. My voice sounded exaggeratedly skeptical.

"Because gorillas sleep in a different place every night, and around this time they start to build their nests out of leaves. They'll spend the night sleeping, and if we get up before them we'll find them in their beds."

"But—"

"Sarah," Gabriel intervened. "Trust Renato. If he says they'll be here tomorrow, it's because they will be."

"And by the way," I said, "where are we going to sleep tonight?"

"Don't worry, sister. There's another shelter uphill, about half an hour from here."

And sure enough, in a clearing surrounded by papaya trees we found a small hut, very much like the one we had slept in the previous night. We dined on huge quantities of the sweet orange fruit with its black seeds, and Gabriel and Renato went to sleep. As for me, no matter how hard I tried, my nerves would not let me get to sleep. Every time I closed my eyes I would see myself coming close to the gorillas like Diane Fossey to Digit in *Gorillas in the Mist*. I was so thrilled at the prospect that the adrenalin stopped me feeling the physical pain and fever which was relentlessly taking over my body.

Next morning Renato shook me in the cot, waking me up when not even the least trace of light was peeking through the cracks in the walls.

"What time is it…?" I asked, half asleep, forgetting that none of us wore a watch.

"Time to leave."

"I'm very tired… I think I'm sick."

"Sister, if we don't leave now, when we get there the gorillas might already be gone."

The magic word had its effect. Invoking the gorillas and getting up happened in a single movement. There was no need to get dressed, because as on the previous few nights I had slept with my clothes on, so that it took me less time than it takes to say it to go out of the door.

As it was not daylight yet, I found myself alone on the threshold in the dark, as though I were blind."Hey, where are you?" I asked.

A tiny flame, that of the guide's lighter, was the signal I needed.

"Come toward the light..." Gabriel said, putting on a sepulchral voice.

"Go to hell," I replied with a touch of early morning bad temper.

"Sister...?" I heard our guide ask.

"Go to heaven..." I tried to rectify clumsily. "With our Lord Jesus Christ, and the Holy Spirit..."

"Amen," Renato said.

I did not hear Gabriel say anything, but I could perfectly picture him pressing his lips tight.

I have no idea how he did it, but the man guided us in utter darkness through the forest and brought us, just as the sun was rising, to exactly where we had been the afternoon before.

A timid orange light was filtering through the proud woody columns, scores of feet tall. It scattered reflections beyond description, from another world, on the shreds of mist caught on the forest floor. Watching that moment of dreamlike beauty, I understood that human beings are as alien to this magical and unreal land as they are to fairytales. Any contact with the world of Oz, whose rules and natural laws we know nothing of, only defiles or destroys it. I understood that we have no right to tread, with our blind greed, on this dream that has become land, wood and life. And yet it was not just we who were there. The never-ending stream of trucks loaded with giant trees we had seen traveling along the road, and the distant sound of mechanical saws (the background noise in any corner of the African jungle) were proof that not content with entering an

Eden which ought to be forbidden to us, we were desecrating, plundering and destroying it, totally and irreparably.

And there, in that landscape out of fantasy, not only existing but forming a part of it, were the black, hairy figures of the legitimate dwellers of that memory of paradise: a paradise which is shrinking daily on its way to irreversible extinction.

I was watching, paralyzed by the moment's overdose of beauty and harmony, when a gorilla stretched noisily. Rising to its feet, it began to walk wearily toward our position. It had not yet noticed our presence.

Renato glanced back uneasily, making signs to us to stay crouching where we were in silence, which we were already doing.

The gorilla advanced nonchalantly, sniffing at a stem here and there, and suddenly its eyes met mine.

There was a second of surprise on both sides. I remained absolutely still, and for a moment the gorilla, baffled, seemed unable to react. Until suddenly it gave a growl of alarm that wakened the whole jungle and made my hair stand on end.

Gabriel and I looked at each other fearfully. More than a dozen black shadows began to appear from nowhere and raise the alarm. I thought I saw at least a couple of females with babies on their backs move swiftly. The gorilla which had discovered us went back quickly to the safety of the group, and then, like a King Kong unchained, a great silverback male came out through the foliage making the ground shake. He supported himself on his knuckles, then came between us and the group with a leap, roaring as I had never imagined a creature could and revealing a row of terrible fangs, huge and sharp.

Fear stunned me. My ankles trembled, and if there had been any liquid in my bladder it would surely have leaked out. The male had stopped a few feet from us, and during the brief moments when he was not roaring, I could hear his heavy breathing.

Just as Renato had said, the gorilla must have been more than six feet tall and well over four hundred pounds. The most massive of boxers would not have dared compare his biceps with the wrist of that titan, with his bowed legs and oval skull.

"Don't look at it!" shouted the guide. "Lower your eyes! Humble yourself!"

I hardly needed to be told twice. I bowed my head like a courtesan before her king, but far from calming down, the gorilla increased his roaring. His tone almost held a note of indignation and reproach. I was getting even more nervous as I could no longer see the gorilla, and his powerful roar made my guts vibrate without letting me know whether he was about to attack. Although there was little I could have done about it in any case.

And suddenly, without an apparent reason, the volume and intensity of the roars began to decrease until they were little more than a succession of booming grunts and huffs. I felt the hitting of the ground with his fists, as if making clear the territorial limits of his patience. I heard him turn round with a final grunt of warning, then go back into the jungle toward the group he was obliged to protect.

That gorilla could have destroyed the three of us without any effort before Renato had had the chance to use his weapon. If he had been a human being, unsure whether we posed a genuinely lethal threat, he would have killed us immediately. However, that supposedly irrational animal had contented himself with warning us not to get any closer, without touching a single hair of any of us.

I wondered whether we were really the *Homo sapiens*, and he the animal.

28

"My God..." I murmured, barely raising my head and trying to get my breath back. My heart was beating furiously. "What was that?"

"We scared them," Renato declared with a sigh.

"*We* scared them?" I repeated. I was still trembling. "I almost had a heart attack!"

"It's their way of telling us not to come any closer. It was really a kind of welcome. Now that they've seen us, it'll be enough if we don't bother them and behave respectfully."

I snorted. "And how do you behave respectfully to a gorilla?"

"As you would do to any other person, sister, just like any other person."

"All right then, what do we do now?"

"We're going to stay very quiet for a while. Then, when they set off, we'll follow them with caution."

"And won't they be frightened and get angry again?" I asked fearfully.

Renato giggled. "Don't worry, sister. They've already seen us, and they are familiar with our smell. If they don't feel threatened, we'll have no problem following them."

"I do hope you're right, my friend," I said, getting up slowly. "Because another warning like that and I'll run all the way to Gabon."

Renato let a sensible length of time go by and then encouraged us to go on. Curiously, from the moment we had been discovered by the group it was advisable to let ourselves be seen at all times so that the gorillas always knew where we were.

Of course we had to keep a safe distance all the time and avoid behaving noisily or harassing them. If we did, they might get tired of our presence and kick us out.

The group advanced lazily through the forest, and sometimes it looked as if each one went their own way, stopping to pick up some fruit within reach or to nibble at some shoot, the way we might with a candy we had found in our pocket. At times the clan spread out so much that we were not sure who we should follow, but in the end they always regrouped around the imposing silverback, who acted like the single and indisputable leader setting the pace the others had to follow.

As we adjusted our own pace to the irregular cadence of their wandering, we entered their dynamic almost without meaning to, gathering some fruit which we ate without stopping more than a few moments, or sitting idly in some particularly sunny clearing. And it might sound exaggerated, or the result of some incoherent Stockholm syndrome, but I felt somehow that I had my place in that great family, like a very distant cousin who might not be particularly welcome but was tolerated. There was a link which had survived millions of years and which I would never have believed possible as an anthropologist. But as a spellbound observer, as part of that incredible experience, I had no doubt that it existed every time I watched and was watched by those gorillas who looked threatening but were really so peaceful and tolerant. And when we crossed fleeting glances in the distance, what can I say? I recognized them and they recognized me, like an old friend from childhood they might not have seen for many years, but in whom they thought they could make out familiar features that invited a second glance.

I now understood the passion of women like Diane Fossey or Jane Goodall who had left everything behind to study primates. A passion that could only be understood if you could see that it was not simply apes they were studying but that they were possibly trying to find the bridge which linked us to the gorillas and chimpanzees and which had become forgotten among the underbrush of our genetic memory.

As the last traces of mist faded in the heat of the morning, the journey became more oppressive. The great exaltation of emotions caused by my first contact with the gorillas was giving way to a rather unpleasant hangover that took the form of feeling deeply unwell.

"Do you feel all right, Sarah?" Gabriel asked coming up to me and lifting my chin."You don't look too good."

"I don't really know what's wrong with me… but my bones ache, my head's booming like a bass drum, and I'd say I've got a fever…"

He put his hand on my forehead and looked at me gravely."I think you have malaria," he said without preamble.

"Malaria?" I asked dumbly, as if he had hinted that I had a third arm.

"Why are you surprised? You know it's endemic in Equatorial Guinea. Or do you think whites don't catch it?"

"No…" I stammered dizzily. "It's just that I… since I got here, I've been taking anti-malaria pills…"

"That might have served to reduce the symptoms so far. But if you catch malaria, you catch it, no matter what you have been taking."

This conversation was making me feel genuinely ill. Up till now I had only seen it as a series of separate ailments, but now the word "malaria" had awakened my fear of that terrible illness which could end my life in a matter of days.

"Then, what are we going to do…?" I asked. I felt suddenly helpless.

"We must get you to a hospital as soon as possible."

"A hospital? Where?"

"In Cogo there's one run by Spaniards," he said. "They'll be able to treat you there, and I don't think they'll turn you in to the authorities."

"Cogo? But that's halfway across the country."

"Sarah," he said, taking me by the shoulders, "you know there aren't many hospitals in this country, and what's more, in the one at Cogo you'll be safe."

"I don't know…"

But I did. Gabriel was right: it was my best, perhaps my only, chance. I cursed my bad luck, wondering what the chances were of so many misfortunes striking the same person.

"All right… let's go to Cogo," I said. I bowed my head, desolate at not being able to go on following the gorillas. "Although all my life I'll be sorry that…that…"

Suddenly I felt my legs losing the ability to support me, my body seemed to weigh a ton, and my sight blurred a second before the world began to spin around me and everything went dark as I fell to the ground like a sack of potatoes.

29

I do not have the slightest idea of how long I was unconscious, but what I do know is that the first time I opened my eyes I was not at the same spot where I had fainted. In fact I had the inexplicable feeling that I was floating in the air, and when I looked up I could see trees moving slowly before my eyes, so that when I fell once again into the twilight I thought I must be in the middle of a pleasant dream.

The next time I opened my eyes, who knows how much later, it seemed to me that I was lying on a soft mattress, surrounded by a small structure of criss-crossing branches and thin tree trunks covered with leaves. The place was definitely small and dark, and there was a penetrating smell of smoke in this shrunken dome. Strangely, I felt comfortable and relaxed. I could not tell whether it was day or night, although the points of light that filtered through the roof suggested the sun was shining outside. Then a familiar voice told me to relax. Even more?

"Take this…" he said next.

Holding the back of my neck with one hand to lift my head, he put a wooden bowl to my lips, and I drank a bitter tisane with a distant aftertaste of tonic water. I tried to refuse it, but did not even have the strength to complain. I ended up swallowing the disgusting liquid, much against my will.

This scene, in which someone held my head and at the same time gave me that unknown liquid to drink, was repeated several times: I could not say whether five or fifty, but time seemed to have stopped its linear course and left me trapped in a repetitive loop. In this I slept, woke up, drank and slept again.

On one particular day just like any other the cycle was broken, but this time for some reason I felt more alert. The structure of the green dome where I was lying appeared more clearly, revealing itself definitely as man-made. I also discovered that this time there was something resembling a skinned guinea pig hanging from the roof. It was being smoked with the aid of a few embers, which also lit the enclosure from inside. Once again I felt a hand at my neck and the bowl at my lips, but this time I had enough strength and clarity of mind to turn my head toward the person who was helping me to sit up.

The dim light and my fragile state made me doubt for a moment what I was seeing. An African face with bulging eyes was watching me with great interest, but what puzzled me especially was how small it was. At first I thought it was a boy of ten or twelve, but looking closely I saw wrinkles which could only be those of a middle-aged adult. The rising line of the cheekbones, the delicate chin and small mop of hair told me I was looking at a woman, which somehow made me feel more at ease. This only lasted a moment, until I made an attempt to smile in gratitude, and she did the same. What I had not been expecting was that she opened her mouth to smile wider, and as she did so the reflection of the burning embers in the hut revealed a set of shining teeth. There was one peculiarity about them that made me start with terror. Every one of those teeth was sharpened like knives. That smile might very well have belonged to a shark.

30

At once the familiar figure of Gabriel came running into the hut, begging me to stay calm. I was huddled against the wall, still shocked, while the tiny woman went on smiling with her white shark teeth.

"It's okay," I heard him say, even though I was not paying attention. "Relax, Sarah, they're good people."

In spite of his soothing words I could not take my eyes off that shark smile, and to cap it all a man as tiny as she was came into the hut with a spear in his hand. He spoke to me in a strange tongue, then made the same grimace as the woman's. At that moment it seemed to have as much courtesy in it as malice. Only Gabriel's presence kept me calm, trying to understand what was happening instead of running away in the belief that I had fallen into the hands of a tribe of cannibals.

After all, I was an anthropologist, what the hell! If I could manage to calm down a little, I could surely figure out how I had arrived there and who those people were. I asked Gabriel to help me to my feet. Then, clumsily because of my weakness, I got out of the soft bed made of leaves and went outside.

The first impression left me dizzier still, because I felt like a giant more than six feet tall surrounded by Lilliputians. I had emerged in the middle of a village, for lack of a better word, formed by nine huts which looked like igloos made out of branches and leaves. Each one had a small hole by way of entrance facing toward the center of the camp. But the most unusual thing was the group of fifteen or twenty individuals scattered through the village who were eying me with uninhibited curiosity. Most of them were idle or engaged in tasks whose significance escaped me; a few seemed absorbed in dabbing the tips of very long arrows with a blackish resin, some honed machetes or knives with a stone. Several women were sitting in a circle gossiping amid laughter when they saw me come out, while a group of children of different ages and surprisingly fair skin stopped their games to stare at me as if Godzilla had appeared in their back garden.

Until that moment, when I had an overall view of the village and its inhabitants, I had no idea what this was. I should have realized sooner just as I should have realized before I came out of the hut that I was only wearing a torn t-shirt that, inexplicably, I had ended up in a small community of the mysterious Pygmies of Equatorial Africa.

My amazement lingered as I looked around me, trying to find some other explanation. But there was none.

It was not long before they offered us a large bowl filled with fruit, yam and roast meat, and I began to wolf it down without any regard for manners. I had never in my life been so ravenous. That feast tasted glorious, and even the meat, with that sweet aftertaste it leaves when it is no longer at its best, was the most delicious I had eaten in years. Gabriel watched me with pleasure, seeing that in addition to my health I had got my appetite back.

Barely raising my eyes from the bowl, I saw that a small – literally – procession had come to sit in front of me. It consisted of three old men and a woman. They were not much taller than me sitting down, and they wore the same loincloths as the rest of the villagers. The only noticeable difference was the advanced age of the three men, so that at first glance I guessed they must be some kind of welcoming committee. The woman remained slightly on the margin, but to my surprise she was the first to speak.

"Well... come," she said hesitantly.

"You speak English!" I exclaimed, delighted.

"Yes... little speak," she said, happy at being able to communicate with me. "Man..." She seemed to think for a moment, as if searching for the right word. "Man with cross teach me when I small." With a smile she clarified, "When I more small..."

"A missionary taught you?"

"Yes," she said, recognizing the word which had eluded her. "Missionary."

"You speak it very well," I said sincerely. Stretching out my hand, I added, "My name is Sarah. And yours?"

She looked at my hand in some confusion, with a glance at the men, seeking their approval. She took it with such gentleness that it was little more than a brush between our palms.

"My name Duyé-Nianu..." she said shyly. "They" – she pointed to her left – "chief of us Djamé-Ngue; medicine man Meke-Lua; great hunter Ipé-Maliki. They say," she added admiringly, "they do, they take care you."

If there had been any doubt, that telegraphic presentation left very clear that this was something like a council of elders, and that I was in their debt, both for their hospitality and the not inconsiderable fact that I was still breathing.

"Please tell them that I am infinitely grateful to them for healing me and taking care of me."

Duyé-Nianu blinked in confusion, and I realized I had spoken to fast.

"Thank you very much," I said slowly, bowing my head with gratitude at the same time. "Thank you all very much."

My interpreter translated the message, although my gesture had been eloquent enough.

The "elders" who showed barely a trace of wrinkles or white hair, and who might equally well have been forty or seventy nodded in acknowledgement. The eldest of them, the one introduced as Djamé-Ngue, made an expansive gesture which took in the whole little settlement, at the same time giving a brief speech that Duyé-Nianu tried to translate for me.

"We... Aka," she said, choosing her words carefully. "Lords of time, lords of earth, lords of everything, give welcome to you. God Kmvum has put you in way of Aka: Aka heal, Aka feed, Aka build *mangulo* for you rest... Aka protect Sarah."

"Thank you," I repeated from the bottom of my heart, moved by their overwhelming hospitality. "And what could I do for you?" I asked spontaneously.

Duyé-Nianu relayed my question.

The three little men stood up as one. The "chief" gave me a condescending smile and said something to the woman, then turned and went back toward the center of the village. The "healer" and the "great hunter" laughed at his wisecrack.

"What did he say?" I asked, my curiosity piqued.

My translator smiled, with the same sharp teeth all of them sported."Djamé-Ngue say, do not die."

31

In spite of my years of study, the information I remembered about the Pygmies was frustratingly limited. I was trying hard to recall a class in my third year in which the professor mentioned how little the world knows about the Pygmies. In fact it seemed that the Egyptian pharaohs had sent some expedition or other to find out whether it was legend or truth that there was a race of tiny men living in the heart of the jungle. The Romans too, if I remembered correctly, had speculated about the existence of that remarkable tribe. Yet it had not been until far into the twentieth century that proof of their existence had been found, and even now, in the twenty-first century, the customs and sociology of the Pygmy people have been left to speculation. There are few serious studies on them due to the difficulty in locating them, since their culture is semi-nomadic and their habitat is deep in that unexplored setting which has always terrified the westerner: the deep rainforest.

I recalled that there were not only Pygmies in Africa but also in Borneo, and perhaps in some other hidden corner of the planet. But without any doubt the most important population even though it consists of no more than two or three hundred thousand individuals is spread throughout the impenetrable jungles of the black continent, always in small clans of no more than fifty souls. Paradoxically, Equatorial Africa's chronic state of war has saved them from harmful contact with western culture, which has already ousted indigenous races throughout the world.

Another debate about the Pygmies involved their controversial because unknown genealogical origin. On that particular occasion, in college, the professor had openly admitted that he had no clue about the origin of that elusive race.

In comparison he pointed out that there was more scientific literature about mountain gorillas than about the Pygmies– with whom, by the way, they shared an ecosystem.

One of the students had called them "the mysterious pocket men" and everybody in the class had laughed at the joke. Needless to say I would choke back that easy laughter today and pay to see that college wisecracker in the middle of the jungle: see whether he had the guts to say it to the faces of these wiry men, with their poisoned spears and arrows.

"How do you feel today?" Gabriel asked.

"Huh?" I said vaguely. I had almost forgotten he was there. "Oh... well enough. Just a little weak."

"It's normal. You were just one step away from going to live with the forest spirits forever. You'd better go back to the hut and lie down. You'll be better tomorrow."

"Yes, I guess you're right," I said resignedly. "Although all this is so exciting for me as an anthropologist that I don't want to sleep, in case it's all just a feverish delirium."

"Well," he said with a shrug, "if it's delirium, then I'm sick too. But it would have to be a recurring dream, because it's been going on for days."

"Days? How long have I been unconscious?"

Gabriel spread his hands, dismissing the question as unimportant. "What does that matter? We're in the middle of the jungle as guests of a Pygmy tribe. Maybe you'd made other plans for the week?"

There was certainly no reason to think about it, so I let him lead me to the hut, where I lay down on my bed of green leaves. When he was about to leave, I remembered to ask him something that had been on my mind. "Gabriel, what about Renato? I haven't seen him around."

"He went back to his village. He's the one who guided us here, and once he knew you were in good hands he decided to go back."

"Did you find my money reserve to pay him?"

"Yes, but he didn't want to take it. I guess when I refused to go back he suspected we weren't tourists... and he said we'd need the money more than him."

The woman who had been taking care of me was not there when I next woke up. I felt suddenly guilty about having acted hysterically, and vowed to apologize as soon as I saw her again. Wondering about what excuses I could find for my behavior, I thought I detected an unfamiliar smell in the smoke from the coals in the center of the hut. Slowly I found myself being carried away by an overwhelming sleepiness, and did not put up much resistance to it.

I had a strange dream, caused I suppose by the excitement of the last days — the days I had been awake, obviously. I dreamt, or perhaps remembered, several dark-skinned naked men, almost completely covered in some white substance which highlighted strange symbols on their skin, giving me a bitter brew to drink. Meanwhile, the one introduced to me as Meke-Lua, the medicine man, intoned a rhythmic chant in his sonorous language as he drew on a small bamboo pipe and blew the smoke into my face. In the dream I thought I could understand what he was reciting in his litany. Apart from constantly repeating the name of their god Kmvum, he seemed to be invoking the good spirits of the jungle to fight against the bad spirits who had taken over my body. The healer, the painted men who accompanied him, the whole village, all seemed to have become involved in the battle being fought inside me.

Slowly the image of the men faded. I was no longer inside the hut, but found myself standing in the middle of the jungle. I could hear the song of every bird, the slithering of every snake, the flutter of every butterfly. I was no longer myself, and my body was no longer flesh but hard wood. Along my bark ran thousands of ants carrying leaves, while my limbs served as shelter to a family of monkeys, and in my crown dozens of nests held little eggs which were about to break open. Then a terrible blast broke the silence of centuries in that forest, and somehow I heard, saw and felt an old friend, nearly a hundred and sixty feet tall, who had been with me for the last two hundred years, falling without any apparent reason. He crashed on the ground, dragging with him all those living creatures whose home he had been. I did not understand what had happened, but I knew he had died, and even without tears or eyes to cry with, I cried.

And as I was crying, a sinister figure armed with a roaring weapon with metallic teeth came toward me. This horrible being, like a man in fatigues but with the claws and face of a hyena, looked up, patted my body and with a perverse smile took a step back and launched his chainsaw against my trunk, ready to cut me in two. I felt those lifeless fangs bite into me and tear me apart while I screamed without a mouth, and my call for help became a moan, in the farewell of an inevitable death.

But then a trumpet of fury made every single one of my branches shake, down to the roots with their deep anchorage in the damp soil, and the whole forest shook when a silverback emerged from the very air and launched itself at the murderous monster. It seized him by the neck with its giant fist, ready to protect me; but then the monster faded into a thick black cloud. With an unclean voice he promised me he would come back to finish me off. Then he broke apart into a million malaria-infected mosquitoes which flew away in every direction, anxiously searching for new victims to infect.

At that moment a hand reached out to me, Gabriel's hand. I was no longer a tree, and I spread my arms to him.

"One day he'll be back," he said, "but for now you're safe. Come back with me."

Once again I was back inside the mangulo. And there were those Pygmies, tattooed in white. I recognized the woman who had cared for me, the chief Djamé-Ngue, the great hunter

Ipé-Maliki, and watching me with evident satisfaction, the medicine man Meke-Lua.

In the small hours of the following morning I assumed that only a day had passed I was awakened by a muffled disturbance. Stung by curiosity, I went out of my mangulo in time to see a dozen Pygmies gathered in a circle, intoning mysterious chants. I looked around and saw Duyé-Nianu sitting not far away, so I went up to her and asked in her ear what they were up to.

"Akas ask Mimbos for help to hunt," she replied softly.
"Mimbos?"
"You don't see Mimbos, but they are... Mimbos in trees, Mimbos in animals, Mimbos in air... if Mimbos don't help, hunt bad, dangerous."
"Are they like... spirits of the jungle?"
Duyé-Nianu shrugged and tilted her head.
"I thought you only worshipped the god Kmvum."
"God Kmvum is god Kmvum. Mimbo is Mimbo."
"I see..." I lied.

Suddenly Chief Djamé-Ngue ended the ceremony and passed his hand over each man's head. After exchanging a few words with Ipé-Maliki the twelve Pygmies, all practically naked, some armed with spears and others with bows and arrows, went into the thick jungle in single file, without looking back.

"Are they going hunting?"
"Yes."
"Far?"
"Yes."
"What about the women? What do you do meanwhile?"
"Gather fish, fruit, mushrooms, yam..."
"Could I come with you?"

Duyé-Nianu giggled. Covering her mouth, she asked the same question of an older woman who was sitting beside her, perhaps her mother.

She also laughed –to be honest, I did not see what was so funny and said a couple of unintelligible sentences to me accompanied by a nod, which made me guess I was accepted.

"When do we leave?" I asked.

"Now," my translator said.

All the women stood up, along with some of the children, and started to walk in the opposite direction to the one the men had taken, so I had no choice but to do the same. Dressed once more in my battered nun's skirt and the same gruyère shirt as the day before, barefoot like my hostesses I took my place at the end of the line. Without losing sight of Duyé-Nianu I went into the jungle again, but this time with the spirit of a cheerful excursion into the country.

32

At first I watched very carefully at every step where I put my feet, fearful of treading on something sharp, or that something might sting or bite me, but as I walked I found myself worrying less and less. At last I decided that if nothing happened to twenty women and children walking in front of me it would be extremely bad luck even though I had had plenty of that lately if anything were to happen to me.

Overtaking a few children who were walking at the front, dressed like aspiring hunters scale models of their parents I caught up with Duyé-Nianu, who was walking gracefully with a wicker basket on her head.

"Where are we going?" I asked, puffing.

"To the river," she said pointing ahead.

"Oh, wonderful!" I said enthusiastically. "I'm dying for a good bath!"

"You die if bathe?"

"Haha! Maybe I will, sweetie, but from pure pleasure!"

The young Pygmy woman stared at me in puzzlement from her four feet or so of height, and decided something must have gotten lost in translation.

I pointed to a tree with threatening thorns sprouting from its trunk. "Do you know what tree that is?" I asked.

"I know, but not know word."

"Oh, it doesn't matter. I was just curious."

But Duyé-Nianu, trying to do better this time, pointed at an upright, fleshy plant."That one called Heal-all."

"Heal-all? Why?" I asked curiously.

"Because it heals all. You cut," she said, pretending to cut her arm, "and tree heal. You pain, and tree heal. You animal sting, and tree heal. Tree Heal-all!"

"I see..."

A few steps ahead, she grabbed a leaf similar to a fern with yellow flowers. "This good to drive away ants from mangulo. Ants bad," she said seriously, "eat our food. And one time eat boy."

"What!? You're saying that the ants ate a boy!?"

"Yes," she said very seriously, and nodded. "One night, mother of very small boy sleep. Ants come, many, many..." – she waved her arm, as though at an imaginary line of ants – "and ants eat little boy."

"Oh, my! That's terrible!"

"Mother only find bones of little boy in the morning..."

"Fuck! I had no idea that ants were capable of that!"

"Ants bad," Duyé-Nianu concluded, and raised her finger in warning.

We went on briskly, following a barely perceptible path, and about half an hour later we reached the longed-for river, which was really little more than a dirty stream. Once there, most of the women made a small barrier with mud and rocks, while others gathered papayas from a tree near the growing dam. When they calculated there was enough water trapped in it, they shut off the other end to the current and opened a gap in the first dike so that the water ran out. At the bottom some tiny fish were left leaping as they tried to escape from the trap. I could not say what surprised me more, the ingenuity of the engineering or the meagerness of the harvest: a couple of dozen of those fish seemed barely enough to make a meal for one person. Despite that, the Pygmy women were happy, singing and laughing. Squatting on the shore, they chased after the tiny, slippery fish, which escaped from their hands half the time. Then one of the improvised fisherwomen waved at me to come and join in the fun, and without hesitation I waded ankle-deep into the mud and tried to grab something I could eat later. All the same, after half an hour I had only managed to catch a couple of fish, and in the process had fallen on my face in the mud, accompanied by catcalls from the other women, who even imitated my clumsiness by throwing themselves headlong into the mud as they chased after an imaginary trout. Inevitably we all ended up laughing, diving into the muddy hole and rolling over like pigs amid jokes and guffaws.

When we tired of the game, we all moved over to a part of the stream where the water ran freely and cleaned off all the dark mud covering us from head to foot. I had not realized until that moment that the children who had come with us had all disappeared. Their mothers did not seem to be missing them at all, but it seemed odd to me. I went up to Duyé-Nianu to ask her what had become of them.

"Children hunt," was the answer.

"So small? Isn't it dangerous?"

She laughed at my incredulity. "Children not hunt elephants."

"But there are snakes and leopards in the jungle…"

"They know," she said, ending the subject. I could not tell whether she meant that the parents were aware of the danger, or that the kids knew how to look after themselves. Whatever the case, I stopped worrying and decided that they knew what they were doing.

Next, I helped clean the fish and gather some coconut liana leaves, which I imagined they would use to make baskets or mats. The work made me thirsty, so I squatted down beside the stream and asked one of the women, with the aid of gestures, whether the water was drinkable. She responded with much hand-waving which could only have meant *don't even think of it*, and gestured to me to follow her. A few steps away she stopped and looked closely at a thick liana. With a stroke from her machete she cut it cleanly and put it to my mouth. To my utter surprise a small jet of clear, fresh water gushed out, tastier than any fancy bottled water I had ever tried in my life.

After a while, tired of gathering fish and fruit, we took a break. Following their example, I sat down on a rock to gulp down a slice of papaya that tasted like heaven. The children came back then, about nine or ten of them, carrying replicas of their parents' weapons, which at first sight might have looked like toys. The impression vanished when I discovered the half dozen birds and the small rodent hanging from their loincloths. The mothers congratulated them joyously, and the children responded by proudly showing off their catches. Some of them were scarcely larger than their victims.

Once we were all reunited we headed back to the village, loaded with food and happy with our productive day. As soon as we arrived the elders and the younger children who had stayed behind came out to greet us. Among them, like a worried giant, was Gabriel, getting clumsily out of a mangulo. He strode forward and stood in front of me, arms akimbo."Where on earth have you been?" he asked, making no attempt to hide his annoyance.

"Why should you care?" I replied, upset in turn by his tone of voice.

He frowned indignantly."What do you mean, *why should I care*?" he said angrily. "You leave without warning me or telling me where you're going, in the middle of a jungle where we almost died, and after I've spent the whole morning worrying myself sick trying to get these grandpas to tell me where you've gone, you ask me why?"

By now all the women of the village had gathered around us without the least sense of restraint. Presumably they were exchanging comments on what was happening, even though they could not understand a word of what we were saying.

I could understand Gabriel's anger, and if he had spoken to me in a different tone of voice I would probably have apologized. But nobody had spoken to me like that since I was a teenager, and I was not going to let him do it, however much he might have fought for me, particularly in front of all those people. On the other hand, the last thing I wanted was for that street theatre cliché of the quarrelling couple to go on any longer, so I pushed him aside. Crossing the village with determined steps, I went to sit by the fire burning in the center, which since my coming back to life the day before I had never seen put out.

Gabriel was left spitting fury amid a circle of Pygmy women who seemed deeply interested in the reactions of what must have seemed to them this furious giant. After a moment of indecision, he went back into the same mangulo he had emerged from – it might have been mine too, but I was not sure – in a huff, probably frustrated at not having a door he could slam in that door less leafy igloo.

Beside the fire the women scaled the little fish and cleaned the yams of any dirt clinging to their tubers, placing the fruits of our labor   or rather, to be fair, of theirs – on top of some enormous green banana leaves, with such care and such a range of foods that it looked as though a banquet was being prepared. And at the moment the women were finishing, with evening nearly upon us, the hunters came back.

With a certain swagger, like that of the children on their return from their hunt, the men, with Ipé-Maliki at their head, came into the center of the village and deposited the product of almost a whole day's work next to the fire: a sizeable warthog which would provide the whole community with meat, and some left over for the next day.

Working together, they all proceeded to skin the animal at once. After cutting it into pieces they skewered it on long poles, and soon it was roasting, flooding the whole village with a delicious smell of grilled pork.

When the feast was ready we sat down in a wide circle around the fire and the food, with the night all around us. Then Djamé-Ngue lifted his hands to the sky and began a kind of prayer. Luckily I was still beside Duyé-Nianu, who translated for me the chief's words as best she could.

"In the beginning was Kmvum..." she whispered in my ear. "I give you all fruits of jungle, all fruits of harvest, all animals that walk, run and fly. I give you and you never hungry in stomach... and the trees are your..." She looked at me for a second, arching her eyebrows with a smile. "I don't know word," she confessed, then went on translating, "and no longer afraid, oh you, most powerful, and no longer cold, oh you most powerful" – the old man raised his voice above the growing murmur of the jungle – "for this we give thanks, oh great Kmvum, who turn among trees, bogs, rivers and roots... for make us masters of time and forest, from beginning to end."

This said, he sat down like any of the others, and with a brief wave of his hand gave the order for the feast to begin.

I turned to my right, holding a fish by its tail. "May I ask you a question?" I said.

Duyé-Nianu, who was already tearing at a piece of meat from its bone, turned and nodded.

"I'd like to know why you all have your teeth so... well, you know, sharpened."

The young woman finished chewing and looked at me in surprise. "You no like my teeth?"

"No, it's not that... it's just that I don't know why you do it."

She went on staring at me as if I had asked her why she walked on her feet. "Aka men like, Aka women like... all like teeth so. Pretty," she said, showing her own sharp teeth.

"Yes," I assured her, "very pretty. You'd start a fashion in my country."

"Your country far?" she asked with interest.

"A little... well, yes, it really is far. And each day it seems farther."

"You want go back to your country?"

"Well, actually I do..." I said. I was suddenly saddened at hearing myself, aware that I was in another world, with very little chance of going back. "I'd give anything to be taking a stroll along the paved streets of old Boston..."

"Boston?"

"Yes, that's where my home is."

"No sad," she said stroking my face at the sight of a tear running down my cheek. "Tomorrow we make new mangulo for you."

That offer, for some reason, only increased my desolation. I felt far, very far away. In time, in distance... as if I were on another planet surrounded by aliens, with no hope of returning. It was then that I understood that distance is not measured in miles or kilometers, as we think. It is measured in tears.

I barely ate anything else, and went to my mat on its bed of leaves in my mangulo. There I found Gabriel lying in his cot, faintly lit by the permanent coals inside.

"I'm sorry about what happened before," I said contritely. "I didn't mean... I..."

"Are you all right?" he asked, sounding sincerely concerned.

"Well, no... not really."

"You look sad."

"I am, Gabriel. I'm afraid of never getting back home..."

Gabriel reached out, pulled me to him and held me gently."Trust me, Sarah," he said firmly. "You'll soon be home, with your family. I swear it."

And I believed him.

And I fell asleep in his arms.

And in that Pygmy village, lying in a fragile hut of leaves and branches, in the midst of a strange, threatening jungle, I dreamt I was walking in Franklin Park with my parents' playful dog. The green gardens dotted with yellow and red flowers and the distant storm clouds on the horizon were announcing spring's imminent arrival in my native Massachusetts... and I prayed, as sleep overwhelmed me, that some day I would be able to see them again.

33

Dawn found us in each other's arms, like two scared kids lost in the forest. Deep down, that is exactly what we were.

The meager light of the jungle dawn crept in through the door of our hut and woke me just before Gabriel woke up. I moved aside, careful not to disturb him, and went out into the morning light.

A couple of early-rising children were running between the huts, several women were busy sweeping in front of their mangulos with palm leaves, and one of the men was in charge of feeding the central fire with small branches, which made me think there must always be someone in charge so that the fire would never go out.

I guessed the feast the night before must have gone on for a long time, because I was surprised to find I was one of the first people up. I took the opportunity to stretch at leisure, in a morning silence broken only by the birdsong and the laughter of the two children. The morning, as always in the jungle, was quite cool, and the worn shirt I had been wearing for days did not provide much cover. As I tried to imagine what I must look like, I realized when I looked at my grubby arms and legs that I had practically no mosquito bites left, and that all those red marks covering my skin had disappeared. The fever and the general seediness which Gabriel had attributed to malaria had vanished as well. Either he had been wrong or these people, in some way I could not explain to myself, really had miraculously cured me. There was no way I could know the truth… but something made me feel the second one was the correct answer.

Incomprehensibly, amid that tribe of little men and women I felt at peace in a way I had not for a long time. I thought in passing that perhaps I could get used to that kind of humble yet full life, away from all the extra complications we westerners love to create for ourselves. Here everything came down to gathering, fishing or hunting on the one hand and eating, sleeping and laughing on the other. And in the end, what do we all long for other than a simple life and the small pleasures which make us happy? Besides, I could not even miss modern medicine, since if he had been able to rid my body of malaria, what could he not do, the *man who heals* in this Pygmy tribe? Duyé-Nianu had explained to me the day before that they extracted remedies from plants for any malady, from a simple headache to the terrible malaria that killed millions throughout the world every year.

But as I was staring at the shreds of blue sky through the thick leafy canopy, I remembered that dream where I had strolled through the fresh green park in Boston, and a sudden impulse made me run back into the hut and shake Gabriel by the shoulders.

"What... what's up?" he asked sleepily.
"We have to leave," I said eagerly. "Now."
"What? Now? Where?"
"Home, Gabriel. I want to go home."

It was not difficult to communicate to Chief Djamé-Ngue, through Duyé-Nianu, that we had to continue our journey. Gabriel explained which way we wanted to go, and after consulting briefly among themselves they offered to guide us for most of our way, since the area we were going to go through was a good hunting ground.

Upon deciding we would leave immediately, I put on my missionary clothes again   after days of wearing only the bare essentials they felt extremely uncomfortable   and with a basket of leaves under my arm which the women had filled with fruit and smoked meat, I joined the hunting party already waiting at the edge of the forest. Gabriel was there too, ready to go, carrying another basket with food and two fiber mats like the ones we had been using to sleep on.

The Pygmy women had gathered to say goodbye, chanting a melancholy song with an air of farewell about it. I kissed their cheeks and hugged Duyé-Nianutightly, thanking her for everything she had done for me, and swore I would never forget them, neither her or the Aka.

"You take much care," she said, stroking my cheek with the back of her hand. "You come back?"

"I don't know," I muttered, on the brink of tears. "Perhaps some day…"

Stepping back, I left the group of women and children. Then the *man who heals* stepped forward."*Nieduwey! Hubuu nog gureu. Maweny, maweny!*" he said in their indecipherable language, but with a clear note of warning.

"What did he say?" I asked Duyé-Nienu for the last time. Meke-Lua's words had brought an unmistakable shadow of worry to her face.

"He say… you have a good journey."

"Well, tell him from me," I said bowing my head, although I was sure that was not what he had said, "thank you for everything. And I hope that one day I might be able to do the same for all of you in return."

The young Pygmy woman did not translate my words, but looked thoughtful. So I bowed my head again and turned to join the group of hunters, who had already started on their way.

I was at the rear and could not help but look back one last time at the little settlement where I had lived through such extraordinary moments. Then I saw what must have been almost the whole village swarming around the healer, apparently accusing or questioning him amid much waving of arms. Something told me I had not been wrong, and that what he had said was a very serious warning.

A warning I wish I had paid more attention to…

34

Ipé-Maliki, the great hunter, walked at the head of the small group of seven Aka, Gabriel and me. All the Pygmies carried a satchel made of fiber over their shoulders, together with bows, very long arrows and a few spears with very sharp tips and smeared in black paste. Compared to the fluid walk of the hunters, I looked as if I were stepping on eggs. I couldn't stop admiring the way they moved with the utmost stealth, totally alert to the least noise or branch that moved above them without any apparent reason. When this happened they would all stop at once, as if obeying an invisible signal, and study their surroundings carefully as they knocked their arrows. Then they would wait a minute or two in absolute silence for the source of the hubbub   a monkey or a bird; in sum, food – to appear through the foliage. At that moment they would release a volley of poisoned arrows.

We walked like this all morning, sometimes at a pace I found hard to keep up, sometimes stopping completely for some time while the Pygmies watched something I could not see, alerted by some sound I never managed to make out. Needless to say, the men's outings were much less fun than those of the women.

The strange, silent walk   I once dared to address Gabriel in a whisper and got reproving looks from the guides   did not stop until the sun reached its zenith, when we took a brief break and had a frugal snack. I had barely taken a bite when we set off again at the same brisk pace, which was already making my legs ache.

After what must have been a couple of hours   although in that jungle time went by irregularly   Ipé-Maliki stopped abruptly and pointed somewhere above his head with his right hand."*Nouegongu,*" he said turning to the others with a smile on his face.

The rest of Pygmies looked up too, and a contagious joy took hold of the group.

Gabriel and I narrowed our eyes to see where Ipé-Maliki was pointing, but we could see nothing noticeable, still less anything that could have elicited that curious wave of good humor.

The Aka left their things on the ground and frenetically began to gather branches from several bushes. Meanwhile we watched the scene without understanding anything at all.

One of them, perhaps the youngest of the group, and the one who seemed to be in best shape, hung one of the empty satchels on his shoulder, lined it with banana leaves and grasped a big bunch of dry leaves the others had gathered. Then Ipé-Maliki took an anachronistic yellow plastic lighter out of his satchel. After a couple of tries, he set fire to the bunch of leaves the young man was holding, and a thick cloud of black smoke began to come forth.

Then, using his legs and holding on to bumps and lianas with his free arm, the young Pygmy began to climb calmly and methodically up the giant tree which rose from our very feet. A few dozen feet up we lost sight of him completely. While Gabriel and I could not stop looking up, intrigued and concerned, the daring climber's companions sat on the ground and talked nonchalantly about this and that, indifferent to their friend's fate. It was truly frustrating not to be able to communicate with them and ask what on earth they were doing.

All the same, when a sudden cry of joy came from many feet above our heads, the Pygmies laid their indolence to one side and began to hop around gleefully. A couple of them even started a kind of dance.

The first thing to reach the ground was the smoking torch, which I guessed he had dropped. Moments later, with both hands now free, the young Pygmy appeared and let himself down one of the lianas that hung to the ground. As soon as he arrived, his companions, completely ignoring that feat of strength and agility, grabbed the satchel and deposited the contents on a mat of leaves. It was no more and no less than a golden honeycomb, with a few bees still moving confusedly on the golden surface.

The seven men, without any regard for manners, fell on the pieces of honeycomb with obvious enjoyment.

"They certainly like their honey…" I said, open-mouthed.

Gabriel said nothing, but he was as amazed as I was.

The great hunter saw us standing watching them from a distance, and waved us over to join in the feast.

I refused at first quite honestly I could not say why but after only a little encouragement from the Pygmy I ended up dipping my hand in the precious loot and stuffing myself with that sweet delicacy I used to love as a child. Just as I remembered, it tasted much better when eaten with your hands, licking your fingers afterward.

When we had all had our fill except for Gabriel, who confessed he did not like honey we wrapped what was left in green leaves, stowed it away and went on with renewed energy.

When the sun had hardly begun its descent toward the horizon, Ipé-Maliki, who always went at the head, stopped again. This time he crouched down, and after studying something on the ground turned to us."*Ibwé nog*!" he ordered. "*Muéatuye, ngadumangulo*!"

We left the unclear path we had been following and came to a small clearing. After leaving their things scattered around, they proceeded to clean it of leaves and bushes.

"What's going on?" I asked Gabriel, who was standing beside me. "It's still nowhere near nightfall. What must have made them decide to stay here?"

"I'm as baffled as you are," he said with a shrug.

To dispel our doubts, while our companions worked on the clearing, we resolved to go back to the spot where the leader had ordered us to stop.

We looked around the area. At first we could not make anything out, until our noses guided us to an enormous fresh mound of dung, surrounded by huge prints, which could only belong to one animal on earth: an elephant.

We reached the conclusion that Ipé-Maliki had come upon the trail of a group of elephants and decided to wait till morning before looking for them, so avoiding the risk of bumping into them in the dark. According to what I had heard, jungle elephants, though much smaller than their cousins of the savannah, were extremely aggressive and responsible for more human deaths than crocodiles or leopards.

"What seems funny to me," I said as we walked back to the clearing, "is the effort they make to keep the fire in the settlement going all the time, considering they have lighters to start a fire whenever they want."

"Well, I don't know for sure," Gabriel replied, "but I think the fire at the settlement has something religious or spiritual about it. It must be like the permanent flame protecting them, something to do with that god of theirs…"

"Kmvum."

"Yes, that one. But that's only what I think," he said with a shrug. "After all, you're the anthropologist."

Puzzling over this, we reached the clearing. We found the look of the place had changed considerably in a very short time.

"They're really hurrying," I said admiringly.

"They must want to go to bed, still tired from last night's feast."

"And what about that? They seem to be building a couple of mangulos, wouldn't you say?" I pointed to four of the Pygmies, who were busy bending some small, flexible trees.

"It seems like too much work for just one night. They're probably simple shelters," Gabriel said, shaking his head, "and besides, I believe the building of the mangulos is exclusively a woman's task."

"And how would you know that?"

He winked at me. "You don't think you're the only one who's been talking to the pretty Duyé-Nianu, do you?"

And to my surprise, like an unexpected knife in the pit of my stomach, I felt the irrational, clumsy and unexpected sting of jealousy.

35

We dined on a good part of our supplies with honey dressing around a small fire amid the jokes and laughter of the Pygmies. After spending the whole day walking in absolute silence, they were making up for it by being as raucous as they could. At first I looked on at the general merrymaking as a mere spectator, because although they tried to include me in the general mood with gestures and mimicry, quite honestly I did not understand anything, no matter how hard I tried. The curious thing was that almost without realizing it I caught something of their good humor and began to smile foolishly. After a while I was laughing my head off without really knowing why, which made them laugh even more. The Pygmies pointed at me, very amused by my way of guffawing, which in turn made me cackle even harder. We all ended up including Gabriel in a fit of hysterical laughter, which must have woken up every living creature for several miles around.

When we had finished dining, with our jaws sore from so much giggling, we went to bed in our shelters. These consisted of a slanting roof of leaves and branches, which leaned on the ground and was held up by a short pole at the other end. Beside it, a piece of tree ants nest burned without a flame, producing a thick smoke that, as I had already learned, kept the insolent mosquitoes away.

"Hey, Gabriel," I said when I noticed that the sleeping place I had been allotted had no wall. "Why don't we change places? I'm going to get wet if it rains."

He looked up, then down at the mat I had spread on the ground.

"Settle down, Sarah… you won't get wet. You're under the roof."

"Yes, but there's no wall beside me. If it comes in from the side I'll be soaked."

"You shouldn't worry about that," he said lying down on his own mat with his back to me. "In case you haven't noticed yet, there's no wind inside the forest."

The truth was I had not noticed. But it was obvious: with so many trees above and all around, it was impossible that—

A sudden laugh from Gabriel interrupted my thoughts.

"What's the matter now?"

"I just realized how funny the situation is."

"What do you mean?" I said, raising myself on my elbow.

"I just remembered," he said, trying not to laugh, "a children's tale my mother used to tell me."

"I still don't understand."

"How many Pygmies are sleeping out there?"

"What? Hmm, seven, I think."

"And so what does that make you?"

It hit me without needing to answer, and I couldn't help a loud guffaw.

Apparently my "seven dwarves" found my cackle very funny again, and began to laugh in their turn when they heard me from their own shelters. Once again we ended up in stitches in the middle of the night in that remote Equatorial African jungle.

This time I did not get a shock when some time before dawn a row of filed teeth glittered in the dark and a hand shook me gently.

"*Wuebuna*," someone whispered. "*Wuebunansé.*"

"Uh, yeah… good morning," I replied as I stretched.

I looked to my left. Gabriel was still sleeping soundly, and I could not avoid the temptation to put my mouth close to his ear and shout at the top of my voice: "Come on, Gabriel! Up! Wake up!"

The next moment the poor man jumped up. With him came the roof of the shelter, the pole holding it and something else that flew out into the dusk and I could not identify. He looked in all directions in alarm, eyes wide as saucers. When all he saw was the silhouettes of the Pygmies gathering their things together, he turned on me and pulled me down on my back. He then proceeded to tickle me until, unable to defend myself, I had to beg for mercy in one of the few moments when I managed to stop giggling and could utter an entire word.

Meanwhile the Pygmies were all ready to leave, and from their short height were staring at me stretched out on the ground, laughing hysterically. Even Ipé-Maliki shook his head resignedly before he offered me his hand to help me up.

We set off at once, first back to where they had found the elephant footprint the evening before, and then following its clear trail of broken trees and branches.

The Pygmies, with their leader always ahead, kept extremely alert, but it was not like the day before when they had scented the opportunity of eating roast bird or monkey. This time they walked much more tensely, with their spears ready in their hands, looking to all sides but never up, no matter how much fluttering of leaves there might be above their heads. Clearly all their senses were focused on the surrounding vegetation, fearing the sudden and unstoppable attack of one of the elephants we were following.

In spite of the attitude of the Aka, I had no way of assessing the theoretical danger of coming across an elephant. I had always seen them as peaceful, intelligent creatures that only attacked in self defense. The stories some natives had told me in Guinea about killer elephants destroying whole villages seemed simply exaggerations or even a justification for killing them for the sake of their precious ivory tusks. Nevertheless, I have to admit that the deeply cautious attitude of those seven Pygmy hunters was beginning to make me nervous.

All these thoughts faded, however, when we suddenly came out of the thick gloomy jungle I had spent so many days in and found ourselves on the edge of an immense clearing. It was made up of a multitude of pools reflecting the blinding sunlight, rivulets of dirty water and stretches of tall grass and reeds where it would have been a pleasure to frolic. In fact, that is exactly what I was about to do when Ipé-Maliki took me by the arm to stop me. With a couple of significant gestures he first took in that whole expanse with a sweep of his arm. Then, with a sinuous wave, he gave a perfect imitation of a crawling snake.

Needless to say, I lost my appetite for running around the clearing and contented myself with following the footsteps of the Pygmy group. I even tried to put my feet exactly where they had put theirs.

The trail went into the boggy area. For a moment it seemed that the Pygmies were hesitating about it, but the great hunter harangued them with a couple of sentences and they decided to go on, albeit not too happy to be going into a terrain that was not their natural habitat.

We were moving along what was undoubtedly a well-trodden path made by the constant passage of fair-sized animals.

"The elephants' path…" I whispered to Gabriel.

"Maybe not," he said pointing to our right above the grass.

I looked that way, but all I could see was a pair of white herons on top of a black rock. I turned to him and shrugged.

"Keep looking," he insisted.

I did, and just when I was beginning to think he was teasing me, the herons suddenly took flight and a huge head crowned by a pair of thick grey horns emerged in the distance, perhaps watching the strange group of hairless monkeys who were entering its domain.

"Fuck!" I blurted out. "A buffalo!"

The Pygmy in front of me half-turned, gesturing me to lower my voice and keep my head down as I walked.

Then the seven hunters dispersed, ready to surround the animal.

Three of them went left and another three went right, leaving the youngest the one who had climbed the tree the day before with Gabriel and me. They moved incredibly slowly, trying not to make so much as a blade of grass tremble, and taking extremely stealthy steps. All this meant that it was some time before they got into position.

I knew I was going to witness an attack on a poor animal that did not know what was coming, and up to a point I wished it would realize it was an ambush in time to run away. But on the other hand I could not stop admiring those daring men, so short in stature and yet so courageous, who had decided to hunt a beast which weighed more than all of them put together and could have killed any one of them with a single thrust of its neck. The situation vaguely reminded me of a scene in Moby Dick, where the animal is harassed by tenacious harpooners led by an implacable Captain Ahab a little over four feet tall. Of course Melville's great white whale did not have those horns, or the unpleasant habit of charging anything which got in its way.

Finally, when the tension was almost unbearable, the imitation of a monkey's call was the signal to attack. The Pygmies, yelling to give themselves courage, got to their feet and ran from all directions, ready to converge on the titanic buffalo, who lowered his horns and readied himself to repel the attack.

36

Confusion took over that boggy meadow. The six Pygmies, leaping over the grass, charged at the buffalo, who found himself surrounded and could not decide who to attack. Then, when they were just a few feet away from the animal, the hunters threw their spears at once. But as the buffalo felt the first sting on his back he broke into a terrified run, so that only a couple of the poisoned tips managed to penetrate the thick, hard skin. It was not enough poison for that powerful ruminant, more than half a ton in weight, running in a frenzy, blind with fear. What really scared me was the realization that the terrified buffalo was running straight toward us.

My first reflex was to run as fast as I could, away from the route the raging bull was taking. But the young hunter who had remained with us seized my arm when he saw what I was intending to do, screaming with his eyes that I must not move so much as a muscle.

That thing was upon us. I could hear his accelerated breathing, and I won't deny that I was shitting myself. The half dozen yelling Pygmies had been left behind, and by now they could not even release their arrows because of the risk of hitting us. So, there I was, with a suicidal maniac in a loincloth who scarcely came up to my shoulder holding my arm, and a freight train with horns which I was sure would run me over in a couple of seconds if I did not move. And just when I was going to twist myself free from the Aka, he let go of me unexpectedly, but only to give me a thrust that threw me to the ground. Meanwhile he stood up very straight, with all his muscles tense.

From where I had landed, surrounded by tall grass, I could see absolutely nothing. But I could clearly feel the vibrations on the ground as it was hammered by the buffalo's hooves. I also heard his snorts just a few feet away from me, which convinced me he was going to be run me over, so I crouched down, half dead with fear.

I closed my eyes.

Gabriel shouted.

I shouted.

The Aka shouted.

And suddenly, with a deafening noise, it was all over.

I was still crouching on the ground with my eyes closed and my hands over my head. An absurd silence had fallen.

Intrigued, I opened my eyes.

I could not see a thing.

I got to my feet slowly, and the first thing I saw was Gabriel, a few feet from me, also buried in the thick grass. From my right, six black figures ran in silence to where I was standing. Then I looked to my left and saw the young Pygmy staring at his feet. I went over slowly, pushing the grass aside with my hands, and it was not until I was right beside him that I saw the great bulk of the buffalo, dead, from a well-aimed spear-thrust in the back of his neck.

I had no idea how the little hunter had managed to kill that enormous beast with a single blow. From what I remembered of the bullfights during a visit to Spain the preening matadors had trouble finishing their victims even when they had been stabbed and were already weakened. And yet that young man who looked like a twelve-year-old had killed that mountain of flesh and horns with nothing but his fragile wooden spear. It seemed to me that all those butchers in their flashy costumes would have a lot to think about if they saw a show of courage like this, without any need of all the assistants who make their job easier.

When the rest of the hunters arrived, they too were briefly dumbfounded, but immediately burst into cheers of joy as they hugged the hero of the day. The most moving moment came when Ipé-Maliki went up to the young man and calmly removed from his own neck a necklace of blue feathers, the only ornament differentiating him from the other Aka as someone important within the tribe. He ceremoniously put it around the young man's neck and addressed him with words which must have meant praise and acknowledgement. The brave young man, who had faced death without batting an eyelash, blushed shyly at being on the receiving end of so much praise in such a short time.

When I went over to him, hugged him and gave him a noisy kiss on the cheek, the poor boy nearly fainted.

Once the congratulations were done with, the Aka hurried to dismember the giant buffalo, cutting it up with their machetes and wrapping the pieces in banana leaves, which they then tied up with flexible lianas. It took them more than two hours to finish the job, and when they did, they loaded the enormous bundles onto their backs.

Until that moment I had not realized that the hunting of the buffalo meant the end of our stay with the Pygmies. Obviously they had to go back to their village with as much meat as possible, which meant that Gabriel and I were to continue our journey alone. The strange thing was that I was overwhelmed with a feeling not of concern or helplessness, but of sadness. A true sadness at leaving that noble tribe of good women and men who had saved my life and who I would probably never see again.

Before he loaded his own bundle, Ipé-Maliki addressed us, pointing to the other side of the clearing with his spear. "*Nomeguwaibwe*," he said, mimicking the act of walking with two fingers, "*Munéna Oveng*."

Obviously I did not understand his words. But the combination of signs and expressions I had heard before made me guess he was saying something like "Follow the path. Oveng is ahead." Of course there was no way of being sure, but as there was no other route in sight I nodded as if I had understood every syllable.

"Goodbye," I said, moved by this farewell. "Thank you for everything, and may the god Kmvum watch over all Aka, protect them and provide them with good hunting."

I bowed my head to show my gratitude. When I looked up, the great hunter had turned around. Picking up his bundle, without looking back, he joined the rest of the group, which like a line of exaggerated two-legged ants was already walking in the direction of their village with enough meat to satisfy them for a long, long time.

Once again Gabriel and I found ourselves alone in the middle of nowhere. The Aka had shown us the way, and I took it for granted that he would not have left us on our own in those marshes if the village of Oveng had not been relatively close. So, with a touch of fear but at the same time trying to breathe trust into myself, I turned my back on the Pygmies, who were already entering the forest they had come from, and faced the spot Ipé-Maliki had pointed out to me.

"Well," I said, staring at the thick vegetation before us. "Let's go on…"

Taking that first step, we headed toward the dark, threatening jungle which awaited us on the other side of the clearing.

37

Again I found myself walking under the dark dome formed by the countless trees filling every available space. Some of them reared high on incredibly thin trunks, little thicker than my own arm, but reaching heights of sixty or ninety feet, using all their energies to rise toward the unattainable blue sky in an invisible death struggle to come by some trace of light.

The environment was the same one I had walked through hours before, but in the absence of the Pygmies the feelings of safety and even jollity had disappeared. Now the forest was once more a gloomy place full of dangers, and only my very slight experience and Gabriel's presence provided me with some vague trust in our chances.

"Do you think this is the same path we were following before we came into this clearing?" Gabriel asked, walking behind me.

"No idea," I admitted. "But it's where Ipé-Maliki pointed to, and it's equally visible."

"He said it was an elephant path, didn't he?"

"That's what I understood."

"So, they come this way..."

"What are you trying to say, Gabriel?"

"I'm not so sure it's safe to walk this way. Suppose we come upon them."

"Well, I know they're pretty violent creatures," I said, turning toward him. "But if we don't scare them, I don't think... you know, I don't think they'll attack us."

"I don't know, I don't know..."

"Anyway," I said with a shrug, "I don't think we have a choice. If the Aka told us to go this way, I think it's what we ought to do."

"All right," he said doubtfully. "I only hope we get to Oveng without any more mishaps."

But his words had already made me feel a little uneasy, and as soon as I noticed the first sounds of branches snapping somewhere out of sight, an untimely restlessness came over me. I began to imagine invisible elephants weighing several tons suddenly charging us.

After a few hours of making progress in the heat we decided to stop to have something to eat and get our strength back. In our satchels we were carrying fruit, smoked meat, and even two portions of honeycomb wrapped in leaves, but as we were not sure how long it would take us to reach Oveng we opted for rationing our supplies and eat just enough to take the edge off our hunger. As a result lunch was brief, and after a short rest we went on.

The path kept going up and down, as we were still in an area made up of more or less high hills, divided by smooth little valleys with winding streams running through them.

"Gabriel?"

"Yes?"

"Are you married?"

He looked at me in surprise before answering. "Not that I know of."

"And do you have a partner, girlfriend, or anything like that?"

He frowned, surprised and amused. "Why do you ask?"

"Oh, I'm just curious. It's just that you haven't told me much about yourself."

"Perhaps there's not much to tell."

"I can't believe it," I said shaking my head. "You have… I mean, you had a good job. You're educated, intelligent, and quite attractive. And… well, from what I've seen in the months I've been in Guinea, it doesn't seem difficult to find a partner."

"Perhaps I'm too choosy…"

"But… you do like girls, don't you?"

"Are you asking if I'm gay?" He turned to me in puzzlement. "Do I give that impression?"

"No, not at all," I assured him. "I just thought that's what you meant when you said—"

"What I meant to say was that I'm attracted to brave women, intelligent, with character… more or less like you." His eyes gazed at me shyly.

I turned away, flushed like a teenager. "What do you mean?" I asked. I could not keep my voice from trembling.

"Come on, Sarah… it's obvious, you know."

"No, I've no idea what you're talking about." Actually I knew perfectly well what he meant, but I found it hard to admit, even to myself.

"Well… for some time now I've had feelings for you."

My heart beat madly, while my stomach seemed to contract every time his words reached my ears. "So… why haven't you told me before? We've been together for quite a few days."

"I don't know. I guess I thought you'd laugh in my face, or you'd stop trusting me," he murmured and lowered his gaze.

"Why would you think I'd do that?"

"Please…" He spread his hands wide. "You're a white woman, and I'm just a—"

"That's nonsense," I cut in. "I don't care whether you're black, white or green."

"I also didn't know how you felt about me."

"You could have given me a clue," I said, coming up to him with my eyes down. "A small gesture would've been enough."

"Sarah…" he said, arching his eyebrows, "for I don't know how many days I haven't moved from your side, looking after you and risking my life to protect yours. Isn't that a gesture?"

"You clearly don't know women…" I said and, coming close to him, I allowed the unwanted feelings that had been growing inside me break through their dams and flood down my skin, neglected of caress. I brushed his neck with the tips of my fingers, and my yearning body searched for his with impatient desire. Gabriel held me by the waist as I stood on tiptoe so that our faces, starved of kisses, finally met. His lips locked with mine, creating an uncontrollable tide of heat which ran though arteries and veins to converge right in the center of my sex.

The noise of the jungle seemed to increase at that moment. The birds tweeted with renewed strength, the monkeys shouted hysterically, and it was not until I felt the vegetation move behind me and a dull vibration under my feet that I realized this was not the result of our passion.

Gabriel pushed me away unexpectedly. Grabbing my arm as if he meant to tear it out of its socket, he pulled me after him and began to race frenziedly across the field.

I neither saw nor understood anything of what was happening. I only heard Gabriel shouting in horror:"Run, Sarah! Run for your life!"

38

I was dragged once again, like a doll, and we leapt off the path. Trying not to make too much noise, we slipped away to some nearby trees, one of which sank its aerial roots into the soil to form an irregular cage with enough space to shelter inside.

"What... what's going on? What are we running away from?" I asked in a frightened whisper from where I was huddling.

Gabriel simply pointed with his finger.

I strained my eyes between the green mesh spread before me without being able to make anything out, until a small tree fell to the ground and a massive gray shadow crossed briefly in front of the gap.

I could not believe it. I had just seen an elephant.

We had hidden a short way from the path, but with the thickness of the forest there might easily have been many more of them, because although I could hear the foliage cracking as the herd passed and the short trumpeting sounds they used to communicate with, I never got to see them at all. I found it unbelievable that these animals which weighed tons and made the ground shake as they walked could remain invisible barely ten yards away. If anything, the occasional bending of a tree trunk as they passed gave their presence away, but I could not even manage to see the reflection of their ivory tusks, or the rough texture of their thick hide. I knew they were mountain elephants, considerably smaller than those we are used to seeing grazing in the Serengeti, and even smaller than the tamable Indian elephants. But what the hell, what mattered was that they were elephants, and oddly enough, those with the worst reputation for violence.

I was pondering as I heard them pass in front of me whether the cause of that aggressive behavior might be the lack of visibility in that environment. They could only rely on their senses of smell and hearing, and when in doubt, naturally, the tendency would be to attack first and ask questions afterward. Particularly in the case of men, because I remembered Duyé-Nianu explaining to me that elephants were part of their diet, and although the Aka were terrified of being attacked by those creatures, surely the elephants felt even more fear when they smelt a human. At any rate, I said to myself, I did not want to pay the bill for that ancestral rivalry between Pygmy and elephant.

During the long ten minutes it took that great group of elephants to pass in front of us, we remained completely still, praying that none of them decided to leave the path, and thanking the appropriate divinity for the fact that the light breeze was blowing toward us and not the other way around. A penetrating smell of musk and dung flooded my nose, but that was better than for my scent of wayward missionary to reach them and give one of them the unfortunate idea of coming to take a peek.

Finally, when the sound of breaking branches came to an end, we agreed with a brief exchange of glances to leave the safety of the tiny hiding place where we were still huddled.

We walked with the utmost stealth, doing everything we could to avoid making the slightest noise. In slow motion we once again reached the path, now filled with mounds of elephant dung and round footprints a foot and a half long, sunk deep into the mud.

"Phew…" I said with a snort, squatting down. "We only just managed it."

Before Gabriel could say anything, a loud trumpet immediately behind us froze the blood in my veins.

I looked in the direction it had come from. A few yards away, perfectly camouflaged even though it was more than six feet high, a grey mass in which all I could make out was a huge eye with thick lashes blinked in disbelief. Only then was I able to distinguish a trunk rising in a clear distress signal, trumpeting deafeningly to warn the herd.

At once a series of trumpets answered the call, and the spongy ground of the jungle began to throb. With identical speed, Gabriel and I began to run desperately uphill with what little strength we had left in our tired legs.

I could not see where I was putting my feet or hands, nor was I even sure my companion was following me. All I was aware of was the ever-increasing crackling of the vegetation being torn up by the roots, and the earthquake which seemed to be pursuing me, and all I could think about was running faster and faster for my life. Luckily the elephants had come from where we were heading to, so that at least I was running in the right direction. Although if that mass of furious feet and tusks managed to catch up with me that would not be any consolation.

I climbed like a lunatic up a steep hill, holding onto trees and roots, slipping on the muddy ground with my sandals, cursing and panting. I heard heavy breathing at my back and assumed it was Gabriel but, to be honest, I did not turn to check. Even if a pack of angry preachers had been after me I could not have run any faster, and if for some reason Gabriel had lagged behind I might not have had the courage to stop and wait for him.

It seemed that I was still on the path, even though I had made a few silly detours and gone up and down a number of slopes. When in utter exhaustion I gave up and leaned against a tree, I could hear nothing but my own wheezing. I was glad to see Gabriel coming up to me, equally exhausted, and not to perceive any trace of movement beyond: no trumpeting sounds, no trees torn up, no sharp tusks reflecting the sunlight.

"I think we've thrown them off," Gabriel ventured as he sought to regain his breath.

"Thrown them off...? I doubt it," I muttered, bending over with my hands on my knees. "But I guess when they saw us running like rabbits... they guessed we didn't pose much of a threat."

"Very true." He nodded. "It wasn't a very dignified retreat, to say the least."

"As a wise man once said," – I panted – "dignity is inversely proportional to the size of the animal that's after you."

"Socrates?"

"My father."

Once we had got our breath back, at ease but still looking around every once in a while, we continued on what we thought was still the same path we had taken hours before. We were slightly worried about the path in question following such an erratic line that we wondered whether we might be going around in circles.

"It occurs to me," I said thoughtfully, "that if this really is an elephant path, then it can't take us to Oveng."

"Why?" he asked behind me.

"Well, I was wondering why would the elephants want to follow a path that would take them directly to a village... to go shopping?"

"Hmm... you're right. Although if this isn't the right way, why did Ipé-Maliki put us on it?"

"He might not have understood we wanted to go to Oveng."

"Where else would we want to go?" he asked, spreading his arms and turning on his heels without stopping. "It's the only village for dozens of miles around. In fact they must have bought their machetes and lighters there."

"Okay...but don't you find it odd, all these twists and turns we're taking?"

"Sarah, we're in Africa. Or had you forgotten?"

"What do you mean by that?"

"I mean you can't give up hope so easily, because sometimes… what you're looking for is in the place you least expect it." As he said this he pointed at a spot to the right, downhill.

I strained my eyes in the direction he was pointing, but was unable to make out anything through that mesh of trees and lianas.

Then a woman wrapped in a loose colorful dress came into sight as she rose from the rock by the river where she had been squatting. Balancing a plastic jug painted in white and blue stripes on her head, she rose gracefully and started down a narrow path. She was twenty yards or so away and did not notice our presence until I started to run down the slope in great leaps, shouting, "*Mbolo! Mbolo!*"

39

We had made it. That was the only thought I had, and it gripped me like a personal triumph I could be everlastingly proud of.

We were in Oveng at last, after crossing the tortuous Alem mountain range which divides the continental region of Equatorial Guinea in two. We had crossed the wildest region of the country, and one of the least explored in Africa. I had survived malaria, an encounter with a green mamba and the blind fury of a herd of elephants. I had never seen myself as a heroine before, nor did I feel a special pride in any of my past actions, but there was no doubt that what I had achieved with Gabriel was quite a story I could tell my grandchildren some day.

Speaking of Gabriel, that... – how to call it, infatuation? – had totally taken me by surprise. Perhaps that was not the right word for what was happening to us. The truth was that an unquestionable feeling had grown during those days without my realizing it... until it fell on me like a bomb, awaking emotions that I had been trying to keep hidden under lock and key.

In fact one of the reasons why I had taken up that post at the end of the world had been to erase all memory of my long and disappointing relationship with John, an architect as gifted at tracing tangents and calculating loads as he was incapable of taking on any type of commitment. Three years of dating without the slightest hint of the possibility of living together was more than I was prepared to accept, longer than I was ready to waste. Enough to realize that he would never suggest it, and that really all we were doing was riding an emotional merry-go-round.

The irony was that I had fallen in love well, yes, those were the right words — with an African. An stranger. A fugitive who would be forced to flee his country to save his life and with whom there was no possibility of sharing a future. Or was there?

"Sarah!"

I looked up and there he was, standing before me, a complete mess, with arms akimbo.

"What's the matter with you? I've been talking to you and I don't think you've heard a single word of what I was saying." He bent over to look at me with a frown. "Are you all right?"

"Well... yes," I muttered. "Well, no. Hmm... quite honestly, I don't know."

Gabriel stared at me, looking intrigued."Well, anyway..." he said with a shrug, "you can tell me when you find out. In the meantime, I managed to get us transport to Cogo."

"Cogo?" I said excitedly. "That's next door to Gabon! The border's just a step from there!"

"Exactly. That's why we're going."

"Although... won't they be watching all the roads?" I said with a shadow of concern. "I don't want to go through it all over again... you know, running away through the jungle to avoid a checkpoint."

"Don't worry, Sarah. That won't happen again."

"But the roads—"

"I never said," he replied cunningly, "that we'd be going by road."

"So have you rented a helicopter?" I said with a grimace.

"No, though that's not a bad idea either," he said, rubbing his chin as though he were considering it. "In fact, we're going by river."

"What? By river? How?"

"In a canoe, obviously."

"You have a canoe?"

"You do," he said, sounding amused. "You just bought us one."

The canoe in question turned out to be an old dug-out tree trunk, long and narrow, somewhat unstable, but surprisingly light. Although on some stretches of the river the rocky bottom was only a few inches from the surface, we never actually touched it.

"Had you done this before?" Gabriel asked behind me. We were dipping the oars gently in the water, letting the current bear us on.

"I've gone rafting a few times."

"You've done what?"

"Rafting, going downriver in inflatable rafts."

"Huh… now I know why you know how to row."

"Maybe. Although rafting doesn't have much to do with canoeing. You simply row like a maniac because you're told to, and you don't have to worry about keeping your balance or steering, and you definitely don't need to watch the banks in case of hippos or crocodiles."

"Relax, there aren't any hippos in this river, and everybody knows crocodiles don't eat white people."

"What?" I said, half turning.

"Haven't you ever seen a Tarzan movie, Sarah? Haven't you noticed that they all start with four whites and forty blacks, and at the end of the movie the whites haven't so much as a spot on their shirts but all the forty blacks, with no exception, are dead?"

"No, but now that you mention it…"

"Lions and crocodiles don't eat whites, the poisoned arrow always hits the black guy, and the possibilities of falling into an abyss go up astronomically if you're an illiterate native. That's the true law of the jungle…" he said, and gave a bitter laugh.

For the time being the river was no more than a quiet stream of dark water a few feet wide. On either side we were prevented from reaching either bank to rest by a solid wall of vegetation more than sixty feet tall whose roots sank directly into the water. To top it all, the few islets of sand and pebbles dotting the river's monotony were invariably occupied by lazy crocodiles enjoying the fleeting sun, with their long and well-toothed jaws wide open. So that in order to rest my back and my suffering butt, I had no choice but to lean back in the canoe and stretch as best I could. An exercise I repeated more and more frequently, since the wooden board I was sitting on was not exactly comfortable   although I could not stop thinking that it would have been far worse to make this journey on foot. At least I was sitting down!

There was a moment when the river widened several dozen yards and the immense trees to either side formed an imposing green dome, a majestic living cathedral which we entered feeling like a couple of insects dragged in by the water. I had never felt so overwhelmed by nature, by her inconceivable scale, by living beings hundreds of years old rising limitlessly to cover the entire sky, harboring an infinity of other beings in their limbs and feeding them with their fruits and leaves. I laid the oar on my knees and let my eyes wander among those benevolent giants, and I could not help but ask myself how long they would remain safe from man's greed.

I was still occupied with these somber thoughts when the stream widened suddenly, while at the same time the trees grew correspondingly shorter. The sun, which had barely poked its nose between the foliage all day long, was now visible, nearing the horizon immediately above the water of a wide estuary which was beginning to open out in front of us. And just after the last bend, unexpectedly   it was the first one we had seen since we started our journey on the river   we saw a small village of stilt houses on the right bank, slumbering in front of a strip of sand and pebbles.

I had been rowing for hours, and although we had done it with the aid of a helpful current, simply holding the heavy wooden oar had worn out my arms and shoulders. In spite of that, without a word needing to be said, the moment we saw it we started rowing in the direction of the village with renewed vigor. It was not until that precise moment that my body began to realize how incredibly tired it was. That tiredness had built up over endless days and, like a huge dam holding back a massive weight of water, it threatened to crack and ultimately defeat me. Even so, with one last effort we reached the beach, and before the prow had even touched the pebbly shore I leapt from the canoe. After a few hesitant steps I surrendered, collapsed on to the rounded pebbles and closed my eyes, overwhelmed by exhaustion.

40

"Sarah, please," Gabriel said a few seconds later. "Help me get the canoe out of the water."

"All good things must come to an end…" I muttered under my breath as I dug my elbows into the pebbles and levered myself up.

"Stop complaining. You spent the last hour stretched out like a cat instead of rowing."

"My back hurt."

"What a lame excuse…"

"You take advantage of the fact that I'm a fragile woman," I whined as I took hold of the canoe at one end.

"Yeah, sure… a princess," he replied as he pushed.

"With that attitude," I said folding my arms, "you're not going to seduce anybody," I said.

"And who says I intend to seduce anyone?" he said also folding his arms.

"Don't play dumb."

"What do you mean?"

"You know," I said raising an eyebrow, "the fact that it was me who kissed you doesn't mean I didn't notice you'd love to do it again."

"Oh… that. The fact is," he grinned impishly, "I'd never been kissed by a missionary like that…"

"Very funny. Well, you can get your next kiss from Mother Theresa of Calcutta."

I suppose that our shouted verbal duel must have made a few heads peer out of the windows of the stilt houses: disbelieving witnesses to a ragged missionary nun raising her voice while she pulled a canoe out of the water, arguing about who had kissed who and why.

When we realized this, we did our best to recover our composure, and greeted the audience. A young man came over to us, with what must have been his wife and small son on either side.

"Good evening!" I said with my best smile. "Could you give shelter to a nun and her companion for one night?

The three exchanged puzzled looks. At last the wife said, "Of course, sister. Our house is yours."

"Thank you. God bless you," I replied. Carried away by my own acting, I even made the sign of the cross in the air as an afterthought.

At this point the man stepped forward with his head bent, as if he were ashamed of what he was going to say. He cleared his throat a couple of times, and addressed me with great formality."Sister," he said, raising his eyes, "surely the hand of God has guided you to this humble village today to relieve our pain."

"Excuse me?"

"You see, sister, we have a little daughter, and she's very sick with malaria, but we're poor and so we haven't been able to get treatment for her, and we beg you to—"

"Treat her?" I interrupted him."I'm sorry, really sorry, but I have no medicines to give you."

"No... it's not that. We would like her to be... at peace with God."

"You want me to...?" I asked incredulous."You want me to perform the last rites?"

"Please... while she's still alive."

Not for a moment, when I borrowed the personality of a nun, did it cross my mind that I might end up in a situation like this. As a convinced atheist I had taken on a disguise to save my life, but now, with the black irony destiny sometimes amuses itself with, I found myself kneeling in front of a cot, looking into the eyes of a dying little girl, while her parents expected a blessing from me which I could not give, and did not even know how to give.

Even the orange evening light filtering through the walls of the hut refused to be a witness of that sad moment. It failed to reach the little girl, barely illuminated by the wavering spirit lamp hanging from the ceiling. The parents, kneeling behind me, joined their hands in silent prayer, while Gabriel, with his head bent, stayed leaning on the doorway of the single room of that hut which smelt of damp and sorrow.

The girl could not have been more than six or seven. She was lying on the bed, looking at me wide-eyed. She seemed to be a little frightened; possibly I was the first white person she had seen in her short life. She wore colored beads in her little braids, as if she were about to go to some birthday party, perspiration pearled her tiny naked body, and her left hand held close to her bosom the battered plastic head of a doll she had probably never had.

"Mommy…" she moaned stretching out her hand.

"Don't worry, my love," her mother whispered. "The lady has come to help you."

The little girl's eyes fixed themselves on me again, but this time there was a plea in them. "Am I going to get well?" she asked hopefully, in the ghost of a voice.

I could barely hold back my tears. I had nothing to do or say here. Any prayer from my mouth would be nothing but a cowardly lie, an insult to these people, and even, for all I could say (although I was no believer), the damnation of that innocent girl.

The only decent thing I could think of to do was to take her little hand in mine and ask her name.

"Luz Marina Ne Mbema…" she recited weakly.

"Luz Marina, what a beautiful name."

"Thank you…" she said, and a faint smile lit up her face for a brief moment.

I glanced at Gabriel, looking for support of some kind but, still leaning against the doorframe, he shrugged helplessly.

I turned back to the little girl. "Are you tired?"

She blinked and nodded.

"Right, but everything is fine... you just rest a while, and soon you'll be better."

"When... when will I be able to play with my friends again?"

"Soon, sweetheart. Very soon."

"Will I, mommy?"

"Of course, my sunshine. And your daddy will go to Cogo and buy you a doll."

"Really, daddy?" she asked incredulous and raising herself a little.

"The prettiest one I can find," he said, and the little girl's eyes widened.

"I want one with a dress..." she said, and then dropped back weakly with her eyes on the ceiling.

"You'll have the doll with the prettiest dress in the world, my treasure."

The little girl's hand, still between mine as if she had forgotten it was there, burned with fever. The malaria was causing her terrible pain, but the little one smiled again feebly, imagining herself with her doll.

I turned to the mother, and her gaze implored me.

I could confess the truth and avoid deceiving these poor people, but after all no real priest was ever going to come that way. A few words of hope would do no harm to anybody, and perhaps might relieve, if not the pain, at least the sorrow of that family.

"Oh Lord, God Almighty," I began to recite without daring to look at the little girl, closing my eyes tightly. "Protect pretty little Luz Marina from all evil. May your hand stretch like a cloak over this family and comfort them in your peace that nothing ill may come to them... and above all, look after their precious little girl, that the beautiful Luz may shine upon us all for many years. But should it be your will to take her," – I whispered, with pity on my lips – "receive her in your bosom… and may your angels fill her with joy, and… may they never forget how much… how much…"

Unable to say a single word more, I burst out weeping uncontrollably. Getting hastily to my feet, I ran out of the door blinded by tears, with my heart like lead inside me.

41

"Are you all right?" Gabriel asked putting his hand on my shoulder.

"All right?" I sobbed. "How can I be all right? Didn't you see what happened in there? I'm not..." I could say nothing more. I simply leaned my head on his chest and let the tears flow.

"Of course I saw, Sarah. And many more times besides this one."

"How do you cope?" I asked, letting myself fall on the pebbles of the beach.

"I don't."

"Something like this... it shouldn't happen," I muttered despairingly. "It shouldn't be allowed to happen."

"People die, Sarah. Even children."

"I know that. But we can't look the other way and let these things happen."

"But they do happen, whether we like it or not."

"They can be avoided."

"Let me remind you that they haven't found a vaccine against malaria yet."

"Well, they should have. I don't know what they're waiting for."

Gabriel gazed at me with something like curiosity. "I'm surprised you're so naïve. Is there malaria in rich countries?"

"You know there isn't."

"Then why do you think a thousand fold more money is spent on research about obesity, wrinkles or acne than on finding a vaccine against malaria, or even an effective treatment?"

"Yes, I know. But even taking into account the indifference of western governments, countries like Equatorial

Guinea might do it. They have plenty of money to finance the fight against an illness which affects them so directly. Or even to give chloroquine to the population so the people don't die!"

Gabriel sat down beside me and shook his head."You don't understand, do you? Do you really think the government of Equatorial Guinea would give a damn if the whole population died of malaria, or anything else…?"

"But… what are you saying?"

"Well now, think about it. What services do the government provide for the people? Nothing! There's no health or public service of any kind, despite the fact that thanks to oil we're the third richest country in the world per inhabitant. The third richest! But the president's clan and his minions keep it all: absolutely everything. Guineans die of disease and malnutrition, while they rob every last cent and make themselves multimillionaires…" He looked at the palms of his hands, then clenched his fists tightly. "Sarah, it would be a wonderful thing for some if the half million Guineans living in what they think of as their private estate disappeared, and the sooner the better. For them we're just so many awkward witnesses of their crimes, an obstacle in their way."

"Isn't there anyone who could do something to stop them?" I asked in exasperation.

"Anyone?"

"I don't know…" I gestured with my hands in frustration. "The USA, the EU, the UN. Whoever!"

"Forget it. Nobody's coming to our rescue."

"But if there's a report—"

"It would be useless," he interrupted me."The biggest oil multinationals are established here. The Guinean government spends tens of millions of dollars a year in the USA alone, to "launder" its image, so that your country's companies and politicians don't have to explain why their profits are deposited directly into Obiang's private accounts. As for the Chinese…

well, if oil were discovered in hell they'd sign a contract with the devil himself."

"But there are plenty of powerful international organizations that aren't at the mercy of the oil industry and its interests. It can't be that just because there's oil here, nobody's going to lift a finger to help."

"Well, they haven't up to now. Doesn't that tell you something?" He breathed out heavily and looked up at the sky, which was already beginning to be tinted with indigo. "I believe Amnesty International made a report, and then several NGOs denounced the atrocities of the regime, but there are too many interests at play to let anyone move out of the picture. When there's so much money at stake everybody tries to get a cut. And nobody's going to risk losing the chance of doing good business just to save a couple of thousand starving blacks."

"I refuse to think like you. There has to be a solution to all this," I insisted, as if I were the last bastion of Guinean hope.

Gabriel shook his head vigorously."You keep thinking like a white person... Not all problems have a solution, the seventh cavalry regiment doesn't arrive at the last minute, and the girl doesn't marry the good guy. Do you really believe we matter to anyone? Do you really believe that even if you went on TV in your country and explained what's happening here, anyone would give a damn?"

I did not know the answer. I had nothing to say. I refused to give in to the sense of powerlessness behind what Gabriel was saying, but I had no words for that feeling. Nor did I have any arguments to refute his statements, as depressing as they were true.

I looked behind me and saw the yellow light of the lamp in the window of the room where that innocent child was dying, an indirect victim of the greed of a group of bastards who did not deserve so much as the air they breathed.

Then my rage and hatred turned, without my realizing how, into an infinite sorrow. My soul ached, the way it only can when it comes face to face with the suffering of those who least deserve it. Slowly the tears slid down my cheeks, one after another, so that there was salt in the corners of my mouth.

At that moment, when I needed someone to hold me as never before, Gabriel came close to me, took my face in his hands and kissed my lips tenderly. It was a kiss of consolation, of understanding... perhaps of love. His lips were hot and the skin of his face very soft. He put his left hand firmly on my back and this contact made me shiver in a way I had not in a long time. Until then I had not been aware of how much I needed the physical touch of another person and the calm it gave me to feel loved, and in some way, protected from the vileness and cruelty which seemed intent on harassing that small, forgotten corner of the world.

42

It was a long, hot night. Little Luz's moaning woke me up again and again, and I even went with Irma her mother down to the river a couple of times, to soak some rags to lower her temperature.

"How long has she been ill?" I asked her as I held a plastic bucket full of rags for her.

"A long time," was all she said.

"And you haven't caught malaria?"

The woman looked at me in puzzlement."We all have malaria," she said weakly.

"All of you? Your son too?"

"In Guinea practically everybody has malaria, sister. Some die, and some are just ill, that's the only difference. I've already lost two children. Children and old people die often."

"And do you think… do you think Luz will be spared?"

"Only God knows that, sister." She paused and gave me a pleading look. "Please pray for her. Surely He'll pay more attention to you than to me. I don't think He listens to us blacks."

With the first light of day, Gabriel squeezed my shoulder to wake me up."Sarah… Sarah…"

"What…?"

"We have to go on."

"Go on?" I repeated. My mouth felt clogged. "Go on what?"

"The boat, silly. We have to go on downriver, to Cogo."

"Can't we wait a little longer?" I said turning my back to him. "I'm very sleepy."

"You can sleep in your next life," he said, patting my thigh as he got to his feet and forced me to get up with him.

We found that José and Irma were already up and had prepared a large basket of fruit for our journey.

"Thank you very much, but it wasn't necessary," I said as I took the gift. "Really I'm the one who ought to give you something for your hospitality."

"Your presence and your prayers are a gift to us, sister."

Once again I felt guilty about lying to them, and perhaps I might have confessed if Gabriel had not pulled my arm, urging me to move.

I turned just as I was about to go out of the door. "How did Luz make it through the night?"

Irma looked at the bed where the child lay. "Now she's asleep. Her fever seems to have gone down since last night."

I broke loose from Gabriel's arm, and in two steps I was at the little girl's bed. I felt an irresistible urge to hug her, but I merely kissed her lightly on her forehead so as not to disturb her sleep.

"Be strong, sweetheart…" I whispered. "You're going to be all right… you'll see."

I hugged both parents and their other child, who had woken up by now, said goodbye thanking them for the last time and went out the door of their hut.

Once again I found myself rowing at the bow of the canoe, letting the current carry me across an ever wider estuary. In fact, a couple of hours later both shores had receded so far that they were not much more than two thick green lines on the horizon. And seeing this, a disturbing idea came into my mind.

"Gabriel," I said turning to face him, "this river ends in the sea, doesn't it?"

"Of course. They all do."

"Don't try to be funny. I say that because I imagine it's not too far to the mouth."

"Yeah, I should think so. Why?"

"Because I've been noticing how strong the current is here in the middle, and I was wondering whether the same current won't end up carrying us out to sea."

He took a few seconds to think about it before nodding firmly. "You're absolutely right!" he cried. "We have to come in close to the right shore straight away. If not, we might end up going on to the island of Corisco."

"But… Gabon is on the left bank, isn't it?"

"That's right. That green line on our left is Gabon."

"Then why don't we go there directly?"

"Because neither of us has a passport, and we haven't got enough money left to bribe the customs agents. And with such a drifter look," he said looking at himself, "they'd never let us cross the border even if our papers were in order. I don't relish the idea either, but we have to reach Cogo. That's where we can get whatever we need to leave Guinea."

We went on rowing, hardly pausing for a break, fighting against the current which was set on keeping us in the middle of the estuary, but by the time the sun reached its highest point over the horizon we had already reached the shore. I suggested we stop to eat and have a rest. That was just what we were about to do when in the distance we saw what must be Cogo pier. We decided to get as close as we could without being seen, with the idea of hiding in the canoe until evening and trying to enter the city unnoticed.

When the sun was nearing the horizon again and the punctual hordes of mosquitoes began to assail us, we rowed quietly to a beach on the outskirts of the city which looked more like a rubbish dump. Trying to stay in the shadows which was not too difficult in a city without any public lighting we slipped through the streets like wandering cats, trying not to attract the attention of anyone clever enough to have seen us.

"Do you know where we're going?" I asked after a great deal of stumbling in the dark.

"I've no idea."

"And that's your plan?"

"Do you have a better one?"

"Well, yes," I replied, pleased with myself. "Ask anybody where there's a religious mission. Maybe they'll help us there."

"Sounds good. I just hope you don't ask a member of the secret police."

"That would be too much of a coincidence."

"You're wrong. There are thousands of them."

"Come on, don't exaggerate. I haven't come across a single one in all the time I've been in Guinea."

"That's what you think, Sarah."

"Well, who cares? Ask a child or some lady who doesn't look like a policewoman, and let's be done with it."

In the end it was an old lady selling roast chicken wings at her house door who told us there was a Carmelite mission a couple of blocks from there. We followed the woman's directions and arrived at the door of the mission. Like the rest of the city, it was dark.

The building was made of brick, apparently well-kept as opposed to the rest of the city, which seemed to be falling apart and had an iron door with a bell that did not work. I banged the door several times with my fist, but nobody came to open it and no voice sounded from the other side of the door.

That, and the absence of light, made me fear I was not going to have the same luck I had had in Luba.

"It seems there's nobody home," I said, disappointed.

"I can see that. I think we'll have to come up with something else."

"Well, I don't know. There are fewer and fewer people in the street now. We have to find some place to hide before we attract too much attention."

"Any other suggestion?" he grumbled.

"Hey, it's not my fault if the nuns are out for a stroll."

"Forgive me, I'm a little tired. How about going up to the church?" He pointed at the building, on top of a hill.

"It'll be closed by now."

"It doesn't matter. There must be a good view of the city from there, and besides, it looks quiet."

"And if we're lucky, maybe we'll find the nuns there."

"Then, there's nothing more to say. Let's go."

Playing secret agents so as not to be seen, we went up the hill to a small, unkempt park beside the church. It had been painted pale yellow years before, but was now covered in blotches of damp and mold. We made our way between trees and bushes, like a couple of unconvincing thieves, to a side entrance. We rang the bell, which was not surprisingly silent, and banged on the door with little enthusiasm. It seemed this place was also abandoned.

"Well… do we have a plan C?" I asked, with my knuckles still on the door.

"I have a few that don't work."

"Any other kind?"

"Does praying count?"

"Maybe…"

"Well, that's the best I've got."

"Great."

Disheartened, we went to sit on the church stairs.

"I'm very hungry, and I'm dying of thirst…" I muttered, contemplating the sparse lights of the city at our feet.

"Oh, you're one of those who eat every day?"

"I used to be."

"Did you know that most people here only have one meal a day?"

"Of course. I've been in Guinea for a while now, remember?"

"Well then, think of it as a cultural experience."

"Since when does hunger have anything to do with culture?"

"In Africa, hunger has to do with everything."

"Huh… well, there are details I wouldn't mind being spared."

"Don't complain, you're still alive."

"But if I don't eat something soon, I'm not going to—"

"Well, well, well!" a voice interrupted us, giving me the shock of my life. "Look who we have here!"

We turned round at once, and I almost died when I saw, lit by the faint lights of the city, the silhouettes of two policemen with their unmistakable flat caps.

43

"Identification!" one of them barked.

Gabriel and I looked at each other, petrified. We had no identification to show them and no money to try a new bribe.

"Come on!" he snapped. "I don't have all night!"

It occurred to me then that they could not be looking specifically for us, since in that case we would have been arrested immediately. So I decided to risk it, hoping that in the darkness they would not be able to get a clear view of our impoverished state.

"I am *Zizter* Cotillard," I said, putting on a ridiculously exaggerated French accent. "*Mon passport* izz in Carmelite mission. But... if *vous voulez*, call zee Governor and he clear all. He know me here in Cogo..."

"Are you French?" he asked. This time his tone was very different.

"*Oui! Izzz ere a probleme?*" I said feigning offense.

The two policemen looked at each other, visibly puzzled.

"Ah... no. It's all right," said the one who had stayed silent. "Sorry to trouble you. Good night."

"*Bonne nuit.*"

Without quite realizing how successful I had been, I saw the two policemen turn around and leave in search of another victim to harass.

"It's amazing..." I murmured when they had left. "After this public and critical triumph, I think I see myself more in the role of a Frenchwoman than a nun."

"Sarah," he said putting his hand on my shoulder, "the way you look now, I see you rather in the role of a beggar in a long battle against soap and water."

"You don't exactly smell of roses either."

"Yeah…" he said, putting his shirt to his nose. "We obviously need a bath and a change of clothes."

"Any idea where we could have them?

"Well, seeing there's no one in either the mission or the church, I can only think of one place where we might find someone to lend us a hand."

"In the World of Oz?"

He pointed at the only building in the city which seemed to have electricity that night."I was thinking of the hospital."

It took us only a few minutes to walk from the church down the hill. Then we set off toward the building Gabriel had pointed out. We did not cross anybody's path in the dark lonely streets until we reached the entrance to the hospital. Here a nurse sitting at a moth-eaten table raised her head and gave us a cagey look.

"What do you want?" she asked grumpily.

"Um... I have a fever," I improvised, "and I'd like to know whether I have malaria."

"High fever?"

"Yes."

"Joint pain?"

"Yes."

"Vomiting?"

"Yes."

"Diarrhea?"

"Yes."

"Then you don't have malaria," she declared firmly, and wrote something in a small notebook she kept beside her.

"Well, I still need to see a doctor. I've been told there are some American doctors in this hospital, it is Red Cross International, isn't it?"

The nurse glanced at me suspiciously.

"Don't you trust Guinean doctors?" she said challenging.

"Oh yes, of course I do… it's just that…you know, I'd like to talk to a westerner."

"So have you come to talk, or because you're sick?"

"And are you here to help or harass patients?" I snapped back. I was in no mood for an interrogation. "Can I see a doctor or not?"

"This is a hospital for Guineans."

"Well, I can see a sign here that says only HOSPITAL, and I'm sick. Doesn't that give me the right to come in and see a doctor?"

"No," she said, delighted to give me this answer.

"Would you rather I died here, at the door?"

"You can die wherever you want."

"Look here, miss," I said angrily, "if you don't let me in, I'll—"

"What's going on out here?" intervened a voice from inside with a definite Cuban accent.

Immediately a dark, tired-looking man wearing a white coat and with a stethoscope around his neck, appeared in the doorway."What's all this racket?"

"This woman. She's getting hysterical," the receptionist said, as if I was not there.

"Hysterical be damned!" I burst out. "I just want to see a doctor."

"So what's the problem?" he asked the nurse.

"She's not Guinean."

The doctor looked at her coldly."You should remember… that it's most certainly not the Guinean government who pays you a salary you don't deserve."

The woman arched her brows as if she didn't care and leaned back in her chair. The doctor, on the other hand, beckoned us to follow him.

"She's a niece of the Governor," he said with a shrug, which explained it all, as we followed him along a pistachio-green passage full of occupied stretchers. Half the fluorescent lights did not work. Together with the moans from dozens of throats, it gave the place a phantasmagoric air.

He led us down a dirty corridor to an office with the name Dr. ROJAS written in ballpoint pen on the door, ushered us in, and sat down behind a table with a mountain of medical reports on either side.

"Well... you tell me," he said, leaning both arms on the table.

"You see..." I had no idea where to begin. "Um... I..."

"Do you have a problem?"

"A very big one."

"And do I have to guess what it is?"

"I'm sorry. My problem isn't medical. It's...with the police."

"We all have problems with those assholes, sister."

"The truth is," I said hesitantly, "that I'm not a nun, or a missionary, or anything of the sort."

"And those clothes?"

"A disguise."

The doctor rubbed his chin, got up from his chair, opened the door and, after checking both sides of the corridor, came back to his seat.

"Well then, explain yourself," he said, as if I were going to tell him about my allergies.

And whether it was the white coat or the sympathy I had always felt for Cubans, or just that I was sick of that whole nightmare and wanted to share it with someone, the fact is that I gave him a summary of almost all my adventures since the day they had arrested me, right up to that same evening. In all, more than an hour talking, while he nodded with his eyes growing wider and wider.

"*Mi amor*," he said, reaching out to take my hand in his own. I realized I had started to cry at some point in the story. "Don't you worry; we're going to help you."

"Really?" I asked, still sobbing.

"Of course we are. Tonight you'll stay here, hiding downstairs in the pantry. When we change shifts I'll come see you before I leave and open the door for you."

"What about my friend? Can he stay with me?"

"Your friend?" he asked, puzzled. "The one who helped you escape?"

"Yes, that's right. He's also running away from the police and the soldiers."

"Of course. The two of you stay here, but make sure nobody sees you hiding."

He stood up and opened the door. After looking to either side again, he motioned us to follow.

"Now go to the end of the corridor, where the toilets are. Go into the ladies' and close the door from the inside until I come back. Okay?"

"What if someone wants to come in?"

"That won't happen," he said sorrowfully. "They never worked."

Just as he had told us, we hid in the toilets which apart from not having water, also lacked sinks and actual toilets and we sat on the floor, leaning on the wall, waiting for Dr. Rojas I had forgotten to ask him his first name to come for us.

I was dead tired , psychologically as well as physically, and it was a blessed relief to be able to unload part of the pressure onto someone else, let someone else deal with it, even though that person was a stranger.

And then, perhaps caught up in the routine of all the bad luck which had been dogging me, I began to wonder about the doctor's motives in helping us.

"I'm wondering…" I thought aloud, "about how nice this doctor has been to us."

Gabriel did not answer.

"He's risking his job, and he might even end up in jail, for helping a couple of strangers," I went on. "Right?"

"That's what it looks like."

"Why do you think he's been so kind?"

"No idea. Ask him when he comes back."

An unpleasant thought took shape in my mind."Do… do you trust him?"

He frowned. "What do you mean?"

"Don't you think it was… I don't know… too easy? You know. He's Cuban. I'm from the US…"

"What I think is that you're beginning to get paranoid."

"What if right now he's calling the police, and here we are waiting like idiots?"

"Are you thinking he's going to come in through that door with a couple of soldiers on either side?"

"He might…"

"Sarah, you've seen too many movies. You're totally—"

At that moment, he stopped talking as we heard footsteps coming down the corridor. It was not just a single person, but at least two or three whose footsteps resounded in the silence of that part of the building.

The steps stopped on the other side of the door.

A fist banged on it, hard.

44

Gabriel and I exchanged a look of panic and jumped to our feet. That makeshift bathroom had a barred skylight which would only have let mosquitoes through, and there was no window to escape through. Paralyzed, we did not know which way to move. We stood there with our backs to the wall as though we were trying to blend in with the dirty tiles.

There came a fresh banging on the door.

"Are you there?" said a familiar voice. "It's Dr. Rojas."

We looked at each other uneasily.

"Are you alone?" I asked after a few seconds.

Silence.

"No," he said reluctantly. There's a couple of friends here who'd like to meet you."

It seemed a prophecy about to come true, but locked in that rattrap the only way out was the door in front of us.

Defeated, I went to the door and slowly opened it.

For a second I only saw the doctor's smiling face. Then I looked behind him for the armed soldiers. In their stead I saw a man and a woman, both blond, wearing white housecoats. They waved at me.

"*Shaquille!*" the woman said in the unmistakable accent of southern Spain. "Whatever happened to you? Did you fall out of a plane?"

I could not help smiling at this. I suppose it was because in some way I felt safe when I heard that friendly voice. All the tension, hunger, exhaustion and fear stopped holding me up, so that I collapsed like a felled tree.

When I opened my eyes, a fluorescent light was shining above me with blue strips of flypaper hanging from it. I was in a room which at some point had been white, lying on a stretcher with a serum drip in my right arm, covered by a well-worn flowery sheet. Around me, trolleys with drawers, metal trays and a large round spotlight in a corner. I was in an operating theater! Although I would say, judging by the dirt piling up in the corners, that it was a long time since it had been used for surgery.

I was feeling strangely fresh and clean, and was amazed when I lifted the sheet and saw that the shabby nun's costume had been replaced by a hospital robe. Someone I trusted it had been a woman, although by now I did not really care had bathed and changed me, then left me in that windowless room to sleep. There was nobody there, nor could I hear any voices, and there was no bell switch hanging from a cord, so I had to either get up and go out in search of the doctors or else stay there waiting for someone to come. But it was so comfortable in that cot, and I was so tired…

"Sleepyhead," someone said beside me. "Come on, time to get up."

I half-opened my eyes. On either side of the bed were the two blond doctors, but this time they were not wearing their white housecoats.

"Hello," I mumbled.

"Feeling any better?" the male doctor asked.

"Much better," I replied, and smiled. "But I'm starving."

"Don't worry, love. That's why we're here," he said as he put a plastic bag on the stretcher, from which he took out a bottle of Coke and a Tupperware container of rice and fried chicken. "There, go stuff yourself!" he added taking off the lid.

I almost burst into tears at the sight of so much food. I was getting ready to dig into it when the woman doctor, following her colleague's example, put another plastic bag at my feet.

"And I," she said happily, with a face straight from Christmas morning, "have brought you a rag or two so you have something to put on." She proceeded to take out a dress, a blouse, a skirt, sandals...

By this point I was no longer able to hold back the tears of gratitude, and at the risk of spilling everything on the floor, I reached out and hugged both of them with all my strength."Thank you... thank you so much," I muttered, weeping.

"It's the least we could do, darling. Walter has already told us your story."

"Walter?"

"Dr. Rojas, the Cuban," she said and, as though suddenly remembering something, added, "I'm Lucia Arias, and he's Pepe, Pepe Arias."

"Are you...?"

"Siblings and residing in the back ass of nowhere."

"In the hemorrhoids of nowhere, you mean," Pepe pointed out.

They both laughed, and I joined in, happy and trusting in a way I had not been for a very long time.

They sat down beside me. While I ate my meal they bombarded me with questions about how I had gotten into all that mess and what I had done to survive.

"They could make a movie out of it!" Pepe said.

"It's true," said Lucia, "Sentenced to prison, escaping through the jungle, the gorillas, the Pygmies... Not even Indiana Jones, *chiquilla*!"

"Quite honestly," I replied with a piece of chicken in my mouth, "I would've preferred a bit less excitement."

"Sure, sure," she nodded. "As for us, we've been here four months, practically without leaving the hospital, and we haven't seen anything of the jungle at all. We've come across the occasional black cobra in the street, the spiders, which are more like cats here, and those bats that come out at dusk and are as big as buzzards." She stretched out her arms as wide as she could.

"Are you hired by the Spanish Cooperation Agency?"

"No, we came as volunteers with an NGO," Pepe explained resignedly.

"And you haven't had any trouble with the authorities?"

"Well… the militiamen like to come every once in a while to mess with us, and the civil servants just want to rob all they can, but certainly nothing compared to you."

"Yeah… I haven't had much luck."

"Hell, you're in one piece, is that bad luck? And besides," – he looked at his sister out of the corner of his eye– "we have another surprise for you."

"It's like it's my birthday! What else have you brought me?" I said clapping. "A voucher to a spa?"

"Better," said Lucia, smiling. "Much better."

"We believe," Pepe said, shaping the words carefully, "we can get you out of the country."

"What? How? When?"

"Calm down, we'll explain."

"But that would be… it would be…!" I cried, overjoyed.

Lucia brought a bench close and leaned on the stretcher in a confidential attitude. "You see, darling, I've been thinking—"

"Ahem!"

"Well, *we*, my brother and I, have been thinking that I could 'lose' my passport, and somehow it could end up in your hands. A few days later I'd report its disappearance to the police, and then I'd go to the consulate in Bata to have a new one made. You'd only have to dye your hair, because they don't even look at the face, pass yourself off as me and try to speak as little as possible to the customs officers so they don't notice your accent. We can lend you the money for the plane to get to Europe, and once there you can go to your embassy and get yourself a new passport." She was silent a second, waiting for my reaction, but I was so overwhelmed that I was left speechless. "What do you think of the plan?"

"It's... you're... I..." I hugged them both again, and once again I burst into tears, but this time they were tears of pure excitement.

"There, that's enough, darling," Lucia said. "Don't cry so much, or you'll dehydrate." But she was crying too.

When I had finally gotten over my fit of weeping and managed to breathe deeply, still holding their hands, I remembered someone I should not have forgotten.

"What about Gabriel? Is he in another room?"

"Gabriel?"

"Yes, of course. The Guinean who came with me."

"Well... I don't know," Pepe said. He and his sister exchanged a questioning look. "There are a lot of people wandering around. Perhaps he's outside waiting."

"Hasn't he been here with me?"

"No, darling. You've been here alone."

"How strange..."

"Maybe he left, thinking you were in good hands now."

It was possible, but I found it unlikely, after all we had been through and what seemed to be going on between us — whatever it was — that he would have left like that, without even saying goodbye. Besides, he needed to leave the country too. It was all very strange, and the immense joy I had just been granted began to fade into a growing sorrow at the thought that I might not see him again.

45

With new clothes, a new hair color and a new personality, I crossed the border into Gabon two days after my arrival at the hospital it was really only a question of crossing the estuary of the river Muni in order to reach Libreville. From there I would buy a seat on the first flight to Europe, to Paris to be more specific, from where I would fly to Boston.

So there I was, sitting just like any other passenger in the packed tourist class of an Air France plane. Around me, dozens of Gabonese were sunk in a certain sadness as they left their country behind, most likely after coming home for a vacation and now going back to cold Europe, where the following day most of them would go back to their respective badly paid jobs.

I was one of the few white people on board, and as if that was not enough to underline the difference, I could not stop smiling.

Finally I felt completely safe from the claws of the Guinean soldiers and their madness. I remembered for an instant the horrible expression on Captain Anastasio's face, and instantly pushed him out of my mind and lost myself in the absurd musical movie, translated into French, which they were showing on the airplane's giant screen. Despite everything, the passengers laughed every now and then, although I could not imagine what was so funny about a famous actor disguised as a fat lady. Or perhaps it was just that I was seeing everything as though through a microscope, bemusedly examining attitudes which weeks before would have seemed perfectly normal to me. As if the human race, its behavior and interests, no longer coincided with mine except at scattered points here and there.

All the same, I came to the conclusion that I was simply too tired and my mind was beginning to wander. So I took off my ear plugs, wrapped myself in the blanket and fell asleep until the captain announced we were approaching Charles de Gaulle airport.

I had called my parents from Paris to let them know I would be arriving in Boston the following afternoon. It was a massive surprise for them, because although they knew nothing of what had happened and were used to long periods between my telephone calls, they had not counted on my return until two months later. And with that intuition parents have when it comes to their children, they immediately deduced that something had gone wrong, although I was reluctant to give them details until I saw them in the flesh.

When I arrived at Logan International Airport, there they were, wrapped in their skiing jackets and waiting by the International Arrivals gate. I was wearing the flowery dress Lucia had given me, with the blanket from the first plane wrapped around me like a cloak, and my only luggage was a palm handbag I had bought in Libreville. In it was the new passport I had been issued at the embassy in Paris, together with the stub of my boarding pass. That was all.

"Good heavens, Sarah! What... happened to you?" cried my mother as soon as she saw me.

"You look like a refugee. Where are your bags?" my father said in the same tone of voice, looking me up and down.

"I'll tell you everything," I said hugging them both, happier at seeing them than I had ever been before. "But now I just want to go home and rest."

"But—" my father ploughed on doggedly.

"Please, dad. Not now."

"Sure, sure, honey," he said taking me by the waist and looking at my mother over my shoulder. "Let's go home and rest. You can tell us whatever you want, whenever you want to."

"Thank you."

Inexplicably, all the excitement I had felt during the journey on the plane faded the moment we touched ground; instead it turned into exhaustion and an apathy which had come from somewhere I could not understand.

In the car on the way home, I did not say a word. I sank into the back seat, enveloped in a strange cloud of silence, unable to find the strength to talk, much less tell them what I had been through. My parents in turn seemed afraid of asking me anything, in case the answer might be too terrible.

Despite their insistence, I assured them I was perfectly well and turned down their offer to stay with them. I preferred my own small apartment: my sofa, my hammock hanging from the wall... my bed. They accompanied me to the door, wrapped me in one of their padded coats and gave me a set of keys to their house, then said goodbye once I had promised I would call them the next day.

Going into my apartment was like travelling back in time. The months I had been away seemed like years when I dropped into my favorite armchair and put my feet up on the table. The first thing I did was reach out my hand and press the switch to turn on the light of the standard lamp. Then I turned it off again. And turned it on. And then off. And on again, marveling at that aspect of daily life which is taken for granted until you come back from a place where that simple act is a luxury within the reach of only a few. I turned on the TV and began to flick through the channels without even giving them a chance. They all appeared to me equally futile and dishonest, so after a minute I turned it off, took off the few clothes I was wearing and took a shower.

I soaped and sponged myself hard, almost vindictively. I felt that Africa had filtered into every pore of my skin, and that

I had brought with me not only the malaria parasite, but also something darker, more indefinable. A kind of hopeless sadness I had never felt before. I felt rage. Fear. Hatred. Love. I was too tired and confused to fight against that turmoil of contradictory feelings. Leaning my back against the tiles, I let myself slide until I was sitting on the floor of the shower, with my head bent and the hot water running down my neck. Helplessly, I found myself being assailed by the memory of Ms. Margarita, slumped in her bathroom, withered away, dying, drenched in the sweat of her fever… and a long-delayed stream of black tears burst out, all the way up from my guts, from my wounds and my memories.

The following day dawned grey, with that cold persistent rain which soaks the bones of the soul, so that you cannot get it off no matter how hard you dry yourself, until summer arrives and the sun makes the fir trees and rivers shine.

I went rather unenthusiastically for lunch at my parents' house, and gave them a G-rated version of what had happened to me, making my odyssey little more than an administrative error.

There was no doubt that my mother, at least, knew that was not all. And I knew she knew. We were partners in crime, and with no more than a shared glance she knew that one day I would fill in the blank spaces and silences. When I was ready. When we both were.

I answered most of my father's questions in monosyllables, until we were having coffee. On the subject of the difficulties I had endured, he said with the conviction that ignorance brings, "Well, you know…in those black countries—"

"What do you mean?" I snapped, taking him by surprise.

"No… nothing…" he said defensively, and raised his hands. "It's just that from what you're telling us, it seems it was better for them when they were a colony, isn't that right?"

"How can you say that?" I said with a fervor which surprised even myself. "It's the European countries who are to blame for the fact that practically the whole of Africa is like that. When they took off, they passed the weapons and the power down to a few bloodthirsty generals in the pay of western multinationals. Instead of carrying out a process of decolonization which would have led naturally to a democracy, the power in Equatorial Guinea was left in the hands of one single family. And even now it's still in power, using terror and force as if they were feudal kings, keeping the Guineans as their vassals and slaves."

"You're not going to tell me now," my father said, ignoring my mother's kicks under the table, "that we westerners are still to blame for everything that's happening, forty years after granting them independence."

"Nobody *granted* them anything," I pointed out. "What happened was that it was returned to them. And I'm not saying that we're responsible for everything. It's not a country of children that you have to look after so they don't hurt themselves. What needs to be done is fight, so that the corporations and some interested governments, like ours, don't keep a bloodthirsty dictator in power at all costs, with the sole aim of exploiting the oil and timber of the country with complete impunity for the benefit of a few."

"But then, why doesn't the country rebel if it's going so badly?" he said. "If it's just one family, why isn't there a revolution there?"

"Do you know what percentage of the Guinean population has been murdered by their own government just for opening their mouths? Ten per cent, dad." I pointed my spoon at him. "Ten per cent."

"Well, but—"

"Look, dad," I said taking his hand as if the roles of father and daughter had been reversed, "you just have to look at the Middle East, and see how for decades all kinds of dictators and kings like the Saudis have been kept on their thrones, thanks to the indispensable help of the USA, and only because they have oil reserves which have enriched a handful of CEOs and oil millionaires. And you more than anybody else," I asserted with my eyes fixed on his, "should understand that."

After that statement, thanks to my mother the conversation moved on to more prosaic topics until it reached the doldrums on the subject of the latest Hollywood gossip. Then, claiming a tiredness I was genuinely feeling, I said goodbye and headed downtown to an Italian café. I always came here when I felt melancholic, to explore the feeling amid the aroma of good coffee.

But that day was the exception to the fucking rule, and I felt lonely.

I took out the cell phone I had not used for so long and called a couple of girlfriends to join me. I thought that maybe with them I might have the chance to bring into the open everything I had left unsaid to my parents.

It was not to be. After a few explanations, leaving whole chapters untold which I hoped would intrigue them and prod them into bombarding me with questions, they just nodded and immediately went on to tell me, one about her latest office promotion, the other about how she could not decide whether to carry on with her present boyfriend or find another one more willing to commit himself.

It was then that I realized that I might never find anyone to share everything I was carrying within me. I had changed so much in the last few weeks that I had become a stranger in my own city, with my family and my friends, even in my own home. I could not even recognize that naïve, trusting young girl who had gone to Africa a few months before in the image my mirror reflected back to me.

Whatever they talked about seemed alien to me, and by now I did not even feel like explaining my deep and disturbing feelings to anyone. Those feelings confused me and dragged me down unexplored, gloomy paths, like that lightless jungle I had spent days walking through.

I tried to think who I might pour all that out to, who would manage to understand me, or at least listen to me in the way I wanted to be listened to.

And only one person came to my mind.

One name.

One man.

A stranger who meant much more to me than I had realized. Than I had wanted to realize.

I wanted to go back to the man I had fallen in love with.

46

The waiting room was like a dentist's. I had imagined a nineteenth-century building, with lofty ceilings hung with candelabra and paintings and photographs of foreign dignitaries on the walls. But that hall with its few chairs upholstered in blue and a table with a couple of old magazines on it did not fit my mental image of the office of the Department of State for Africa.

An assistant had taken me here, and now I was waiting for the head of the department to come for me, a Mr. Mowell, whom I had arranged to meet more than a week before.

After almost half an hour of boredom, a tall, gaunt man in a grey suit with skin to match came striding into the hall toward me. "Good morning," he said in a neutral voice, without offering me his hand. "I'm under-secretary Mowell. Please come with me."

I followed him to an office as grey as its occupant, with a photo of the president beside the flag and an elegant map of Africa in sepia tones occupying a whole side wall. The man sat at his desk, keyed something into his computer, and only then gestured to me to sit down. "So," he said leaning on the table. "Tell me."

I was surprised by this family doctor approach, and I could not miss a certain impatience in his manner.

"Well, I sent you an email a few days ago with a detailed account of everything that happened to me in Equatorial Guinea and what I was expecting from the State Department."

"Ah, yes," he said, looking at his computer. "You're Miss…"

"Sarah Malik," I murmured.

"Hmmm... I see," he said, moving his mouse and apparently opening my message. "You're the lady who wrote me that dreadful tale about militiamen and police, aren't you?"

"Tale?" I said with some annoyance. "It's not a tale; it's what happened to me just a few days ago."

"Oh, yes, of course. Forgive me." He turned back to the screen.

He read — or pretended to — for a couple of minutes of uncomfortable silence. Then he clicked on the mouse, pushed it to one side and sat back in his executive chair, tapping the fingers of his left hand on the desk. "Very well, Miss Malik. What can we do for you?"

"I need your help to get the man who saved my life out of Guinea. He's in great danger there."

"I see. And this gentleman—"

"Gabriel Biné."

"Mr. Biné. He's an Equatorial Guinean, right?

"Of course. I said so in the message." I glanced at the computer out of the corner of my eye.

"In that case, unfortunately, I don't see how we can help you."

"What?"

"You see, we can't demand of any country that they hand over one of their own citizens."

I leaned on the desk. "You don't understand. You don't have to demand anything from anybody. You just have to order the American Embassy in Malabo to help a man escape from his country."

"We can't do that either."

"But you can give him the status of political refugee, can't you?"

The civil servant closed his eyes for a moment. "Miss Malik," he said wearily, "we can't hand out political refugee status to anybody. It requires several complex processes and very special circumstances."

"Don't you regard it as special that they want to murder him for criticizing his president in a bar?"

"That's what he told you…"

"Are you implying that he lied to me?"

"Put yourself in my place," he said, spreading his hands wide. "It's his word against a jury's."

"A jury? Are you serious? You know how they judged me! You've got to be kidding me!"

"Every country has its own legislation, and there's nothing we can do about it."

"But he's innocent!" I cried standing up.

"Sit down, please. You have to understand that as far as we know he could be a serial killer. We can't help a fugitive to escape just because you believe he's innocent."

"But he's being persecuted for his political views! Why don't you ask the Guinean authorities for a report on the case?"

"That wouldn't be appropriate."

"Appropriate? Don't you think it's *appropriate* to save a man's life?"

He sighed deeply. "Miss Malik, things are not so easy in that part of the world… as you've experienced for yourself. And more specifically, our relations with Equatorial Guinea are going through a delicate stage which we might… jeopardize, if we tried to put our nose into matters of internal politics."

"You're talking about the granting of oil contracts, aren't you?"

The under-secretary's face changed from an expression of indolence to one of clear hostility. "I haven't said anything of the sort."

"But that's what it's about, isn't it? Oil in exchange for lives."

"That's a slogan, Miss Malik. And I believe it's been overused." He ran his hand through his hair, impatient to be done with the whole thing. "International politics are very complex, and I'm not going to try to explain them to you now, but sometimes we have to prioritize, in the interests of the country… and we have no choice but to make sacrifices."

"Sure, particularly if it's just a black man, or ten of them, or a thousand, right? Screw Human Rights!" I cried angrily, leaning over his desk. "Screw the damn blacks! Where's that contract? Did you sign it directly in blood, or you still use ink?"

"Miss…"

"Don't you fucking *miss* me!" I was beside myself. "I bet you haven't even sent a complaint about an American citizen being tortured and nearly murdered. Am I right?"

"I'm sorry," he said. He got to his feet and indicated the door. "I have other matters to attend to now. The interview's over."

I picked up my coat and threw the heartless puppet one last furious glare."You're a bunch of crooks!" I shouted, and slammed the door. But not before hearing the under-secretary's last word.

"And you're so naïve…" he murmured, loudly enough to make sure I heard.

47

I left the building, my jaw clenched with fury, imagining that miserable bureaucrat enjoying a vacation in a Guinean prison. I was so furious I almost forgot the appointment I had arranged for that same morning at the office of the Association for Freedom for Equatorial Guinea. I did not think this second interview would be much use, apart from sharing bad experiences and frustrations with some exile or other, but since I had made the trip to Washington I had nothing to lose by talking to these people. Perhaps through them I would somehow be able to contact Gabriel. And in any case the walk down to Canal Street, where they had their headquarters, served to soothe my agitated spirit.

On my way I stopped at a café where I asked for an herbal tea, and had it sitting outside so that the mild winter sun could warm my face. I amused myself by gazing at the deep blue Washington sky, so different from the Guinean one, always veiled by that desert sand which crossed half a continent to end up in the Gulf of Guinea, where the evenings offered the kind of glorious sunsets that cannot be imagined in any other continent.

Pedestrians walked by my table, their minds on their morning business. Most looked worried, bestowing on their small problems a scale which was out of proportion. All of them must have had water, electricity, gas, telephone, a roof to live under with all the home appliances their salary could buy them, plus a level of health that three-quarters of humanity would want for themselves. And yet there they were, apparently unhappy as part of the elite we call the first world, the west, or some euphemism of the kind which skirts round the fact that that we are the privileged rich and the rest, the hopeless poor. An infinite number of television marathons would need to be organized to raise enough money to launder that definition's conscience.

It is strange how before I went to Africa and in spite of my career as an anthropologist I too was one of "them". I had never really thought deeply about the subject. Even knowing for sure that sixty or seventy per cent of the world's population has no fresh water, electricity or public health, living as we do in opulence and waste, I was simply not capable of understanding that fact any more than I was capable of understanding the Catholic concept of the Holy Trinity. When an alien reality like that is involved, our brain may be capable of filing away the data and the figures, but the heart cannot react to that stimulus. That is why the look on our faces is the same whether we hear that a thousand children die every day from malnutrition or that the Dow-Jones has gone down half a point. In both cases it sounds like gibberish to us, just as if it were happening on another planet. But for me, all that had changed from the moment I set foot in Africa.

Walking along the muddy streets of Malabo just a few days after landing I found little children, naked and with swollen tummies, playing in the fecal waters as if they were at the beach. Something inside me clicked. Unexpectedly, some forgotten neuron made the connection and I had the same epiphany many others had had before me, which is: we are the exception. It is we, the privileged minority, who live in a distant planet, and they, the disinherited, who are the true inhabitants of the earth. We are so used to living as an anomaly, in a bubble of wellbeing and safety, impervious to the tears of others, that we find it impossible to glimpse the reality of the human being and of our civilization.

For good or ill, I had been able to glimpse, through the curtains of my sanity, what I had not known before. And now, sitting at that table outside that café in a downtown street beside the Potomac, I watched the passers-by as if they were ghosts, halfway between the physical world and a beyond world of mortgages, bonuses and discounts.

When I felt that my wrath had gone down to a reasonable level and that I was no longer dreaming of torturing under-secretaries, I paid the tab and headed for my next appointment.

In a few minutes I was standing in front of the buzzer, where only the initials FGE in ball-point pen on a piece of paper stuck with Scotch tape indicated the floor the association was on. I rang, they asked my name, and after a short wait I was invited to come up.

When I knocked on the second door on the third floor the bell did not work a lady of about fifty, unmistakably Guinean, in a colorful, typically African costume with a matching scarf around her head, opened the door and gave me a friendly smile, showing perfect teeth."Hello!" she said as she shook my hand. "Welcome to the association. My name is Clara."

"Hi, Clara. I'm Sarah Malik."

"Of course. Come in, please." She closed the door after me."Would you like some coffee, or tea?" she asked as I followed her down a corridor.

"No thanks, I just had one."

"Ah, right." She indicated a chair in the room we had just walked into. "Please take a seat."

"Did you get the email I sent you?" I asked as I sat down.

"I did." She sat down on the other side of a small table. "I read it, and I assure you that I'm very sorry about everything that happened to you in my poor Guinea."

"You don't need to apologize. The only responsible party for what happened to me is the Government of Guinea."

"Of course... they're also responsible for the fact that we're here."

"Did you have to flee Guinea?"

"Naturally. Whether it's for political, economic or family reasons, not a single Guinean exile is so by choice. We love our country, the people are wonderfully kind—"

"I can vouch for that."

"They are, aren't they?" She nodded, smiling. "I don't say this because I'm a Guinean myself, but Guineans are the most hospitable people in all Africa. And if it wasn't for those who've taken power and their henchmen, no Guinean would have been forced to migrate. Did you know," she asked, drumming her index finger on the table, "that in 1968, just before Guinea became independent from Spain, thanks to the exports of cocoa, we had the highest per capita income in all Africa?"

"Before oil was found?"

"Yes! Long before! Just imagine! And now there's oil as well. But because of the Obiangs we've become one of the poorest countries in the world. If I'm not mistaken... let me try to remember..." – she rubbed her chin – "we're in the 120th or 130th place in the world in the UN development ranking; 151st out of 163 in corruption, according to Transparency International. And we're fourth in the world for censorship... and we're on track for the bronze medal," she added with a sour smile.

"I had first-hand experience of it," I said. "The pretext for putting me on trial and finding me guilty was that I'd written some notes criticizing the government in my personal journal. And Gabriel, the Guinean man who helped me so much, was arrested for making a comment while he was having a beer at a bar. It would drive anyone crazy!"

"Yes. Unfortunately, in Guinea that's very common. Torture, rape, extortion or murder on the part of the government are our daily bread. And as far as you're concerned, and don't misunderstand me," she added more confidentially as she reached out to take my hand, "you've been lucky."

"I wouldn't say that…"

"Of course not. That's because you've suffered it in your own flesh and bones, and it's still fresh in your memory. But seen from the outside, and knowing how most of the detainees there end up, you can believe me when I say you've been very fortunate."

"What about you?" I said to change the subject. "What is it you do in this association?"

"Well, we help each other. We also have craft workshops, an exhibition now and then, classes of Bubi and Fang for the children who are born in the US. We also advise newly arrived Guineans on how to get their papers, find a house, a job and all that."

"And could you help me get Gabriel out of Guinea?"

Clara sat back in her chair."Well now," she said, putting her hands together. "We might be able to help him get out of the country, it wouldn't be the first time we've done that. But after reading your email… I think we have a big problem."

"What's that?"

"Very simple. We have nothing about him: not his full name, nor his age, identity number, a photo… And what's even more important, there wouldn't be a way of locating him!"

"But… don't you have contacts over there, in Guinea? Perhaps somebody knows him."

Clara leaned her arms on the table thoughtfully. "We can try," she said shrugging. "But if, as you say, the police and the militiamen are looking for him, he won't tell anybody his real name for fear it might be the secret police. And you also have to consider that he might already have crossed into Gabon or Cameroon, or even…"

"Even?"

"Well... he might have been captured. You said yourself that he had disappeared in the hospital in Cogo. He might have been caught there."

"I'd rather not think of that possibility."

"Right... I understand you."

A few seconds of leaden silence settled on us.

"So," I insisted, "you don't believe you can find him, and get him out of Guinea?"

"Without at least knowing how to contact him..." She shook her head slowly. "Are you sure he didn't mention any address, or a phone number...?"

"Nothing. Absolutely nothing."

"You see, don't you? We don't have a single clue. In fact we couldn't even recognize him physically. You're the only one who knows what he looks like."

The interview ended shortly afterward, with an honest look of consolation. But that was the only thing I brought with me when I boarded my flight back to Boston a few hours later.

My trip to Washington had been useless. I had only been able to find out, on the one hand the hypocrisy and unscrupulousness of international politics, and on the other hand the good intentions but limited resources of those who had a disinterested concern for their fellow human beings.

I was even more disheartened than I had been before those interviews, which I had put all my slender hopes on.

There seemed to be no hope.

And yet...

48

Clara's last sentence filtered through into my subconscious, surreptitiously, and would not stop haunting me for the remainder of the day. And the following day too, and the next, and the one after that…

I tried to convince myself there was nothing I could do unless the State Department or the FGA Association gave me their backing, so that for the whole week I tried to occupy my mind with less dramatic things.

I wrote a devastating report for the UNICEF commission which had sent me to work in Guinea, adding an annex in which I detailed everything that had happened to me personally. I did not really believe the association had much scope to exert pressure on the Guinean government, if any. And in any case, they would make a formal protest via some trivial communiqué, since after all I was only an external employee, begging that nothing of the kind would happen again, and blah blahblah… The best I could hope for was that the said protest would end up in the wastebasket beside the fax machine in some office in Malabo.

I devoted myself to cleaning my apartment in depth, restocking the fridge, moving the furniture around… all activities which kept me busy without making too many demands on me. I met my girlfriends again a couple of times, trying to pretend polite interest in their concerns, making an effort to get back into the life I had been enjoying just a few months back. But no matter how much I tried, the things they talked about seemed to me so insubstantial that there was no way I could reconnect with them. The Sarah Malik of the spring did not have much to do with the Sarah Malik of that cold fall moving on inexorably toward winter.

I wandered through the streets downtown, through the park, and even around my apartment. Without purpose, with no interest in anything or anybody. I even surprised myself by dialing John's phone number. I hung up straight away, just before I keyed in the last digit.

I tried to get rid of this feeling of emptiness, of impotence, of knowing that every day that passed without my doing anything someone was suffering with no chance to defend themselves, while at the same time the Guinean dictator and his clan kept filling their pockets in the face of the ignorance or indifference of the whole world. But to be honest with myself, what affected me most was not knowing what had happened to Gabriel: whether he was in Guinea or whether he had succeeded in leaving the country, whether he was free or in prison, alive or dead…

The following Sunday I went back to my parents' house, in response to a firm invitation from my mother, who had heard from my girlfriends about the rough time I was going through.

The table was set when I arrived, and there was no mistaking the fact that the enormous honeyed turkey occupying its center had been cooked in my honor. They knew it was something I really loved.

"Thanks, mom," I said, knowing she would know what I meant.

"You're welcome, sweetheart," she replied, and gestured me to a seat.

The meal was accompanied by congratulations to the cook and smiles, and when we came to the dessert, my parents exchanged looks and then my mother turned to me.

"Sarah," she said with sudden solemnity.

"Yes?"

"Since you came back from Africa we've noticed, and your girlfriends have confirmed this, that you're rather unhappy. They believe you might be suffering from depression, and they've even suggested that we refer you to a psychologist."

"They talk too much," I said, annoyed, "and they don't even know what about."

"They know you spend the day walking on your own, or shut up in your apartment. And that's not a good sign."

"I don't feel much like talking to anybody."

My mother sat back more comfortably in her chair. "We know you went through a terrible experience in that African country—"

"Equatorial Guinea," I said.

"Whatever it's called." She waved as if putting the name aside. "What matters is that it's affected you very much, and we don't like seeing you like this."

"I don't like it either, but this is how I feel."

"That's the point I'm trying to make." Again she exchanged glances with my father. "We think we might be able to help you."

"Help me?" I was puzzled. "How?"

"We understand it's been a very sudden change and you miss the tropics, and particularly that African friend who helped you so much…"

My heart leapt. Surely my parents couldn't really want to help me to… or could they?

"In a nutshell, we've booked you a plane ticket for this week." Her smile stretched from ear to ear.

I was listening in disbelief. Thrown off key by that daring initiative on the part of my parents. "But…" I stammered when I managed to come out of my stupor, "I… how could I—"

"How could you?" my dad interrupted me cheerfully. "You just have to board the plane, obviously."

"What about the visa? And anyway, I can't go back to Guinea with my own passport. I'd be arrested the moment I set foot in the airport."

My father looked at me flabbergasted."Guinea?" he said spreading his arms wide. "Who said anything about Guinea? The booking's for a week in the Bahamas!"

My mother joined in at this point."We think a week on a nice beach, under the palm trees and the Caribbean sun, will heal all your troubles." Winking, she added, "Maybe even those of the heart."

I had gone from discouragement to enthusiasm, and from there to disappointment, in less than twenty seconds. My parents had acted with the best intentions in the world, but they were very far from understanding my deep feelings and the pain which had my soul in its grip.

"I... I'm very grateful, really. But I can't go to the Caribbean… that's not where I want to go."

"Then," my father said, "feel free to choose any place in the world you want. We'll pay for everything, right?" he asked my mother rhetorically. "So tell us, Sarah. Where would you like to go?"

At that exact moment, like a revelation which had spent days trying to break through, a clear idea took hold of my mind.

And I knew where I wanted to go.

49

"A fake passport?" Clara asked incredulously at the other end of the line.

"That's right."

"But... we don't do that kind of stuff..." she argued warily.

"All right, but I bet you know who does."

During the next five seconds of silence, I knew Clara was debating whether to help me or get rid of me with a polite excuse.

"I might..." she muttered, still warily, "know someone who knows someone who does... you know, that sort of thing."

"You needn't be so careful when you talk, Clara. I'm not the police, and I'm not recording this conversation."

"It's not you."

"Well then?"

"We know we're being watched. They check our mail, our phones are tapped..."

"Clara, the police can't do that without a court order. And it would be very difficult to get one without some very good reason."

"It's not the American police that are watching us."

It took me several moments to understand the implication of this. "You don't mean..."

"Yes, *them*. Here as well."

"But how...?"

"Anything's possible with money. And they have all the money they need."

"I can't believe it..."

"Well, you'd better. We've been threatened several times before."

"But why?"

"Why do you think?" she exclaimed. "For denouncing those assholes. Are you there?" she suddenly asked of the ether. "That's for you, bastards! I'm spelling it out to you because you're such morons you might not even understand me!" She sounded like she had gone crazy. "Forgive me, but sometimes I can't help indulging myself."

"Sure," I said, not altogether convinced. "Go ahead."

"Well," she said in the end, "we'll help you."

"Oh, thank you! Thank you so much!"

"Don't thank me yet. What you're asking is going to cost you dearly."

"I trust you."

"Good. I'll call you from a public phone as soon as I hear something, I guess in a couple of days, three at the most."

"That's wonderful. Thanks."

"You're welcome. I wish you all the luck in the world."

"Thank you, and I'll see you soon."

"See you."

Sitting on the plane, I propped my new passport wide open on the tray in front of me. I was staring at the photo of a young woman with bags under her eyes and hair dyed blonde, and it was difficult to recognize myself. Beside the photo a counterfeiter with a peculiar sense of humor had decided my name would be Karen Blixen, taking for granted that the customs officer would never have read *Out of Africa* and that I would be creative enough to invent some Danish origins. To say I was nervous at the prospect of passing the rigorous police check with a fake passport would be like saying that Marie Antoinette was slightly worried as she went up the steps of the guillotine.

When the plane started to descend we were still over the Atlantic, and it was not until seconds before landing that the luxurious vegetation of the island of Bioko appeared on the other side of the window. It reminded me, just in case I was not sufficiently aware of it already, that there was no going back, and that in spite of the ferocious opposition of my family and friends and of my own common sense, which had sounded all the alarms I was going willingly into the wolf's den. A wolf which would love the chance to bite my head off and chew it at leisure.

When the plane stopped near the new terminal the old one had been nothing more than a building in ruins the passengers jumped like springs from their seats and crowded out of the front door. Usually I would wait for everyone else to go out before I do, but this time it seemed more prudent to mix with the rest of the passengers and not be the last in the immigration line. Although clearly, as the only white woman among more than two hundred black-skinned Africans, it would not be easy to pass unnoticed.

Holding my small handbag I waited patiently for my turn at the immigration line, but what with the heat and my nerves, I could feel great drops of sweat running down from my forehead to my chin and down the tip of my nose. I could see the only policeman who was checking passports a few yards away from me inside his booth, checking in detail, page by page, not only the personal data of each traveler but also the stamps of the places they had visited before. Finally he spent some time comparing the photo with the owner of the passport, made some comment or other I could not hear, then reluctantly ended up stamping any page at random.

When my turn came, after almost an hour of sweat and nerves, I took out my passport as nonchalantly as I could. With my most seductive smile I handed it to him through the glass opening that separated us.

My heart was beating like a wild horse while the official skimmed the pages with deep interest and studied them first on one side and then on the other, as if he had never seen a passport before in his life. "Purpose of your visit?" he asked at last, without looking at me, and without hiding his displeasure.

"Tourism," I replied in a rather shaky voice.

He looked up suspiciously. "Nobody comes to Equatorial Guinea for tourism."

"Then I'll be the first."

"What else are you going to do in Equatorial Guinea?" he insisted.

"Tourism," I repeated, still smiling, as I took my camera out of my handbag. "Only tourism."

He stared at me for a few seconds and went back to checking my passport page by page, as if he had dropped something in it. "Where will you be staying?"

"Tonight I'm staying at the Hotel Ureka. Tomorrow we'll see."

"You don't know where you're going to be?" he asked warily.

"I've already told you, at the Ureka. If I like it, I'll go on staying at that hotel. If not, I'll move to another one."

"The Ureka is a good hotel."

"In that case I'll stay."

He did not reply, and went on checking blank pages. Surely the man must be terribly bored for the rest of the day, and he did not care in the slightest about the long line at my back. When he came to my photo he gazed at it in absorption, raised his eyes a couple of times to compare me with it and concluded, "The woman in the photo isn't you."

"Excuse me?"

"I said," he repeated, putting the passport in front of my eyes, "that this isn't you."

"Of course it's me!" I said, taken aback. "This photo isn't even a week old!"

"The woman in this passport," he said with perfect assurance, "has her hair tied up and is wearing different clothes."

I could not believe what I was hearing. "Are you serious?"

"You can't enter the country with this document," he said, making a feint to give it back to me.

"Wait a minute, wait a minute…" I muttered, trying to make sense of this absurd situation. "The woman in the photo is me, but the day it was taken I had my hair up and I wore a coat because it was cold."

The policeman looked over the passport page after page a third time and then I realized what was happening.

"May I have my passport back for a moment, please?"

The customs officer gave it back to me. I lifted my blouse slightly and took a twenty dollar bill out of the fanny pack I carried close to my body, folded it, put it between the pages of the passport and gave it back to the policeman. He opened it at the page in question, openly put the bill in his shirt pocket and stamped my entry permit for Equatorial Guinea.

50

The highway which separates the airport from Malabo appeared deserted from the yellow Renault 12, its windows lacking glass and its door tied with cord to the hinges. I let my eyes wander along the dense jungle passing by on both sides of the road, interrupted only by fabulous mansions surrounded by high walls, owned by the president's family who could not be totally confident about their situation, as it was notable that they were all just a step from the airport. The warm, humid wind, so different from the one I had left behind a few hours before, struck my face, bringing the smells of the jungle with it, and I felt as though I had never completely left that place. As though I never would.

"Do you know a comfortable hotel," I asked the taxi driver, "that isn't too expensive?"

"That's quite difficult, miss," he said, swaying his head from side to side. "A lot of foreigners come to do business with oil and timber, and as they don't have a place to stay, some of them pay hundreds of dollars for rooms without running water."

"Okay, great," I muttered. "Is there anywhere you could recommend that won't cost an arm and a leg?"

"Well...I could take you to a friend's house, she rents out rooms. There's no water either, but at least it's cheap."

"Is it far from the center?"

"Oh no, not at all. It's on the road to Basilé, ten minutes from the square."

"Wonderful. Let's go there."

We left the highway or to be precise, it left us and went into downtown Malabo, the small capital of Equatorial Guinea. There was a succession of two-storied houses, more or less derelict: most made of wood which had originally been painted in lively colors, a few of brick or ugly grey concrete with anonymous stains. The whole city seemed sunk in an apathy of neglect, as if there was no other way it could possibly be, so that once the building was erected, its upkeep was left in the hands of fate. Only a few of the stores seemed to have anything to sell, while the majority showed nothing more than a lady yawning behind a plain counter, watching the few passers-by who dared move under the gentle late afternoon sun along streets which had been foolishly stripped of their trees. The vehicles were almost as scarce as the pedestrians, and they were all destined for the scrap yard just as much as the one I was in, except for the occasional striking exception we passed on the highway in the form of the latest model Lamborghini or Bentley. I did not bother to ask the driver who owned those jewels of the road.

Just as the taxi driver had promised, the guest house was a few blocks from the center, and although it was not a place I would have recommended even to the worst of mothers-in-law, by Guinean standards it was quite acceptable.

Rosa, the owner, a rotund woman enveloped in a huge dress patterned in orange, with her hair tied up in a scarf, was washing clothes in the backyard. When the taxi driver introduced us I offered her my hand, but she gave me her wrist so as not to get soap on me.

She showed me the "best room of the house," painted in dirty bottle green, with a small window looking out on the courtyard, a water drum with a bucket floating in it, and a bulb of undefined wattage hanging nakedly from the moldy ceiling with its covering of cobwebs.

"How much?" I asked with a grimace.

"Forty dollars a night."

"Okay… Does the fan work?"

"Sometimes, when there's electricity."

"Is there any at night?"

"Hmm… yes. Until about eight."

"I see… but I can't pay you so much for the room, I'm just a tourist."

"How much can you pay?"

"About… ten dollars," I ventured.

"Thirty is the least."

"Twenty and I'm staying."

"Twenty-five."

"All right, let's leave it at that," I said. Looking around the miserable room, I thought that in Asia, for that amount of money I would have a beach-front bungalow with a hammock.

Rosa accepted, and she was already leaving the room when she turned at the last moment. "Um… in case you haven't noticed, the room has no key."

I looked at the place where the doorknob should have been, and it was true: there was only a hole. "But—" I began, pointing at the door.

"Don't you worry," she interrupted with a wave. "Nobody steals things here."

"If you say so…"

"Well, no one," – she smiled – "except, you know…" She raised her eyebrows as if pointing up with them.

"Yes, of course," I nodded indifferently, not risking sounding too enthusiastic, just in case.

Once I was alone in the room I stuffed the hole in the door with a plastic bag, washed with the bucket floating in the water drum and changed my clothes for others better suited to those latitudes. Then, pulling a hat down over my eyes and wearing dark glasses, I went out into the street.

I was not really going anywhere in particular, I just wanted to stretch my legs and get out of my asphyxiating bedroom, but I began to wander aimlessly until I found myself at the half-derelict pier when the sun was beginning to set, and I stayed there, leaning on the concrete rail, to watch it. The great swarms of fruit bats, which I had already seen several times before, seemed more numerous in that region of Bioko, and shaded much of the sky with their black wings. They gave sharp cries as they let themselves fall from the tops of the palm trees, which in that part of town flanked the sidewalks. The disc of the sun burst into flames when it touched the horizon, and by the time it had sunk completely into the ocean, twilight had fallen on the streets and only a few scattered street lights allowed me to see where I was going. I went on walking down Independence Avenue until I reached the cathedral, possibly the tallest building in the city and certainly the most attractive. Although its pastel-colored façade showed the effects of mold and apathy, like the rest of the city, it still stood out with its twin bell towers and wide windows amid the monotonous urban mess of Malabo. In front of the cathedral, built by the old settlers in honor of Saint Elizabeth of Hungary, patron saint of the city, the arrogant Independence Square offered its benches and palm trees as an oasis for the wanderer to rest. And so I sat down on one of those benches to gaze at the railing in front of me, which separated the civil city from the presidential compound: a sizeable chunk of Malabo which had been amputated by the country's first president, requisitioned by decree for government use and never returned to the capital's citizens. I was thinking that on the other side of those gates were the ones who were responsible for nearly all the misfortunes besetting Guinea, and that it did not seem as if it would be so difficult to take that Bastille, in the event of an unlikely revolution which without any external support would be bound to fail.

     I walked back toward the guesthouse, and sat down at a small diner to have dinner. A huge and loud-voiced lady had her eyes on a television set and took a good ten minutes to come and take my order.
     "What do you have for dinner?"
     "Crocodile soup or porcupine."

"Okay... I think I'll have the soup."
"Anything to drink?"
"A 33, please. Very cold."

Some time later she brought me the beer, which was far from cold. I sat back in the plastic chair and passed the time, while I waited for my food, watching the ever livelier street. The women brought out their improvised grills to sell chicken wings on the sidewalk. The Nigerian vendors walked around with their strings of handcrafted necklaces and bracelets, and even the cars began to drive by more often. In one of them, one of those exceptions, a black Ford Explorer with tinted windows, a man was driving nonchalantly with his elbow out of the window and incongruous mirror glasses when the sun had long since set. It was fairly dark and the car was six or seven yards away as it passed by, but I recognized the man's face and my heart missed a beat.

Once again, as if fate were trying to tell me something, I had come across that sadistic face I would never be able to forget.

51

Captain Anastasio, driving his black SUV, chased me through nightmares all through the endless, asphyxiating night. During this, sheltering inside my mosquito net, I discovered that when Mrs. Rosa had said there would be electricity until eight o'clock, she did not mean eight in the morning.

At first light, impatiently and with my backpack on my shoulder, dragging my lost sleep through the streets which were just beginning to stir, I went to the corner where the vans for Luba left from. I got on the first one with an available seat. Quickly leaving behind the outskirts of Malabo, we took a road which went through virgin jungle and old abandoned cocoa plantations, perhaps those same plantations I had escaped into from that military truck, guided by Gabriel's hand. We went through small villages like Basupú or Bataicopo, and near Arenablanca the road edged close to the coast bordering the wide bay of Luba, until we reached the village of the same name. At the village's only identifiable hotel, an almost abandoned white building on the edge of the water, which in colonial times had been a nautical club, I found an empty room where I could leave my things. After a naïve attempt to get water from the shower, I decided to go to the convent of the Franciscan nuns where it now seemed like something from a previous lifetime– they had helped me so much during my escape.

This time it was daylight, I was not fleeing from death, and when I knocked on the door I was expecting to find the three nuns, to hug them like old friends and thank them once more for all they had done for me. But instead it was a young Guinean novice sister who opened the door."How may I help you?"

"Hi, good morning. I'm looking for Sisters Julia, Cecilia and Antonia."

"Who wants them?"

"Just tell them I'm an old friend from America."

The girl scratched her head under her headscarf.

"Well… those sisters aren't in this mission any longer. They were transferred."

"Transferred? Where to?"

"I think it was Cameroon."

"But… do you know why? Did they have any trouble with the authorities?"

"No, I'm sorry. I just arrived a few days ago, and I don't know anything about it."

I was worried by the possibility that they might have been expelled from the country on my account. "Isn't there anybody in the mission who knows?" I insisted.

"All this week I'm here by myself, I'm afraid."

"It's all right… Thank you."

And so, disappointed as well as worried about the possible punishment the missionary nuns might have suffered because of me, I turned round and went to the ever empty Jemaro restaurant, which belonged to the Lebanese who claimed to prepare the best *bisu* in the whole of West Africa. Although I had eaten here a number of times, the owner did not recognize me with my blonde hair under the hat and dark glasses. This put me at ease, as it showed that my simple disguise was more effective than I had imagined.

As soon as I had finished my lunch I went to the upper part of the village, looking for Maria and her daughter Paula's house, for lack of a better word. The streets were more like gullies, where the water from the mountains came down in dirty rivulets on its way to the sea, and the dwellings, all similar in design and wood and nipa construction, made it hard to guess which one of them I had hidden in. I wandered about for nearly two hours, going round the same streets again and again, until I got tired of wandering aimlessly and knocked on the door of one of the huts.

And old woman with an inquisitive look in her eyes appeared in the doorway.

"Good afternoon. Could you tell me which house Mrs. Maria and her daughter Paula live in?"

The woman went on scrutinizing me, and at last asked, "The one who has a daughter with HIV?"

"Yes, that's the one. Can you tell me which is her house?"

"Oh… not there any longer," she said, spreading her hands wide.

"Who's not here? The lady?"

"Not the lady, nor her house, nor her daughter…" she said sadly. "They took them away, and pulled down the house."

"And… you haven't heard anything more about them?" I asked, although I already knew the answer.

Sorrowfully, the old woman shook her head.

"The militiamen?" I insisted.

She shrugged her narrow shoulders. "They said they were terrorists."

Although this was the answer I had been expecting, I could not help feeling a knife piercing my heart. "Oh my god…" I muttered under my breath.

The woman nodded slowly, and I took my leave with a brief wave, turning away with tears in my eyes, weighed down with anger and powerlessness.

I walked without thinking where I was going, my sight blurred from pain and a feeling of guilt I could not escape from. I remembered that it had been me they were looking for that night. I knew perfectly well that if Maria and Paula had not come back by now, they never would.

I was sorry I had not had the courage to grab a knife from the restaurant table the night before and sink it in Captain Anastasio's throat.

I had nothing left to do now in Luba. The women I had come to see and to whom I owed so much had disappeared, some of them for good... and all of it because of me. I thought for a moment of asking for Gabriel among the old neighbors, but I rejected the idea immediately for fear of getting anybody else caught up in my nightmare, and above all, because of the possibility of attracting too much attention and getting myself into trouble again.

My footsteps led me back to the hotel, with my head spinning and my spirits dragging themselves along behind me. Not only had I found out nothing about Gabriel, I had also discovered that my pursuit by the militiamen had taken two innocent victims whom I had unpardonably involved. And the reward for those women's kindness had been deportation and death.

While I had been getting ready for my trip, in Boston, I had been sure that everything was going to turn out well. I would arrive in Luba, find Gabriel's trail, follow the thread until I reached him, and leave the country with him.

Now I saw how naïve I had been, and realized that that particular dream was not going to come true.

52

Remorse for all the evil I had caused, however unwillingly, to those who had helped me in any way took away any chance of sleep, and until I took a sleeping pill I did not manage to nod off that night.

When I woke up, well into the day, the waves were beating hard against the rocks the hotel was built on. With the lack of running water making it impossible to take a shower, I went down to a small black sand beach close by, and at least was able to lather and refresh myself, even though I knew that the salt of the water would end up being as annoying as the dirt I was trying to clean off myself. On the way back to the hotel I could not help a grimace when I passed a curious official sign which demanded, literally: ATTENTION TO TOURISTS, UNDER PENALTY OF FINE. Just one of those Guinean things.

There was no sense in staying there any longer, so I packed my bag and went to what should have been the reception desk, but it was as empty of people as it was of furniture. I remembered that the day before, when I arrived, a woman at the door had directed me to my room, but now there was no trace even of her. In fact I realized I had seen nobody else, either hotel employees or guests, in the twenty-four hours I had been there – which could mean the hotel was abandoned and would explain the lack of light, running water or bed sheets. So without bothering to wait for someone to pay for a nonexistent service, I slung my backpack over my shoulder and took a bus back to Malabo.

As soon as I arrived I went to the only central travel agency, on Independence Avenue, and bought a ticket for Bata on the evening flight. During the van journey, in spite of the disappointment of the visit to Luba, I decided that now that I had travelled all the way to Guinea I could not leave, no matter how slim my chances might be, without at least trying to locate Gabriel on the mainland, where I had last seen him.

I left my bag at the agency and, to while away the time, decided to take a stroll through the suburban slums of the city, which I had barely got to know. I went up 3 de Agosto Avenue, and on my left I saw the sprawl of the Lamber district: a labyrinth of tin-roofed huts and winding streets with streams of sewage running along them. Without a second thought I went into it. A poor neighborhood, on the outskirts of a calamitous city, in a country sunk in poverty. The real Africa, the Africa of the Africans. Wandering along those streets was the same as in Nairobi, Lagos or Freetown; it is where the majority of the population is clustered, a long way from the national parks with their tourists or the central business districts where the plunder of a whole continent finds its way out. A reality that the "civilized" world is incapable of even imagining, although it is the everyday life for the immense majority of Africans.

As I walked past that succession of walls made of used cardboard, garbage rotting on the corners and surreal posters with Obiang's image under the motto "FOR A BETTER GUINEA" pasted on pathetic huts which could barely manage to stay upright, a series of depressing articles I had read on the web a few days before came to my mind. One of them explained that child mortality in Africa was eleven times higher than in Europe, and that life expectancy had plummeted across most of the continent. For many countries it was around forty years of age, almost half the American average. And that was the length of time it was calculated that Africa needed, simply to regain the extremely poor standard of living of the seventies –assuming, that is, that it could hold back its determined descent into hell.

On one corner of the dusty street someone had set up a sort of pavement café with a couple of lame tables and some plastic chairs. I sat in the shade of the rusty porch and asked for a beer, which made me remember that refrigerators are a rarity in Guinea.

A small brown dog of indefinite ancestry and sorrowful eyes limped over with its head lowered, expecting something or someone that would never come. A boy of six or seven, stark naked, with a red cord around his bloated belly, approached the dog and laid a hand on its head, like old friends and comrades. They were both watching me with the same curious, wary look, and when I raised my hand to wave at them with a smile they both ran off as one: the one barking, the other laughing.

Meanwhile an old man had come over, supporting himself with a worn stick. He sat down on the free chair and leaned on the table to examine me openly.

"*Buenos días*," I said in Spanish.

The man gave a start, raising his eyebrows. "Are you Spanish?" he asked.

"Well... no. From the United States. But I took Spanish at university." I was amused by his attitude. "Why do you ask?"

"Well, I *am* Spanish," he said.

"Are you serious?" It was my turn to be surprised.

"Of course! All Guineans are Spanish!"

"Oh... I see. But as far as I know, you got your independence years ago, didn't you?"

The old man brought his head closer, confidentially. "They fooled us, you know?"

"Who did?" I said, as if I did not know.

"All of them... The Spaniards, the Americans and the French who wanted the country for their companies. Macias Nguema who wanted the country for himself and his family... until Obiang, the nephew, killed him and made himself president. But they're both the same..." He leaned back in his chair and gestured around him. "When I was young, we had electricity, running water, cinemas, hospitals, schools... we were the envy of Africa. And look at us now..." He pointed sadly at himself.

"You're talking about colonial times, aren't you?"

"The Spaniards were not good to us, you know? They treated us like idiots, and some of them called us monkeys... they only remembered us in the ads for powdered chocolate. We were *aquel negrito del África tropical...*"

"Do you miss those days?" I asked in puzzlement.

He raised his voice. "Of course I do! We were a thousand times better off than now! Even though we were the poorest of all and they saw us as cheap labor, we were citizens with certain rights. But now we have nothing. They fooled us when they said, the Spaniards are taking away your money; when Guinea gets its independence you'll live like the whites. And look at us now..." He looked around. "We're still waiting."

"I'm truly sorry..." I muttered sincerely.

"Everybody is to blame," he insisted. "If they hadn't treated us like slaves, who knows, we might not have voted for independence. And we wouldn't have let ourselves be fooled by those bastards..."

"Well... we'll never know."

"But, tell me," he said, this time more cheerfully. "What's a pretty American like you doing walking around Lamber?"

"Nothing, really. I'm just filling in time before my flight to Bata."

"Pity!" he said with a wink. "I'd have taken you dancing. I'm a very good dancer."

"Oh, I'm sure of that," I nodded, smiling.

"And what brought you to Equatorial Guinea?"

"Tourism..." I said, a little doubtfully, taking a swig of my beer. "I'm a tourist."

"Nobody comes to Guinea as a tourist," he replied skeptically.

"I've been told that before... and in part, they're right. I'm also looking for a friend."

He winked at me again "Ah...now I understand. I won't do?" he added roguishly, with a toothless grin.

I could not help but feel a sudden sympathy for the old man."Sorry," I said contritely. "But my heart's already taken by the person I'm looking for."

"A lucky lad, surely. I might even know him. Does he live in Bata?"

"I really... don't know where he lives."

"How are you going to find him if you don't know where he lives?"

"To be honest, I don't know that either."

The old man rubbed his chin, deep in thought."You know? Perhaps I can help you... Equatorial Guinea is very small and everybody knows everybody. If you tell me his name I can ask friends and relatives, and perhaps when you come back from Bata I'll have found him."

"That would be wonderful," I said bringing out pen and paper from my bag. "I'll write down my friend's name," I said as I did so, neatly, "and my email and my phone number. If you help me find him I can assure you I'll compensate you generously."I handed him the piece of paper.

"What I don't understand," he said, looking at what I had written, "is that you've come from the United States, looking for someone... without knowing where he lives or how to find him."

"The thing is," I said trustingly, "that he's in trouble... and I believe he might be in hiding."

The old man looked at me inquisitively."For political reasons?"

"Something like that..."
"Bubi or Fang?"
"Bubi."

The man pursed his lips, as if undecided about explaining something."There's a place..." he said at last, hesitantly, "in this same neighborhood, where the Bubis persecuted by Obiang usually meet."

"And you think my friend—"

"If he's a Bubi and in trouble, they might know him there."

"Then... you think I could ask them about Gabriel?"

In answer, the old man leaned on his stick and got to his feet determinedly."Better than that, miss. I'll take you to them."

53

"My name is José," the old man said as he walked beside me, limping visibly.

"Mine is Karen... Sarah."

"Pleased to meet you, Karen Sarah."

"No, just Sarah."

"All right, Just Sarah."

"No, excuse me, my name is..." Out of the corner of my eye I saw the old man holding back his laughter. "Hasn't anybody ever told you it's rude to laugh at a lady?" I asked, pretending to be indignant.

"Forgive me, miss, "he said, with laughter still lingering in the corners of his mouth. "But it's not often you get the chance to make fun of a white person."

"All right then, "I conceded, smiling. "Enjoy the moment."

We went on our way, going deeper into what could compare to the derelict version of a favela. With each step, poverty assailed my eyes with depressing visions of children playing with the plastic skeleton of what had once been a toy fire engine, women feeding babies from shriveled breasts, or vultures feeding on dead rats in the middle of the street.

"Do you live here?" My voice sounded low-spirited.

"No... I have a small palace in the suburbs, just beside Obiang's."

"I'm glad to see you haven't lost your sense of humor."

"There's not much of it left, my dear. It's the last trench against despair."

"I can understand that."

"No, you can't understand it," he said listlessly. "Nobody who doesn't spend their whole lifetime here among the garbage, with no present or future, knowing their children and grandchildren will live and die in this garbage dump, could understand anything. No," he repeated to himself, "they couldn't."

After a winding walk   perhaps with more turns than necessary   down alleys with a sweet smell of rot hanging over them, we stopped in front of a hut much like any other. José called out to a certain Augusto, a voice answered from inside and a man   presumably, Augusto   appeared at the door. He had to blink a couple of times when he saw me to convince himself that his eyes were not deceiving him.

I realized then that my presence might not be welcome among a crowd of fugitives. There was no doubt that a white woman at the door of the house was hardly likely to go unnoticed in that neighborhood. The feeling was reinforced when the man began to argue animatedly with my companion in a language I could not understand but supposed it was Bubi.

The man's body language made it very clear to me that I was not welcome and that he was not at all happy to see me at his house. After a heated discussion, the man appeared to relax a little and looked at me directly, without hiding his distrust and hostility."What's your name?" he asked without preamble.

"Sarah Malik."

"Who are you looking for?"

"Gabriel Biné."

"I don't know anyone by that name."

"Isn't there anybody else we can ask?"

"No," he said bluntly.

"But—"

"I said no."

Obviously it had not been such a good idea after all."All right, I won't bother you more. I'm going now."

Without even saying goodbye, he turned and went back into the house.

José looked at me despairingly and shrugged.

"Don't worry, you've done all you could," I said.

"I'm sorry. I thought they might help. I didn't expect him to be so angry."

"Well, after all, his attitude's quite logical."

"I'm sorry," he repeated.

"Let's not dwell on it," I said, trying to sound unconcerned. "Come back with me to where we met and I'll treat you to a beer. How's that?"

"That's fine, my dear. I think that'll be just fine."

The way back was much shorter – which confirmed my earlier suspicions – and ten minutes later we were back at the same table, sipping lukewarm beer.

We had a good time going over the various evils of Guinea, and José gave me an overall description of the turbulent days of decolonization. "We were an autonomous region until 1964," he said, "but the United Nations put pressure on Spain to leave the country so that the oil companies could negotiate with a corrupt dictator instead of the Spanish government. So without being prepared for it, and with a lot of Guineans thinking things were going too fast, there was a referendum in 1968 and the "yes" won. Then just a few months later came the elections that Macías won, and he became president on October 12 of that same year." José paused to sip his beer, letting his gaze wander over the roofs of Lamber. "That same day the riots began. They burned churches, pulled down statues, and attacked some of the thousands of whites who lived and worked in Guinea."

"Is that when the colonists left?"

"No, that was about a year later. Macías went raving mad and the Minister of Foreign Affairs tried to stage a coup, which cost him his neck. But Macías was convinced Spain was behind it all, so he started to set the people up against the

Spaniards, until the police even got as far as killing one or two of them."

"Fuck!"

"Yes, it really was a bad time. In the end most of the colonists had to flee, protected by the Civil Guard."

"It must have been horrible."

"Just imagine it. Some of them had lived here their whole life… and they had to leave with nothing but the clothes they were wearing. Since that day, Guinea's gone down the drain," he said firmly. "We were left without businesses, without trade, without plantations… and the government, now there weren't any awkward white witnesses, could spend their time doing what they did best: stealing."

The old man went silent, his gaze distant.

"It's a sad story," I said in a low voice.

"Very sad," he agreed.

And then, as if he had suddenly remembered an urgent appointment, he leaned on the table and stood up. "Well, there you are, my dear. I won't go on boring you with my stories."

"You're not boring me at all, you're very interesting. Although I'm surprised that you talk so freely about certain subjects with a stranger."

"Well, you don't look like police… and besides, I'm very old. One of these days I'll die so I'd better make the most of it now and say what I please. I no longer care about what the militiamen might do to me."

"You're a brave man."

"Thank you for your kind words to an old man," he said, trying to smile. "I wish you all the luck in the world in finding your friend."

"Thank you. Take care."

With a nod he went away, limping down the street.

I finished my beer and realized it was already time to head for the travel agency to pick up my baggage and go to the airport. I took my handbag from the floor and when I looked up, I found a pair of green eyes staring at me in amazement.

"I liked you better as a brunette," said the mouth under those eyes, and then kissed me passionately.

54

"But... how?" I finally managed to stammer, broken-voiced.

"Easy," he said, putting his hand on mine on the table. "I was actually at the house you went to."

"But that man—"

"Augusto doesn't know my name. Like everybody else fleeing Obiang and his minions, I changed it. As far as they're concerned I'm Leo."

"Why?"

"You never know who might be listening."

"And...is Gabriel your real name?" I asked suspiciously.

He let out a brief burst of laughter. "Of course! I'd never lie to you."

"Ah, but you did abandon me in that hospital in Cogo!"

"That has nothing to do with it."

"Well, for me one thing is as bad as the other. Why did you do it?"

"I don't like goodbyes," he said spreading his hands wide.

"Is that your excuse for leaving me stranded?"

"I don't know what you mean by stranded. As far as I could see, you were in good hands."

"But you can't just disappear like that!" I said angrily. "You didn't even leave me a phone number, or an address where I could find you."

"I'm sorry," he said, stroking my back with his hand. "At the time I thought it was the best thing to do... I didn't think you'd ever want to see me again."

"Well, you see... that's the kind of fool I am."

He pinched my chin. "Don't say that. It's a miracle you're here."

"The real miracle is that we've found each other. I still can't believe it!"

"That's true," he said, and smiled happily. "I thought I'd never see you again." He kissed me softly.

I was happy too. More than happy, in fact. I was exultant, overwhelmed by such a feeling of joy I had never known before in my whole life.

"But tell me," I went on, unable to erase the smile from my face, "how have you managed till today? Why did you come back to Malabo?"

Gabriel sat back in his chair, and made a face."I tried to hide in several places on the mainland," he said in a tired voice, "but as you know, I'm Bubi, and the people on the mainland are Fang."

"So?"

"Well, people were staring at me. It's very unusual for a Bubi to leave the island of Bioko, and at any moment I could have attracted the attention of the police or of a snitch… and then I'd have been lost. So I decided to come and hide in Malabo, among my own people, where I can pass unnoticed."

"And didn't you try to leave Guinea?"

"I did try. But without papers or money it was impossible even to get anywhere near the border. So I had no choice but to stay and hide."

"At least it allowed me to find you." I smiled."I guess it must be fate."

"Maybe."

"The important thing is that we're together again," I said, taking his hands in mine, with my heart leaping with joy. "And you can't imagine how happy it makes me."

We spent more than an hour celebrating our reunion at that small bar. I told him everything I'd done, first to get him out of the country, and then to come looking for him myself. And he told me of the difficulties he had had in getting back to Malabo on the same ship we had taken the other way. He knew nothing about Mrs. Maria and her daughter Paula either, but he agreed with me that given the age of the one and the health of the other, they would hardly have passed the test of the Guinean prisons.

Reluctantly, we parted while I went to pick up my backpack at the travel agency before it closed. We decided that the best thing would be for me to go alone to avoid being seen together, then I would take several taxis so that nobody could follow me, and we would end up meeting at that same bar an hour later.

Exactly one hour later, I was back. Gabriel was still waiting at the same table, and together, we took a room at a miserable guest house in the same neighborhood of Lamber, a building which only a spirit of extreme generosity could have called a hut. But I did not care.

The owner looked at me in disbelief when I rented that room without any kind of light, water or bathroom. The cardboard and reed walls let in smells, noises and mosquitoes by the battalion, and it was certainly the dirtiest bed I had ever slept in. But it did not matter.

I closed the door behind me, left the backpack on the floor, and sat down on the edge of the bed.

Gabriel did the same. "Thank you for coming to look for me," he whispered in my ear.

"Thank you for waiting for me," I replied, immediately realizing how silly my words sounded.

We both laughed from sheer joy, and embraced, letting ourselves slide onto the bed. There we stayed for what felt like hours, entwined in silence, with no need to say anything because words would have said less than the mere whisper of our breathing. During that long while I think I cried a couple of times, and laughed as often for no reason. We kissed. At first very slowly, tasting our lips while we stroked one another's faces, unable to believe we were together again, exactly I now realized as I had imagined it every day we had been apart.

Gradually the intensity of our kisses increased, and the passion I had held contained for so long began to break the knots of sanity, escaping the control which had been with me in all my previous relationships. Now I was in Africa, in the arms of an African, and common sense dissolved in the heat of the night and of our bodies, ever more stripped of clothes and inhibitions.

We were naked before I even realized. I was only partly aware of a mouth sowing kisses all over my body. First my neck, where he lingered with gentle bites, making the soft hair on the back of my neck stand on end and a stream of pleasure run all through me, down to my toes. After exploring around my shoulders, he went down to my erect nipples, softly running the tip of his tongue along the contour of my breasts, circling up to their summit and finally kissing them hungrily, exciting me to unbearable limits. Then he went down my stomach, lingering around my navel on his way to gently nibbling my pelvis, which produced a strange mixture of tickling and irresistible pleasure. From there his deft tongue covered the short distance to my pubis and, after a series of artful kisses, made his way between my legs and climbed up to my level. I felt a part of him entering me as if I had been waiting for him all my life, reaching my innermost places, pushing me on to delirium amid sighs and moans of pleasure.

Many hours later, lying surrendered on the bed, I let my gaze wander among the reeds of the roof and the damp stains on the fragile walls. I did not want to think, I was happy there and then. With one of Gabriel's arm and leg over my body – he was resting face down beside me– I was afraid that any thought passing through my mind would only serve to spoil that instant of exhausted delight.

But unexpectedly, it was Gabriel who spoke first."So now what?" he asked straightforwardly.

The question would have sunk me into a deep sadness if I had not had a good reply to hand."Wait," I said jumping off the bed. "I have a gift for you."

"A gift?"

"You'll see, you're going to love it."

I opened my backpack, and by touch alone found my lighter and a little Swiss knife. Carefully, since I was doing it with a single hand, I tore the double lining inside. Then, I put the knife on the floor, inserted my hand back in the backpack, and brought out a small envelope wrapped in plastic. Gabriel watched me with puzzlement and interest while I unwrapped the packet. Finally I took a small blue notebook from the envelope with the words *United States of America* engraved in gold on the cover.

"What's this?" he asked, astounded.

"What does it look like?" I said, laughing.

"It's an American passport. But... I don't get it." He opened it and saw the face of a black man, and a name beside the photo that was not his own. "And who's this?"

"That's you, from now on," I said cheerfully.

"But the man in the photo isn't me."

"He looks quite like you and that's enough, nobody looks like themselves in their passport photo. You'll have no trouble at customs. It even has the Guinea visa and a fake stamp of entry. With this," I said enthusiastically, "you'll be able... we'll be able to leave Guinea and go to the United States."

Gabriel looked at it carefully for a good while. At last he closed it, put it back in the envelope and handed it back to me."I'm sorry," he said heavily, "but I can't accept it."

I heard what he said, but could not believe it."What? Why not?"

"I can't leave Guinea."

"But, with this passport…" I brandished it in front of him.

"What I'm trying to tell you," he murmured, getting on his knees on the bed and holding my hand, "is that I don't want to leave Guinea."

55

"Come on, Gabriel," I said, trying to stay calm. "Will you please just explain what's all this about not wanting to leave? Are you insane?"

"I'm sorry, Sarah. But I already made that decision."

"Do you realize I've come from the United States, risking falling into the hands of the militiamen again, just to come and save you?"

"Of course I do, and you can't imagine how happy you make me."

"But you don't want to come away with me."

"No... I mean, yes. But not yet."

"Not yet?" I was baffled. "Why? Do you have to pick up laundry?"

Gabriel lowered his gaze and pressed his lips together. "Do you know what happened to my parents?" he asked after a while. His stricken face told me it was nothing good.

"No... no, I don't."

"Nor do I, Sarah. They've disappeared from the face of the earth, without a trace. Do you know what that could mean?"

"I can imagine..."

"Then do you really believe I can leave, just like that?"

"But what else can you do." It was more a statement than a question. "Turn yourself in."

"I thought about it, but I don't believe they'd let them go even with that... that is, if they're still alive."

"Then what!" I exclaimed. "Are you going to attack the prison all by yourself? Are you going to kill the president?"

When I said this, he looked up and his eyes shone coldly.

"You're crazy," I said, as if all of a sudden this man were a complete stranger.

"Maybe," he said with a shrug.

"They'll kill you like a dog, before you even get anywhere near."

"Perhaps."

"We're talking about murder!"

"Say it louder, I don't think they heard you in the police precinct."

"Gabriel! That's not right… it's not right. You're not like that. That'd be… it'd be… terrorism."

"Terrorism?" he repeated, suddenly angry. "How can you say that? You've seen what happens in this country. If nobody does anything to stop it, the Obiang family will go on inheriting power for generations and plunge Guinea even deeper in its misery."

"But killing is just sinking to their level."

"That's nonsense," he retorted, even angrier. "He's a thief and a murderer, and I'm going to try and stop him in the only possible way."

"There has to be another way, Gabriel. Violence only begets violence."

"Please stop repeating clichés. Do you really believe that rabble would step down from government if I asked them nicely?"

"But—"

"Sarah," – he sighed wearily – "there's no other way. Nobody's going to help us get rid of these parasites from outside, and we don't have a true democracy either. Either we kill him, or else he'll kill us just as he's been doing all this time."

With us both sitting on that filthy bed, this conspiracy to carry out an assassination seemed unreal. We were like a couple of children scheming to change the world.

"I see, Gabriel. I understand your reasons and if I were in your place... perhaps I'd do the same, but it's not as easy as that. What's the guarantee that whoever takes his place won't be even worse?"

Suddenly Gabriel gave a soft laugh. "Don't you remember that time when we were sitting on a bus and I asked you the same question?" he whispered, gazing into my eyes. "You told me you didn't know, but that at least we ought to try. And you were right, we can't live in fear. If you're burning in the fire, better to jump off, even at the risk of falling into the coals, than stay still, right?"

"Now it's you repeating clichés."

"It doesn't matter, I know my decision is the right one. The arguments are the least important thing."

"I'm sorry, but I don't think arguments are ever the least important thing."

Gabriel seemed to ponder for a moment. "You know who Nelson Mandela was?" he asked at last.

"Of course. He was president of South Africa and was given the Nobel Peace Prize."

"Did you admire him?"

"I admire what he did for his people."

"Well, he once said, 'a government which uses force to maintain its rule teaches the oppressed to use force to oppose it.'" Pointing his finger at me, he concluded, "That's one argument."

"If we're going to start on historical quotes…"

"It's not that at all. I want you to understand that the great changes and revolutions have always had to use violence to achieve their goals. Do you really think the *sans culottes* would have been able to take the Bastille with flowers and guitars? Or that the Thirteen Colonies would have thrown out the English just by asking them nicely?" He snorted. "When a really oppressed people wants to break free, they'll always be forced to use some form of violence. It's the only thing left for them, and they're driven to it by precisely those same people they want to overthrow. I wouldn't want to risk my life to put an end to anybody, but I look around and I see friends, relatives and strangers dying of hunger and sickness, while all they do, those who are supposed to govern us justly, is humiliate us and give free rein to their own malice with impunity." He lay down on the bed on his back, with his hands behind his neck. "No, Sarah. It can't be permitted. Someone once said that the only thing necessary for the triumph of evil is for good men to do nothing. And I don't know whether I'm a good man, but what I am sure of is that I don't want to be one of those who do nothing."

I saw I would never be able to convince him to change his plans, but even so, my fear of losing him overcame any other feeling of justice or morality. "And if they catch you… or kill you," I said, "what am I supposed to do without you?"

"I'm sorry, Sarah. You can't imagine what it means to me that you've come, and what you say you feel for me is similar to what I feel for you. But sometimes you have to do what you have to do…"

"I don't see myself in the role of a disconsolate widow."

"Nobody's asking you to do that."

"What I mean," I said more firmly than I had expected, "is that I'm not going to sit with my arms folded, watching you get killed. You haven't altogether convinced me with your arguments, but in the meantime… I'll help you."

"What did you say?"

"I'm saying that your fate is mine. Whatever it is that you're going to do, we'll do it together."

"Oh, no!" he protested. "There's no way I'm going to let anything bad happen to you because you've followed me in this."

"I didn't say I'd follow. We'll do it between us. I'll take care of you, and you'll do the same for me. We'll be a team."

"I think you've seen too much television."

I offered him my hand. "Do we have a deal or not?"

He stared at me, trying to guess how serious I was. "This isn't your war," he said feebly.

"It is, from the day they tortured me."

"But—"

"Come on, my hand's getting tired!"

"This is crazy."

"Then we'll share the craziness. I'd rather die with you for a just cause than live a long empty life without you."

Gabriel stared at my hand thoughtfully and at last, he took it in his own.

56

There were no restaurants nearby where we could have breakfast, or anything of the sort, so the woman who had rented us the room produced some boiled rice, and along with a chocolate bar and a bottle of orange soda we ate it as we sat on the bed in our frail hiding place.

"I've been thinking," he said.

"I thought you looked strange," I teased.

"Ha, I see you're in a good mood."

"I'm happy. For the first time in a long while, I feel happy."

"Do you like playing conspirators?"

"I like being with you. And about what you want to do—"

"What *we* want. We're a team, remember?"

"All right, what we want. Well, I've been thinking about it… and I believe you're right. But what I can't decide is whether all this is based on a desire for justice or revenge."

"If what you intend to do is something helpful for the vast majority, do personal reasons matter that much?"

"Of course they do!"

"Oh, really? Are there police in your country?"

"Don't ask silly questions."

"All right. Do you believe they work for money, or for high-minded concepts of order and justice?"

"Well… probably both. Yeah, I see the analogy. But what we're intending to do is still a crime."

"My dear innocent Sarah," he said as he gobbled a spoonful of rice. "Calling something a crime or an act of liberation is only a question of dates. Today I might be a would-be assassin, then a few days later a national hero."

299

"Or vice versa."

"I don't think this is the case."

"I certainly hope so… and by the way, how have you thought we'll… you know, do it?"

"With a bomb."

"A bomb? But that could kill other people!"

"Relax. It'll be a small bomb that will explode when his official car goes by. I'm not a butcher."

"Couldn't you do it some other way? I don't know… from a distance, with a rifle?"

"Impossible. He's always surrounded by a human shield of bodyguards, and the car has bulletproof windows. Besides, do you have a sniper's rifle?"

"Do you have a bomb?"

"Not yet."

"*Yet*?"

"We'll have to make it."

"Do you know how to build a bomb?" I asked in disbelief.

"No," was his nonchalant reply.

"Well then?"

"*You* are going to build it."

We decided that going everywhere together would attract attention and be too risky, so we divided the tasks between us. I was in charge of finding out on the internet how to build a homemade bomb. To my surprise, not only were there dozens of sites which explained in detail how to make one, but it was appallingly simple, provided you had a few chemicals which would be easy to pick up in drugstores and pharmacies.

Considering what we were trying to do and the means at our disposal, I was inclined toward the classic option: dynamite, very powerful and easy to make from a few ingredients. I copied the recipe sitting at a computer in the lobby of a hotel. Then, pretending to be working for an oil company, I dedicated the afternoon to pleasantly criss-crossing Malabo in a taxi to buy all the necessary ingredients.

Meanwhile Gabriel had spent his time finding somewhere discreet and out of the way where we could live and work without raising any suspicions. When we met, he took me to what would be our home for the moment, an abandoned house with cement walls in the San Fernando neighborhood. Here we unloaded everything we were going to need to make the explosive.

We spent that first night going over the process for making it and checking we weren't missing anything. The warnings I found in the text explaining how to make dynamite laid great stress on the dangers of the process.

First we had to prepare nothing less than nitroglycerine from sulfuric and nitric acids, then add glycerin and try to keep the temperature from going over 86°F, since in that case the mixture would explode with devastating effects. For that reason we left everything ready for the following night, when it would be less hot and there would be less chance of being interrupted.

The night was warm and humid, like all nights in Guinea. Perhaps because we were sweaty in that small bed, aware that every night together might be our last one, we threw ourselves on each other in a primitive sexual struggle, without tenderness, searching for each other with insatiable hunger in a paroxysm of sweat and pleasure that was almost brutal, each seeking the other's exhaustion without any consideration for restraint or limits.

When we were sated, locked in a silent embrace, with my intimate parts still throbbing, I had the horrible feeling that fate had already numbered the remaining nights we would share.

The following day we tried to forget our worries, so like any ordinary couple we went to the beach. To avoid arousing any unwanted curiosity, we went separately, in two different taxis, and met at the idyllic beach of Seis. It was low tide, so that a substantial strip of fine black sand was revealed, watched over by stately palm trees. Hand in hand we walked along it as far as the end, where after crossing a shallow river we found an ancient rusty ship stranded between the rocks.

The whole scene was very beautiful, and even the sea of that small bay showed a calm face, with gentle ripples which approached to caress the island's shore. As the water was hot we decided to take a swim, and as there was no one around, we went in naked.

"It's hard to believe," I murmured, floating languidly beside Gabriel, who was playing dead, "that we're still in Guinea. This calm seems strange to me."

"It's a shame all this has happened to us. If we'd met under different circumstances, who knows? We might have even been happy here. Guinea is a beautiful place, a paradise ruled by the devil."

The sun was at its highest, and letting myself drift with the faint current, I saw a flock of what looked like seagulls flying in formation above. "Do you think we'll succeed?" I asked, more to the sky than to Gabriel.

"What do you mean?"

"Everything. Get rid of the tyrant without being caught. Survive."

"That's something only God knows."

"I didn't know you were a believer," I said, without changing position.

"Only when I'm scared to death."

"Huh… like everyone else. By the way, the day after tomorrow is Christmas. What do you usually do to celebrate?"

"I'm not in the mood for celebrations."

"Well, I am. I'd like to know what the typical Christmas dish is here, what songs you sing… you know, all that sort of thing."

"The songs are Christmas carols the Spaniards brought, and the food is anything that will satisfy your hunger. Here we don't have turkey or seafood, nougat candy or chocolates…"

"How about toys?" I pressed on, ignoring his tone of voice. "Do you give toys to the children?"

"When I was little," he said bitterly, "I once got a bottle of Fanta on Christmas Day. Does that count?"

"All right, if you don't want to talk about it…"

"No, I don't want to talk about it. What I want," he said coming up behind me and holding my breasts hard, "is to make love to you on the beach."

At nightfall we went back to our lair and spread all the ingredients for making dynamite on the floor. In the middle of the room was a large tub full of ice, with another smaller one inside it, like a double boiler in reverse. Using gloves and protective masks, we poured out the nitric and sulfuric acids in the appropriate proportions. The thermometer we had bought at the pharmacy showed 80°F inside the mixture, but the surrounding ice had its effect and slowly lowered the temperature to 57°F. Then, with the greatest care, using a dropper, we began to pour in the glycerin very slowly so as to get the nitroglycerine which is the basis of dynamite. What the instructions had not warned us about was that the temperature of the mix would go up again. When I realized, it was already at 70°F and rising rapidly.

"Gabriel!" I shouted as soon as I realized. My voice came out distorted by the mask.

"What is it?"

"Look!" I pointed at the thermometer, which was now over 72°F. "We've got to add more ice! If it reaches 86°F we'll be blown up!"

"Ice? And where do you think I can get ice at this stage?"

"Fuck, we have less than a minute!" I cried in terror when I saw the mercury bar passing the 77 mark.

"Well, there's no ice!"

"Then let's run!" I said grabbing his arm. "Let's get out of here!"

"No! Wait a moment!" he said, breaking loose from my grip. "I have an idea!"

"There's no time for experiments!" I protested, seeing the thermometer was already showing 82°F.

Ignoring me, he leapt toward the kitchen and came back with a pack of salt we had bought that same afternoon. He took off his mask to bite off a corner of the pack, and poured all the contents into the tub of ice.

The temperature went on rising as far as 88°F, while I watched, paralyzed by fear, convinced that everything would blow up at any moment.

Then, miraculously, the temperature stabilized and slowly began to go down: 84, 80, 75, 68...

I fell on my butt, sweating profusely, unable to believe I was still alive.

Gabriel did the same, and from the floor he gave me an exhausted smile. "That was really close," he said with a gasp.

"I still don't know what happened... What did you do with the salt?"

"I poured it on the ice. That way it acts faster."

"I thought we wouldn't live to tell the tale..."

"In the end it was funny." He smiled. "You should have seen your face..."

"Fuck you!" I said, but I could not help a nervous giggle.

And absurdly, we ended up laughing, celebrating the fact that we were still alive, and our laughter must have been audible far away in the silence of the Malabo night.

57

In the small hours of the morning we were able to appreciate the final result of our deadly work. A dozen newspaper cones with a thick handcrafted fuse sticking out of them lay innocently on the kitchen table.

After the big scare while making the nitroglycerine, the rest of the job was a lot easier. We just had to mix the nitro with a solution of baking soda and water to neutralize the acid, and then make everything into a dough. To this we added sand and gunpowder cotton, which is nothing more than regular cotton soaked in nitric and sulfuric acids and left to dry. Finally we wrapped the result in multiple layers of paper, added the appropriate fuses, which were also made of gunpowder cotton, and the dynamite cartridges – or rather, dynamite cones – were ready.

I had never in my life imagined I might be able to do anything of the kind. Not only that, but to feel proud about it and a little impatient to use it.

Was it me doing this? Had I changed so much without realizing, or had I always harbored a murderer inside me without knowing? Who was the real me? The one before, or the one now?

I woke up before Gabriel, who was sleeping like a log. I dressed in silence and went quietly to the door, but when I opened it the rusty hinges creaked.

"Sarah?" he said.

"Sorry to have woken you up, it's this door that—"

"It doesn't matter, sweetheart. Where are you going?"

"Downtown, for supplies."

"All right… I just wanted to remind you that I love you."

"I love you too," I said, and closed the door behind me.

Feeling happy, almost singing under the morning sun, I headed downtown. I had decided to make some special Christmas dish, no matter how bad-tempered it might make Gabriel, and the only place I could get something that did not smell rotten was the Lebanese shops on the 3 de Agosto Avenue six blocks long and as narrow as any other street. Unbelievably, I found Christmas sweets and Catalan cava at an exorbitant price as well as some packed veal fillets which did not look too bad I could not remember the last time I had eaten veal and some seasoning for the meat. We would have a Christmas dinner, no matter what.

On the way I took a detour toward the market with the idea of looking for some seafood, or perhaps even a lobster. The roof without walls that was the Malabo market, very unlike what happened in the rest of the country, was bursting with vendors spilling out all around its four open sides. Most of them were offering local fruits and vegetables, of which I bought a couple of pineapples and some mangoes. Already quite heavily loaded, I approached the fish market, and that's all I could manage. The place gave off a stench of decay which filtered through my nostrils and seemed to get as far as my very brain. I don't think I had ever smelt anything so disgusting; not even rotting meat smells in that particular way. Obviously I gave up the idea of seafood. I was sure I could prepare a delicious dinner with what I had already.

With a couple of plastic bags in each hand I walked quickly back home. Incredibly, evening was already setting in while I was thinking I had only been out for a couple of hours, and my camera I could not recall how it had got into my handbag was beginning to feel heavy. I was thinking I would have to go back for more ice for the cava when I unlocked the padlock on the door which I did not remember having locked.

"Hello, love!" I said, as I came in.

There was no reply and I was convinced that he was still sleeping.

"I can't believe," I said, "you're still in—"

But there was no one in the bed. I looked around and saw that his clothes were not there either.

"I wonder if he went looking for me..." I said aloud.

My blood froze when I saw something I had not noticed when I first walked in. Or rather, when I did not see it: The dynamite was gone.

In less than a second an endless series of explanations went through my head, and none of them was good. Terrified, I searched the place for clues, convinced that the police had come to arrest Gabriel and found the dozen cones of dynamite on top of the table. But why had they bothered to lock the padlock again? It made no sense, unless... With a dreadful feeling I saw that my backpack too had disappeared, and my clothes were lying in a pile on the unmade bed. Above the bed head was a note stuck to the wall.

Slowly, as if there were lead in my shoes, I walked over to it, took the piece of paper with a trembling hand and read: *I have to do it on my own. I love you. Gabriel.* He had drawn a little heart next to his name.

Overwhelmed, lost, dead... I could not keep the note in my fingers, and it fell, swaying, to my feet. So did my sanity, shattering against reality.

I hurried out into the street, without even bothering to close the door. I ran like a stray dog, up the street and back down again, sniffing at every corner and indiscriminately asking anybody if they had seen a man with a big green backpack. Nobody could help me. Out of my wits, I went downtown, examining every door, tracking every possibility, scanning every face.

I must have searched every inch of the city in two despairing hours, with my heart running wild and the agonizing feeling that I would never see Gabriel again.

I was exhausted. The sun had just gone down into the ocean, encouraging hordes of bats to come out in search of food amid shrill shrieks in a huge, ominous black flock. A shop here and there gleamed with blinking Christmas lights, standing out amid the general sobriety and in contrast somehow making me feel much worse than I really was. Every wink of those bulbs felt like a mocking laugh to me.

Finally, not knowing where else to go, I stopped at an open air bar and, in the absence of any relaxing herbal tea, I ordered a beer. I tried to regain my lost calm and begin to analyze the situation as logically as I could in the circumstances.

The fact that Gabriel had disappeared with the explosives did not necessarily mean he was going to use them immediately. Perhaps his plan was to hide until the opportunity arose, and then make the attempt. If that was the case he might wait days or weeks before doing anything, which would give me time to find him. If I had managed it once I convinced myself I could do it again.

The cold beer sliding down my throat had the desired calming effect, and by the time I had finished the whole pint I was already seeing the situation less dizzily and more confidently. I had time and money, so I would certainly manage to find Gabriel before he did anything foolish.

Realizing this, I relaxed in my chair and let my gaze wander round the premises until it settled on a small black-and-white TV set. It was broadcasting a mute image of Obiang reading a speech.

"What's he talking about?" I asked the owner of the bar, pointing at the TV with my bottle.

"I guess he's giving his Christmas speech," she replied, looking at the TV out of the corner of her eye from where she was leaning on the inside of the counter. "But who cares…"

"You don't seem to like him," I said, even managing a smile.

"Him?" she said angrily. "How's anybody going to like him? They're a family of rogues, from the first to the last. If only the whole church would fall on them tonight."

"The church?"

"Malabo Cathedral," she said, pointing at the temple rising a few blocks away. "Tonight the whole clan's gathering together for midnight mass. If the church exploded," she fantasized dreamily, "the whole bloody government would go on a visit to Satan at the same time."

58

I took the first note I found in my purse, left it on the table and stumbled in the direction of the cathedral. Surely... no, without any shadow of doubt, Gabriel would be there. It was the opportunity he had been waiting for, the best he could have. Could he have had it all planned out while we were making the dynamite? Had that last *I love you* from the bed been a goodbye? Had he used me? I could not stop thinking about it all as I walked at a light pace, trying not to attract too much attention.

In a few minutes I reached the vicinity of the cathedral, only to find militiamen in their dress uniforms already barring access to vehicles and people. I went round the block behind the cathedral, but they had also cut off access from the other street, and there was no other way of reaching the building and its immediate surroundings. In that case, could Gabriel be walking the adjacent streets carrying his deadly load? Or had he gone into the cathedral before the checks had been set up and the street closed? I searched for his face among the people approaching the railings with curiosity, but the street lights barely let me recognize the nearest faces, and although I began to circulate amid the growing crowd, trying to make out those familiar features in the gloom, I got nowhere. Except that I aroused the interest of a police officer here and there as they watched the strange wanderings of a blonde woman among the throng.

I had no choice but to leave, before anyone came over to ask what I was doing. I walked to the nearby pier beside the sea and set myself to think how I might find Gabriel before midnight and stop him from blowing up a whole cathedral full of worshippers.

I guessed he must already be inside the perimeter which included the cathedral and the Independence Square, since it would be impossible to go through the police check with a dozen dynamite cones on his back. The obvious drawback was that I was the one left outside, and a mere tourist would certainly never be allowed to attend that mass which, as the woman at the bar had said, was exclusively for the president's clan and his acolytes. Clearly my skin color would not let me pass myself off as a distant cousin. Perhaps they would let some ambassador's wife in, or a senior executive of an oil company, but I was neither of those, and nor could I hope to pass for one of them with the clothes I had brought with me from Boston.

However much I thought about it I could not come up with any way of getting in there. Unless, of course…

A crazy idea began to form in my head. I went back to the house as fast as I could, convinced that this was the only chance I had of finding Gabriel.

I had lost track of time during the previous few hours, and by the time I took a taxi back to the cathedral it was nearly midnight. For a fleeting moment I thought that if in the jungle I had been a kind of Snow White with my seven Pygmies, now I was more like a stressed Cinderella whose midnight deadline was almost up. Although the derelict taxi carrying me through the solitary streets of Malabo was not exactly a carriage pulled by spirited horses, I trusted I would not turn into a pumpkin and that my humble disguise would not disappear into thin air.

I was wearing my father'sD40 Nikon camera round my neck, a prop I had brought in the country for my role as a tourist. I did not even know how it worked, but combined with a photographer's vest also my dad's on whose top left-hand pocket I had hastily written the word *Press*, and a reasonably tidy appearance, I trusted I would be able to cross the security perimeter in the guise of a photojournalist.

The taxi stopped a few yards from the entrance. I paid the driver double for the speed he had taken and went determinedly toward the soldier watching the only entrance in the railings. "Good evening, I need to get through," I told him, with as much self-assurance as I could muster. Without even stopping I walked on to the door, showing a confidence I was nowhere near feeling.

For a second I thought I was going to get through with no trouble whatsoever. Then the soldier's hand reached out and grabbed my arm."Identification," he demanded sternly.

"I'm a press photographer," I said showing him my camera.

"Identification," he repeated as if he had not heard me.

"Look," I said feigning impatience, "I have to cover the mass, and if you don't let me through I won't be on time."

"You can't come in unless you show me some identification."

"But… I was in such a hurry I left it at the hotel, and I don't have it on me."

The soldier squeezed my arm more tightly and raised his hand."Sergeant!" he shouted. "We've got someone without papers here!"

The sergeant strode over and studied me with an unfriendly gaze."You don't have identification?" he asked, rather as if I had said I had no lungs.

"I already told the soldier that I left it at my hotel."

"Don't you know that foreigners always have to carry their identification papers on them?" He added ominously, "You'll have to come to the police station with me."

A chill ran down my spine."Look, sergeant," I said slowly, drawing on all the calm I could muster, "I'm the special envoy for an important news agency, here to cover this event. I know I ought to be carrying my papers on me, and I apologize, but if you don't let me through I won't be able to do my piece on

President Obiang and his family, and tomorrow you'll have to explain, perhaps in person, why I wasn't able to do my job."

The soldier seemed to lose a little of his poise. "But with no identification…" he said, wavering.

"All right," I bluffed. "Take me to the police station or do whatever you want, but start thinking up a good excuse to give your president to explain why he won't see his photos in the New York Times tomorrow."

The sergeant stared at me, visibly angry, but unsure. In the end, after frisking me thoroughly and making sure I was not carrying any hidden weapon, he gave me an unfriendly nod and let me through.

The cathedral was almost full, with all the pews at the far end occupied by people in their Sunday best accompanied by their haughty wives. I had checked the outside of the temple and the small park in front, and had seen no sign of Gabriel. There was only the cathedral itself left to check.

I went in through the main door like the other attendees and walked down the central aisle, feeling I was the focus of attention. I did not recognize anybody, but there was the whole Guinean government with their families, on the left and right, sitting on the long wooden pews.

"Press!" someone cried behind me. "Hey! Press!" they insisted, and then I realized they meant me. I swallowed and turned.

A man in a suit, with a prominent belly, had risen from his pew.

"Yes?" I asked him.

"Why don't you take a photo of us?" he said, indicating the woman who must be his wife, sitting between a boy and a girl. "Or are you only going to take photos of the boss?"

"No, of course not. Get ready and I'll take the photo."

Apart from not knowing how it worked, I had not even checked that the battery was charged; if it were not, they might suspect my cover and I would be in serious trouble. *It'd be ironic,* I thought, *if they ended up finding me out because of something as stupid as that.* So my heart was tight as I pressed the *on* button, and held my breath until I saw the green light of the flash go on.

I tried to focus as best I could, and in the small screen of the camera I saw the four members of that family smile. Although the parents might be undesirable people – something I could not be sure of – the girl of eleven or twelve with her pink gown and two cute pigtails and her younger brother with his gap-toothed smile were not guilty of anything, and obviously did not deserve to share the fate of an old dictator simply because they found themselves under the same roof for an hour.

I pressed the button, the flash went off, and I convinced myself that not only did I have to find Gabriel, but stop him at any cost.

I watched the result on the screen, surprised by the good shot I had taken, when as I put the camera to my eye I saw a face I knew in the photo, a couple of rows back. I nearly dropped the camera when I realized it was the face of Captain Anastasio Mbá Nseng.

I turned quickly and began to walk away toward the front rows. Several more people asked me to take photos of them as well, which I refused with the excuse that I had to change the battery, but that I would be back shortly.

The uniformed guards posted every few yards were not paying me the least attention, no doubt thinking that I would not have been there without the appropriate permit. Pretending to fumble with the Nikon, I discreetly checked every pew until I reached the first row, desolate at not having seen Gabriel.

"Young lady," a deep voice said beside me. "Aren't you going to take our picture before the service begins?"

I turned around to repeat the excuse of the battery, and I found that the person addressing me was very familiar. In fact his photo could be seen on every corner in Malabo, and was framed in every shop or office of the country. I did not need to see the presidential sash across his chest to know who I was facing.

"Oh, sure! Of course!" I stammered. With trembling hands I took a step back and lit up the nave once again with the flash. "Done," I said foolishly.

"It's all right, young lady," he said, half-closing his eyes behind tortoiseshell glasses. "I didn't know the press was invited to the mass."

"Um... well I don't know. I was given a—"

"It doesn't matter," he interrupted with a wave of his hand. "I'll speak to the press manager later. You may go."

"Thank you..." I mumbled, with the parody of a curtsey. "Have a nice..." I realized I was babbling and Theodore Obiang Nguema had not taken his eyes off me. "Anyway... good evening."

I turned on my heels and headed toward the nearest wall. There I saw the wooden door to an adjoining room, went hastily in, closed it behind me, and immediately leant against it. I was soaked in sweat.

After breathing deeply a couple of times to recover my poise, I looked around and realized I was in a small side chapel, completely empty. When I was about to leave I saw another door. I went across to it, opened it with an effort and found a steep spiral staircase going up to what must be the roof of the cathedral.

I nearly dismissed the idea, but I told myself I had to search everything, so I started off up the metal stairs. A few minutes later, panting, I reached a small iron door.

I opened it and found myself in the open, looking out from the domed roof of the cathedral. In spite of the darkness of the night, studded with stars and veiled by the harmattan, I made out a man crouching with his back to me on the highest point of the dome. He had not seen me.

I went up to him stealthily and called out his name when I recognized him. He turned, with a lighter in one hand and one end of a fuse in the other, and looked at me in astonishment.

59

"What…? What are you doing here?" he asked, stunned, as he straightened up.

"You're asking me that?" I spat out, suddenly furious. "What the fuck are *you* doing here? Do you really mean to blow up the fucking church with everybody inside?"

Gabriel came over to me, and I noticed he was wearing an old police uniform, washed and sewn many times over.

"Don't touch me!" I said as he tried to reach out to me. "You abandoned me again! What do you think I am, a fucking dog?"

"Calm down, Sarah. Please…"

"Calm down?" I repeated, and laughed disbelievingly. "You leave me without a word, you leave with forty pounds of dynamite, I find you trying to kill hundreds of innocent people, and you're asking me to calm down!" I took the camera off my neck and slammed it hard on the floor.

"I understand you, Sarah. Forgive me, but I'm doing what I have to do."

I took no notice of this. "And here I am like a fool, believing all that crap about being a team, that you wouldn't do anything without me…"

"Listen to me, please. Believe me or not, I love you. I hated myself for leading you on, but I had no other option."

"You could have told me the truth."

"I didn't want to put you in danger.Besides," he added pointing to the dynamite, "would you have helped me to—"

"Of course not! This isn't what we'd planned."

"I had to improvise."

"But you're going to cause a massacre! Why?"

"You know perfectly well why. Why kill a single snake if I can get rid of the whole nest at once?"

"What about the dozens of innocent people who're going to die? There are children down there! Did you know?"

"I can't do anything for them," he murmured, lowering his gaze.

"You can't?" I exclaimed. "Don't blow up the dynamite, that's what you can do!"

"I have to do it, Sarah," he said, picking up the end of the fuse again. "For every innocent who dies tonight, hundreds will be saved later on."

"You don't know that," I replied. I was nervous at seeing him with the fuse in his hand again.

"True, but at least I'll have tried."

"And this attempt is worth two or three hundred lives?"

Gabriel's expression hardened. "That," he said seriously, "is less than what they kill in just one month."

"Yeah, and you want to compete with them."

"Don't say that. You know it's not like that."

"And you're telling me this with a dynamite fuse in your hand?"

"It's the only way to get justice. Don't you remember everything they made you go through?"

"Of course I remember! But killing others won't make me feel better."

"Perhaps not you. But it will the half million Guineans who've had to put up with them for thirty years, I can assure you."

"It's a very high price."

"Freedom doesn't come for free, Sarah. Innocent people die in any revolution. It's sad, but unavoidable."

"But it *is* avoidable!" I pleaded, seeing him light the fuse. "Don't light that fuse!"

"Sorry, there's no going back. Get ready to run."

"No! Don't do it!" I shouted.

At my back, a rasping, mocking and unpleasantly familiar voice asked, "What is it you don't want me to do, Miss Malik?"

60

I turned around. Behind me, in dress uniform, with a gun in his hand, stood the sinister soldier. There was a macabre smile on his scarred face.

"What do you think you're doing?" he asked, as if he found it amusing.

"Me? Nothing…" I said, terrified.

Captain Anastasio came a few steps closer and scrutinized me."Then, what are you doing with that… sort of rope?"

I looked down at my hands, not knowing what he meant. In my right hand there was no doubt that I was holding the fuse for the dynamite."I don't know…" I muttered, honestly surprised, "how it got here."

The captain followed the line of the fuse with his gaze until he noticed the bunch of paper cones tied together. Then he raised his gun and aimed it at my head."You damn terrorist," he said under his breath. "I knew that's what you were. Drop that fuse at once and move away from the explosives!"

Stunned, I did what he said."I swear… I wasn't intending to do anything," I protested timidly. "I wanted to stop it!"

"Do you take me for an idiot? I catch you red-handed and you still have the gall to deny it? I ought to kill you right now!"

Puzzled, I looked around for Gabriel, wondering how he could have vanished so fast.

"Who are you looking for, terrorist? There's only you and me up here. Nobody's going to come to your rescue, and you won't be so lucky as to escape from a moving truck again. Did you know you're the only one we couldn't catch?"

Obviously he was lying. Gabriel had escaped with me too.

"I've told you the truth." I was trying to buy time, imagining Gabriel would be hiding somewhere and would jump on the soldier at any moment. "These are explosives, it's true, but I can assure you I was trying to stop them being used."

"Do you know you're completely nuts?" he said, staring at me with what was almost compassion. "There's no one but you here, don't you realize? I followed you when I saw you taking photos. I climbed the stairs after you and I've been watching you from the door." He shook his head with a cruel smile. "You've been arguing all by yourself for five minutes."

"But... what are you saying? You're just trying to confuse me."

Captain Anastasio laughed heartily."Why would I want to confuse you? You're so crazy you haven't even realized. I was enjoying myself watching you shouting and waving your hands as if you were talking to someone. In fact until you took out the lighter I hadn't made up my mind to arrest you."

Instinctively I put my hand in my pocket, only to find, with a sudden shiver, that there was a lighter at the bottom of it."I... I don't understand," I muttered.

"I'll explain it to you," he said, showing his teeth. "You're absolutely crazy. But don't you believe for a second that it will stop you facing the firing squad. Being wrong in the head is no excuse here for evading justice."

Unaware of his voice, my memory was retracing the trail of the last minutes, days, weeks, in fits and starts... going over and over each of the moments I had shared with Gabriel, as though in a slideshow. And inexplicably, in each one, his face, his voice, his presence faded in my memory, escaping like smoke between my fingers... as if he had never been there.

With a shiver, I realized I had never once seen him interact with other people. In fact, when I came to think about it, even when I talked to him in front of others I had noticed puzzled expressions and never known the cause.

How was it possible?

Had I come back to Guinea looking for Gabriel... or could it be a dark part of myself that had driven me on to that roof?

I was trying desperately to evoke some possible situation that could refute what reason was screaming at me.

For goodness' sake! I had made love with him! How could anyone imagine that?

What about everything he had told me about Guinea? Had I already known? So who had dragged me through the darkness of the jungle on that first night? I refused to believe it had been myself... had I needed to have someone by my side so badly?

I did not want to admit it. I could not.

And yet deep down in my brain a desolate certainty was struggling to make its way through, trying to tell me there had always been something which did not quite fit.

But if that was the case, it meant that I—

"What is it?" he asked mockingly, interrupting my thoughts. "Are you coming to realize just how demented you are?"

I could not believe... no, it could not be true. It had all been real. How could Gabriel not exist? I had fallen in love with him!

Even so, that inner voice kept insisting that this despicable individual was right.

I could not believe it, did not want to believe it... and yet the more I thought about it, the surer I was.

The man I loved and for whom I was ready to kill or to die... was nothing more than an illusion, a mirage, the hallucinatory desire of a mind which on the brink of the abyss, to retain its sanity, had conceived a hope that took me by the hand in the form of a black-skinned archangel.

And the final result was that I had ended up on the roof of a cathedral, surrounded by explosives.

Gabriel had turned out to be a vengeful archangel.

And I had gone crazy.

61

I raised my hands. "But…" I murmured in bewilderment, "I… didn't want to kill anybody. It's the truth, I swear ."

"Oh sure. What's in the cones?" he asked, pointing at them.

"It's… dynamite."

"Were you planning to bring the cathedral roof down on everybody?"

"No!" I hesitated for a moment. "I mean… I don't know. I don't understand what's going on."

"I'll tell you. You're a terrorist, sent to kill our beloved president, and I've caught you in the act."

"I guess you're right," I admitted feebly, and collapsed on the tiles of the domed roof. "I don't know how, but you were right, right from the beginning." I hugged my knees and gave a sigh of resignation, thinking about the insanity of it all.

"Sure," Captain Anastasio repeated. "I'm always right." He walked over, keeping his gun on me, to study the newspaper cones more closely. "Are they homemade?"

"Can't you tell?"

He was so absorbed in the explosives that he let the question pass."Did you make them by yourself?"

"No," I said with a sad grimace. "a ghost helped me."

He glared at me again with his cold, cruel eyes."I'm glad to see you have a sense of humor," he said in an icy voice. "Because starting from tomorrow… you and I are going to have a lot of fun together."

A while ago that threat would have made me cringe, but now it left me indifferent. My whole world, my very essence, had collapsed on itself as that dome nearly had. I had become brutally aware of my true mental state, losing in a single moment not only the ghost of a man I thought I had fallen in love with but the woman I had thought I was. And when you lose everything, including your reason, who cares about all the rest? I was no longer Sarah Malik; this tired body was not that of the woman who months ago had arrived in Guinea full of dreams, the girl who had played with her dog at her parents' home, the teenager who had got away to the beaches of Cape Cod on weekends, and above all I was not the convinced pacifist of old. So who was this woman who saw the world through my eyes? How long had she been there? And in any case... did it matter anymore?

I looked up, my gaze and my mind equally lost, and saw the captain examining the explosives closely."This is very good..." he was muttering, "really well done."

"Do you like them?" I said. "You can keep them as a present."

He looked at me out of the corner of his eye for a moment and turned back to the cones."How long does the fuse burn for?" he asked, apparently guilelessly.

I was about to answer him when I guessed the possible, and chilling, implications of that question."You couldn't be thinking of...?"

Captain Anastasio straightened up, with evil flaming in the depths of his eyes.

Shaken, I jabbed my finger at him. "You want to use the bomb!"

"Isn't that what you wanted to do a moment ago?" he asked sarcastically.

"No! I already told you I was trying to prevent... well... myself from detonating it." I felt my stomach turn.

"Listen, you're completely insane. So, not only will you be blamed for the attack, but you'll look guilty as well."

"You're an asshole!"

Instead of getting angry, he laughed under his breath."And I'll be that for many years to come, while you rot in one of our prisons."

The strange thing was that this man's threats were beginning to affect me less and less."But… why?" I wanted to know. "What will you gain by killing all those people?"

He laughed again, like a hyena, shaking his head."A captain's pay isn't bad at all," he said, standing tall and raising his jaw. "But I think a president's would be even better…" He laughed for the third time.

The murmur of prayer reached me through the soles of my feet, giving the moment a greater feeling of unreality, if such a thing were possible."You're crazier than I am!" I heard myself say. "You'll never be president, and you'll be tried for murder!"

"Oh yes?" He sounded amused."And who's going to judge me? The whole government and all the senior officers are down there. I must be the highest-ranking officer who isn't at that stupid mass right now, so if they all died because of a tragic terrorist attack… there'd be a need for a firm hand to take the helm of Equatorial Guinea."

"And you intend that hand to be yours," I said in disgust.

"Can you think of anyone better?"

"I may have lost my mind but you… are a monster."

"And you'll be my whore," he said. He brought his face close to mine. "As from tomorrow, you'll see what's waiting for you in—"

I did not let him finish the sentence. I had found the strap of the camera by touch and when he came close thinking that I was unarmed, I hit him on the temple with the Nikon with all my strength. It weighed almost a pound.

He put his hands to his head, moaning with pain and rage, and I leapt down the dome toward the door. As I went through it, with my heart hammering in my chest, I heard him shouting furiously, "You fucking bitch! I'm going to kill you! I'm going to kill you!"

But I was already running down the spiral staircase as fast as I could, barely touching the steps.

In a few seconds I reached the chapel, crossed it and appeared all of a sudden in the nave of the cathedral, stumbling right beside the parish priest who was officiating at the mass.

A few isolated cries of surprise came from the front pews, and I was immediately approached by four soldiers aiming their guns at me.

I grabbed the microphone from the astonished priest. "Listen to me, please!" I shouted desperately. "There's a bomb in the church! Get out of here right now!"

The congregation, far from taking any notice of me, were looking at each other and murmuring aloud.

The soldiers reached me. Two of them grabbed my arms and dragged me brutally off the pulpit.

"Listen to me! There's a bomb in the roof!"

Almost everyone looked up, but obviously saw only the damp-stained frescoes.

There were a few outbreaks of laughter.

"Take this lunatic away!" someone shouted.

The soldiers went on tugging at me relentlessly, dragging me down the central aisle, while I struggled uselessly.

"Get out of here!" I shouted again, and when I saw the children I had photographed before I cried, almost out of my mind, "For God's sake get the children out of here! Get the children out!"

But nobody moved from where they were.

I had nearly reached the door by now.

And then the roof exploded.

In the following tenth of a second the wave of expanding air hit me directly in the chest like a hammer, driving all the air out of my lungs. Just before the blast of the explosion arrived, the windows of the cathedral were hurled out, shattered, while the solid walls and the ground itself trembled as though in an earthquake. By the time the first pieces of rubble fell from the roof a hundred feet above, the dull boom of the cave-in was already mingled with the shrill cries of panic from the throats of three hundred men, women and children who saw death plunging toward them amid a dirty cloud of stone and dust. All of a sudden I was free from the soldiers who were dragging me; they were looking up in disbelief at the sky which was collapsing on their heads. There was still time for me to throw myself on the floor and cover my head with my arms in a gesture both instinctive and useless. The first thing to hit me was soft but lifeless: a human body, perhaps one of the guards. Paralyzed by terror, clenching my jaw so hard it seemed to me my teeth would break, I waited for the downpour of rubble which came like a hailstorm, hitting every inch of my back and legs. One especially heavy piece hit me on the side and made me howl with pain; it felt as if it had crushed my ribs and splinters of bone were tearing me apart inside. I also had to bear the trampling of feet as people stumbled over me, fleeing in the thick darkness of dust and smoke which made it hard to breathe. I was trampled by dozens of maddened beings in search of a way out which undoubtedly did not exist anymore, screaming. Parts of the ceiling and walls kept falling, often on soft targets.

And as abruptly as it had begun, the cave-in stopped, although it would still take a long time to disappear from my eardrums, and even longer from my memory.

An unreal silence fell. For a few seconds it seemed that everyone was quiet, rapt before the miracle of a world that had finished its collapse.

And then, when a strange peace seemed to bring relief to the senses, the pain became intolerable. Thrust forward by an invisible hand, I fell helplessly into the dark well of unconsciousness.

In a state of shock, my blood-smeared hands are the only thing my sight and mind can hold. Is it just mine, all this blood sliding warmly and thickly down my wrists as far as my elbows?

I try to move my head from side to side, but I can't.

I try to get up, but I'm caught under the weight of a now uninhabited body, and my muscles don't belong to me. I'm strewn on to the ground. Yes, that's it... but what's happened?

An unbearable buzzing stops me hearing anything and crushes me with the certainty of fear and helplessness. Although, wait a moment... in the distance, as if from miles away, I think I can hear moaning. No, there's something more. There's screaming. Wrenching screams of pain, barely uttered, but cutting their way like knives through the shrill deafness.

But who's screaming?

I think I know that voice.

Oh, no... it's me.

Oblivion

It is the end of the southern fall. An increasing rain hits the windows of the café I come back to every evening in the Plaza Serrano of Buenos Aires.

I came here to finish writing this story which has so disturbed me, seeking to get away from anything that reminded me of Africa, and I type these last lines in my laptop after glancing at my notes, hoping I have been faithful to the words and the silences which Sarah dictated to me over three long, moving weeks.

She survived the explosion in the cathedral with a few fractured ribs and countless cuts and bruises, unlike more than a hundred people for whom that was the last night of their lives.

The dictator Teodoro Obiang Nguema was urgently whisked to a clinic in Switzerland in his private jet and treated for his wounds there. His limitless bank account guarantees that he will live for many years longer, healthy and unpunished, and currently continues as the inevitable president of Equatorial Guinea. As for Captain Anastasio, all suspicions about the assassination attempt fell on him, and one day he simply disappeared, I suspect as the victim of the judiciary system he was a part of for so long.

I never heard from Sarah Malik again.

She stopped writing a long time ago. Perhaps she decided that her relationship with me, my frequent questions or my mere existence, brought back all she was seeking to leave behind.

Then from some dark corner of the café Carlos Gardel sings *Volver,* and I seem to see her again with her hair still dyed blond, framing her expression of weariness as she travels back into the past, leaning on the counter and downing her beer, waiting for Gabriel to come back and hold her in his arms once more.

But when in the final verse the old tango regrets all that *living... with my soul clinging to a sweet memory that I cry over once again,* I recall the last time I saw her, in the lobby of that Libreville hotel where I was staying. She had come to say goodbye. I thanked her for the last time and we said *till the next time*, lying through our teeth with the implication that we would meet again.

Then, she turned around and walked out of the hotel and out of my life forever.

But as I watched her walk out of the door, I noticed a mulatto boy of six or seven who appeared to be waiting for her, sitting on the stairs of the hotel and eating an ice-cream.

Sarah went over to the child and pointed in my direction as she lovingly ruffled his hair.

The boy looked toward me and smiled, and it was only then that I noticed he had green eyes.

OTHER BOOKS BY FERNANDO GAMBOA

THE LAST CRYPT
Ulysses Vidal Adventure Series Book 1

Diver Ulysses Vidal finds a fourteenth-century bronze bell of Templar origin buried under a reef off the Honduras coast. It turns out it's been lying there for more than one century, prior to Christopher Columbus's discovery of America. Driven by curiosity and a sense of adventure, he begins the search for the legendary treasure of the Order of The Temple. Together with a medieval history professor and a daring Mexican archeologist they travel through Spain, the Mali desert, the Caribbean Sea and the Mexican jungle. They face innumerable riddles and dangers, but in the end this search will uncover a much more important mystery. A secret, kept hidden for centuries, which could transform the history of humankind, and the way we understand the universe.

BLACK CITY
Ulysses Vidal Adventure Series Book 2

An ancient mystery.
An impossible place.
An unimaginable adventure.
Professor Castillo's daughter has mysteriously disappeared in the Amazon jungle. Determined to find her, he begs Ulysses and Cassie to go with him. Unable to dissuade him and not wanting him to go on his own, they both accept to help their old friend in his crazy attempt at her rescue. The three embark on an incredible journey to a place which should not exist, the Lost City of Z.
A journey nobody has ever returned from.

NO MAN'S LAND
The Captain Riley Adventures

NO MAN'S LAND takes place at the end of August of 1937, in the days prior to the Battle of Belchite in the Spanish Civil War, but is in no way a novel of war. It is a thrilling tale of adventure full of humor, starring Alex Riley and his loyal friend Joaquín Alcántara, volunteers in the Lincoln Batallion, who unintentionally find themselves mixed up in a daring rescue mission under the very noses of Franco's Army

CAPTAIN RILEY
The Captain Riley Adventures Book 1

It is 1941, and Captain Alexander M. Riley and his crew of deep-sea treasure hunters believe they're setting off on yet another adventure—to find a mysterious artifact off the coast of Morocco for an enigmatic millionaire with questionable motives. Part-time smugglers, world travelers, and expats who have fought causes both valiant and doomed, Riley and his crew soon find themselves in the crosshairs of a deal much more dangerous than the one they bargained for. From Spain to Morocco to an Atlantic crossing that leads to Washington, DC, Captain Riley must sail his ship, the *Pingarrón*, straight through the eye of a ruthless squall and into a conspiracy that goes by the name Operation Apokalypse—a storm that only he and his crew can navigate.

DARKNESS
The Captain Riley Adventures Book 2

From European shores to the heart of the African jungle, Captain Riley's *Pingarrón* embarks on new action-packed adventures.

On their last mission, Captain Riley, his loyal crew, and his girlfriend, Carmen, bravely averted a global disaster. Now, while World War II rages on, they hope that they are on more solid ground working for the US Navy. But when a job goes awry, the team finds itself taking a treacherous journey deep into the Belgian Congo. There, within the jungle, they will come face-to-face with wild animals, cannibals, and dark forces that shroud a decades-old mystery. They defeated the terrifying Operation Apokalypse that nearly destroyed them, but can they survive this?

AUTHOR'S NOTE

What you have just read is a novel, a fiction I thought it was necessary to write in order to describe the chilling reality. What I set out in it is the fruit of my own experience in Equatorial Guinea, of testimonies gathered personally, and of full reports from a variety of organizations such as Global Witness, the International Lawyers' Association, Transparency International, the Committee for the Protection of Journalists, The Alternative Commission for Africa, Amnesty International and the UN.

From this point on, dear reader, we let go with our hands. Whatever you decide to do or not to do with what you know now is entirely up to you.

www.gamboabooks.com

ACKNOWLEDGEMENTS

I wish to thank my parents, Fernando and Candelaria, and my sister Eva, for their permanent support, as well as to all my friends and beta readers for their patience and accurate suggestions, and above all, my eternal gratitude to the thousands of readers who decide to embark with me in each new adventure.

Thank you.

Fernando Gamboa

Made in the USA
Columbia, SC
23 November 2017